The Pursuit
of Elizabeth Millhouse

Amanda Barber

[Handwritten note: Younger sister of Monica Parker (she & Jason were church planters in Colorado.) High Country Baptist Church, Colorado Springs, Colorado]

A**X**IOM
PRESS

Mobile, Alabama

The Pursuit of Elizabeth Millhouse
by Amanda Barber
Copyright ©2013 Amanda Barber

All rights reserved. This book is protected under the copyright laws of the United States of America. This book may not be copied or reprinted for commercial gain or profit.

ISBN 978-1-58169-456-7
For Worldwide Distribution
Printed in the U.S.A.

                      Axiom Press
       P.O. Box 191540 • Mobile, AL 36619
                800-367-8203

I dedicate this novel to my family—
Mom, Dad, Monica, Jeremy, Justin,
and all the various extended family
who have always cheered me on
and encouraged me in writing
from the time I was eleven years old
until now.

I also thank Michael Collins
who encouraged me to finish this book
and gave me his unbiased, constructive criticism.
I could not have written this first novel
without his help.

Introduction

Most of the time, the memories from when I was a little girl are vague and nondescript. Others are as clear as crystal. Those are the short ones—phrases, words, the expressions on a person's face. My memory from a certain church service is vague and nondescript, but one phrase a pastor spoke at that service is as clear as if I heard it yesterday. "The Hound of Heaven." Besides the fact that I knew it was the name of a poem, I don't remember anything else that was said. There was something very mysterious about that phrase, but still strangely familiar considering the fact that I'd never heard it before. Still, I knew instinctively that God was the Hound of Heaven. As I grew up, that phrase would come to my mind at various times and give me an odd mixture of pain and happiness deep down inside that was nearly impossible to describe or put into words.

I was seventeen or eighteen when I finally typed that phrase into a Google search, printed out the poem, and read it for the first time. Then I read it again. And again. And again. As I read, it seemed to put many missing pieces together in my mind. Growing up, I often experienced an incredible longing to fit in, to belong, to be admired and loved. Whether my perceptions were correct or not, I often felt that goal was just beyond my grasp. I never had a lot of friends. My personality was not glittery or charismatic. I was never the popular girl that everyone gravitated to. I was the other one, leaning awkwardly against the wall, wishing I had something to say or do that would make them all like me, severely regretting the thick glasses that were forever sliding down my nose. I often complained to my parents about my situation. Then one day, my dad said something similar to this, "You will never be happy unless the only person whose good opinion you really care about is God's. If you are God's child, He will keep taking things away from you, stripping away friends and your best hopes until you learn to love and rely on Him completely. And He does this out of love because He is the only one who can satisfy you."

When I read the poem, I saw the truth of what my dad said worded in a different way. Here in the poem was a man who ran from the Hound of Heaven in fear, grasping for love, friendship, the beauty of nature, while the Hound tore all of those things away systematically in an apparent cold-hearted disregard for the man's sorrow and loss. It is only at the end that the man, who has finally lost everything, realizes the Hound's motivation and his own blindness to it—love. "Thou dravest love from thee, who dravest me," says the Hound, as he tenderly lifts that miserable man out of the mound of ashes his life has become. God is love, and we can only experience that love in Him. Nothing else will do. Nothing else will satisfy. Nothing else can take its place. And nothing else but an unconditional surrender of our own will to God's can ever give it to us.

I began to think how I had been blessed with parents who loved me and taught me of the love of God. What about someone who did not have parents like mine? How would someone like that ever become convinced that God was love? It seemed so impossible. And then I remembered that God is the Hound of Heaven. He is the one that does the convincing, that pursues us throughout our lives. At that point, I began to write *The Pursuit of Elizabeth Millhouse*. The poem plays a prominent part in Elizabeth's life, appearing for the first time when she is a little girl and entering her thoughts throughout her life. Like the man in the poem, Elizabeth mistakes God for a cruel tyrant until she realizes what I did—that God's love is not manifested only in pleasantries. Often it is present in the most excruciating pain, through the best work that He does in our hearts.

Here, nearly a decade after I began writing Elizabeth's story, is the fruit of my labors. Take your time and enjoy.

Chapter 1

My name is Elizabeth Millhouse Brown. At one time, I made a name for myself, so perhaps you've heard of me. I was born to very wealthy parents on May 10, 1898, in a small college town in Pennsylvania. From a young age, I formed the impression that my birth must have been a mistake because my parents never seemed to care for me or for each other. A stony, icy set they were. The most affection I ever received from either of them was a dutiful kiss on the cheek or a pat on the head.

My mother reminded me of a picture of Rapunzel, the beautiful fairy-tale princess in one of my picture books. She was tall with a fair complexion and beautiful long blond hair that reached below her knees. My father was tall, dark, and handsome. They looked like a couple out of a fairy-tale book like Cinderella and Prince Charming perhaps. But whether they really loved each other was a debatable matter. The only testament to their love resided on the fourth finger of each of their respective left hands. I never saw them exchange so much as one fond look toward each other. They were continually at odds with one another, but always in a very dignified, respectable sort of way.

Mine was not a pleasant upbringing. I felt as if I were being held at arm's length or examined through an eyeglass. My first memory is of my nanny, a grim woman, lifting me out of my crib and washing me properly. Then she took me down to my mother's dressing room where Mother was sitting in front of her desk, writing.

She glanced at me and remarked, "Did she eat all of her breakfast this morning?"

"Most of it, ma'am; she didn't seem very hungry," Nanny said.

"Pale as usual," Mother remarked. "You'd better change her stockings. There's a stain."

On rare occasions, when my father was home from business, they would sometimes call me to the drawing room in the evening. Nanny would put on my best pinafore and take me down there. When we arrived, the following pattern would happen like clockwork every time.

Father would look up from his paper and say, "Good evening, Elizabeth."

"Good evening, sir," I'd reply.

Then I would kiss mother's cheek and sit in a chair, waiting until such time as one or the other of them looked up at the clock and noted that it was past my bedtime. Then Nanny would come and take me off to bed. On those nights, I had a lot of time to watch my parents. Mother read books sometimes, but most of the time she stared into the fire. Father, on the other hand, always read the paper. He would read everything to do with politics and the economy. Last of all he would read the column by Alexander Stonely, and it would always make him angry.

When he finished that column, he'd toss the paper on the stool, snort, and say bad words. I knew they were bad because Mother would lift an eyebrow and tell him that I was in the room. I wondered if maybe Mr. Stonely was the reason Mother and Father didn't like each other. Then Nanny took me to Mother's room where there were always letters addressed to Mr. Stonely on her dressing table. I never understood why; it was a puzzle to me.

My parents never showed any emotion besides a chilly sort of anger. There was nothing my mother hated worse than an emotional display. I learned never to cry or stamp my foot in anger when she or my father was present. I didn't laugh very often because there was seldom anything to laugh about that I could see. But on those rare occasions when I did want to laugh, I learned to follow the correct protocol. At the Christmas and New Year's Eve parties that Mother and Father hosted for example, they both laughed a great deal, but it was just polite laughing. I could tell from where I stood on such occasions, peering around the corner or through a keyhole that they weren't really laughing, not like the cook did downstairs when she was tickled about something.

When the guests left late at night, their voices floated up to the nursery and through the window where I lay in bed.

"What a charming woman Mrs. Millhouse is!"

"Oh, indeed. And my how well she plays the piano!"

"Didn't she look lovely in that gown?"

"Yes, I've heard she has one daughter, but I've never seen her. I wonder if she's as beautiful as her mother."

"I doubt it. She's probably an ugly duckling. Why else would they keep her out of sight?"

"Perhaps you're right."

I heard such comments all the time and I used to cry about them in my bed and pinch my cheeks and bite my lips to make myself look pretty. I thought that maybe if I was pretty, my parents would like me better, but it was no use. I was always getting sick, it seemed, and I spent a good portion of my first six years of life in bed. I was pale and skinny and tired most of the time.

By the time I was six, I'd given up all hope of being pretty, and I'd resigned myself to the fact that my parents would probably never love me.

So I looked for consolation in other things. I learned to love books, and having little to do but read, I learned rapidly. Nanny taught me to read the Bible first, and that was all I read for a year or so. For some reason, the story of Jonah and the whale held a kind of morbid fascination for me. I suppose it was because Jonah couldn't hide from God no matter how hard he tried. To me, the thought of God being everywhere and seeing everything was frightening.

I finally asked Nanny about it one day. "Nanny," I inquired, "is God really everywhere like the Bible says?"

"Of course he is." Nanny snorted.

"But how do you know? What if the Bible is wrong?" I persisted.

"Don't ever say such a thing again, Elizabeth! It's blasphemous."

The look on her face was enough to curdle milk. I was too afraid to utter another word, she looked so angry. For the next half hour, Nanny shifted uncomfortably in her rocker as she knitted. She kept looking at me and opening her mouth as if she wanted to say something but then shut it again. I think she felt badly for scolding me. But later on, she stood up, pulled the Bible out of the cupboard, and began paging through it.

"I remember this passage from Psalms," she said, more to herself than to me. "Whither shall I go from thy spirit? Or whither shall I flee from thy presence? If I ascend up into heaven, thou art there: if I make my bed in hell, behold, thou art there. If I take the wings of the morning, and dwell in the uttermost parts of the sea; even there shall thy hand lead me, and thy right hand shall hold me. If I say, surely the darkness shall cover me; even the night shall be light about me."

When she was done, she paused and looked at the clock, then declared, "Eight o'clock, Elizabeth. It's bedtime." She helped me into my nightgown and tucked the covers around me. She was about to take the lamp and close the door, but she hesitated and came back. She laid a hand on my forehead and asked, "Are you feeling all right, dear?"

"Yes, Nanny," I answered.

"Would you like me to leave the lamp until you fall asleep?" she asked.

That was a strange question for her. She'd never asked that before.

"Yes, Nanny," I said.

"Very well, then. Goodnight." She bent and kissed me and went out.

I felt tears coming to my eyes, but I wouldn't let myself cry until Nanny turned down the lamp and closed the door. From then on, I always felt as though I had a true friend in Nanny. She was grim and she was cross with me sometimes, but I think she did love me in her own way.

When I was seven, my health began to improve. Nanny took me for walks in the park and my color came back, although I stayed quite thin.

I saw my parents more often then, much to my dismay. Meals were such miserably silent affairs, and I felt like every move I made was being watched and scrutinized by my mother. Father didn't notice me much, however.

Mother began to set aside regular hours of study time for me. Besides my reading, Nanny taught me arithmetic, spelling, and writing, and I caught on quickly. Once a month Mother called me to her and fired question after question at me to see how I was coming along.

On one of these occasions, when I was eight years old, I remember Mother gave me more questions to answer and more problems to figure than usual. After I'd answered each one correctly, she leaned back in her chair and said, "She's not stupid."

She stared at me a while longer before she finally dismissed me. I knew that things were about to change. For one thing, the tension between my parents increased decidedly. The air between them seemed thick enough to slice. Whatever the problem was, they finally reached some sort of agreement. Mother called me to her about a week later.

"Elizabeth," she announced, "I've decided to send you away to school. I think you have the potential to become a good scholar."

She looked at me as though she expected me to say something, so I said, "Yes, ma'am. Will Nanny come too?"

Mother smiled and explained, "No. I've given her notice."

I went up to my room with a heavy heart. I wasn't especially attached to my home or my parents, but they were all I knew. The prospect of living in a strange place with new people was frightening, and I wouldn't see Nanny again, at least not for a very long time.

Mother went through all my clothes the following day, putting aside anything she thought was unsuitable for me. Then she had a dressmaker come in and fit me for a new wardrobe, and that was rather exciting. I'd set my heart on pink silk, but mother thought it was vulgar and chose material she deemed acceptable. I'm sure she was quite right in that respect, but it was hard to give up the idea. I let myself be measured and fitted and fussed over for about an hour. Then I grew tired of it and disappeared into the nursery to read *Alice's Adventures in Wonderland*. Nanny had given it to me as a farewell gift. I lost myself in Alice's adventures and almost forgot to worry about the future.

Two weeks later, my trunk was packed and ready to go. I waited by the door, dressed in my new coat, knowing that Mother would come soon. When she did, she took my hand and led me outside where Father helped us into the carriage. He told me to be a good girl and learn my lessons well. Then we were off to the train station.

I spent a long, silent hour on the train. Mother read a book the whole hour, and I stared out the window at the flashing scenery. I began to get a headache so I leaned back in my seat. The next thing I knew, Mother was shaking me awake. She took me by the hand and steered me through the crowd of people milling about at the station. From there we drove several miles out of the little town along winding roads. I assumed that the boarding school would be in town. But as the buildings and streets of the city gave way to fields and countryside, I began to feel as though I was entering a different world. I'd rarely traveled more than a few miles from home because of my precarious health, so I'd never been in the country before. I wasn't sure if I liked it. It was windy and cold, and leaves swirled down from the trees while the bare branches they left behind scraped against each other.

By the time the school came into view, it was beginning to get dark and I was chilled to the bone. I was too tired to pay much attention to the outside of the house. I only knew that it looked terribly big.

A man came outside and shouldered my trunk as Mother marched me up the steps after him. As soon as I walked in the door, I felt a hand on my shoulder so I looked up into a smiling pair of eyes. It was a woman about the same age as my mother, but she was so different.

"Mrs. Millhouse?" she questioned as she held out her hand.

"Yes," Mother said, returning the handshake.

"I'm Mrs. Woodward," she said, "and this must be Elizabeth." She shook my hand saying, "How are you, dear?"

"I'm fine, ma'am," I answered politely.

"Mrs. Millhouse, you have a beautiful daughter. You must be very proud of her."

Mother smiled briefly. "I would like to clarify a few particulars."

"Oh, yes," Mrs. Woodward said, springing into action. "Goodness me, I'm forgetting my manners. Won't you sit down?"

"I'm afraid not. I have to be back at the station in a half an hour."

"You won't be able to have a tour of the house then!" Mrs. Woodward looked terribly disappointed.

"That won't be necessary," Mother replied. "You've been highly recommended."

"Well, at least allow me to call my husband. He teaches science, grammar, and mathematics. I teach literature, history, geography, and etiquette, of course." Then she turned and shouted, "James!"

A door opened to the right and a man's head popped out. His hair was tousled, and his spectacles were on crooked. Girlish voices chanted pronouns in the background.

"James, would you come out here and meet our new pupil?"

"Certainly," he said.

"This is Elizabeth Millhouse," Mrs. Woodward said.

"Pleased to meet you, Elizabeth," he said as he shook my hand.

I wasn't sure why, but I decided that I liked Mr. Woodward the best. He had bushy eyebrows and hair that flew every which way. He had kind eyes, and his air of forgetfulness was comforting. As soon as he'd exchanged a few words with Mother, he excused himself and went back to his class.

"I'll be going now," Mother said. "Goodbye, Elizabeth. Learn your lessons well and be respectful." She bent down so I could kiss her cheek, and then she was gone.

I lay in bed that night, staring up at the ceiling. The wind whistled around the corners of the house, and tree branches made frightening shadows on the wall. But through the grate in the floor a light glowed, and I heard Mr. and Mrs. Woodward talking softly to one another. They sounded happy to be with each other. The girl in the bed next to mine was already asleep, and her soft, even breathing calmed me. I stared at the glow and felt warmed by its light and I slept.

Chapter 2

Mr. and Mrs. Woodward were a little astounded at all the information I carried in my little head. It took them only a few days to realize that I was far ahead of the other girls my age. Twenty girls, ranging in ages from six to sixteen, lived at the establishment, and I was ahead of girls two years older than me.

Most of the girls didn't know what to do with me. I kept to myself most of the time, but when I felt like being friendly everyone seemed to enjoy my company. But then the notion would pass, and I would be just as unfriendly as before. It was not the best way to win friends, but I didn't care. One particular girl tried to tease me into talking to her, but I got angry and gave her such a withering look that I scared her. After that, no one ever teased me again, and all the girls, even some of the older ones, were a little afraid of me.

In spite of it all, I had two friends that I always knew I could count on. The first was Genie and the second was Mr. Woodward. Genie was my roommate and she was the same age as me. She was a happy little girl who wouldn't be intimidated by my haughtiness. No matter what I said or did, Genie responded with a smile at best and a big hug at worst.

Mr. Woodward was a different kind of friend. Of course, I couldn't be haughty with him. I remember the first day I spent at school. I wandered around the house exploring and I came to an open door and looked in. There sat Mr. Woodward scrunched over his desk, squinting to read a manuscript because his spectacles were perched on top of his head instead of his nose. The room was, for all practical purposes, bursting at the seams with books.

I was going to go quietly away, but I sneezed, so he looked up and saw me standing there. I stared at him without saying anything wondering if I had done something wrong, but he smiled cheerfully and beckoned with his hand.

"Good morning!" he greeted me. "Now let me see if I can remember your name."

He furrowed his brow for a minute and said, "Emily?"

"No, I'm Elizabeth," I told him.

"Oh, that's right," he said. "Elizabeth, my God is bountiful."

I wrinkled my nose and cocked my head at him with a questionable look.

"That's what your name means. Did you know that?"

I shook my head.

"It's a beautiful name and a beautiful meaning. God is indeed bountiful. He gives so many things."

"What things?" I asked curiously.

"Well…that lovely blue sky," he said, pointing out the window, "the food we eat, that pretty dress you're wearing. Hmmm?" he mumbled as he tried to think of more things.

I bit my lip thoughtfully. "I don't know. I thought my parents bought it for me."

He threw back his head and laughed. "So, they did! What I mean is, that God gives us the air we breathe, the strength in our bodies, and the mental capacity to work and earn the money that buys things like that dress." Then with a sober look he added, "…in Him we live and move and have our being…" but he trailed off at my perplexed expression.

"Well, at any rate," he said, changing the subject, "how do you like Woodward's School for Girls? Are you homesick at all?"

I smiled slightly and replied, "No, sir."

"Good, I'm glad to hear that."

"You have a lot of books," I stated.

"I do at that," he chuckled. "Do you like to read?"

"Yes sir!"

"Maybe you'd like to have a look at them," he suggested as he searched the drawers of his desk for something.

"Yes, I would," I said. "What are you looking for?"

"I seem to have misplaced my spectacles," he answered, lifting a stack of papers to look underneath.

"They're on top of your head," I pointed out with a smile.

"So they are!" he laughed. "Now I think that my most favorite book when I was younger was Robinson Crusoe. I know I had it here on the desk just yesterday. Where are you, Robinson? Ah, there it is. I really must learn to put my things away. How would you like to try it?"

"Please!" I responded with enthusiasm.

"Here you are, then," he said, placing the book in my hands. "But don't go just yet! I have to give you something else. I'll find it shortly, you'll see."

He searched his drawer, then his trouser pockets, then his vest pocket. His efforts were almost painful to behold. He thumped his head and then his face brightened. He walked over to the closet and looked in his coat pocket.

"Here we are!" he announced. "Hold out your hand and close your eyes."

I felt something round and smooth in my hand and when I opened my eyes, I saw a piece of peppermint candy!

"All right now, out you go," he said, laughing at my delight. "I've got work to finish!"

So out I went, clutching my book and sucking my peppermint. From that day forward, I was a welcome guest at Mr. Woodward's study. Sometimes I just sat and chatted with him about this or that. When he was too busy to talk, I was content to read a book while the clock ticked and his pen scratched away at the paper.

I really don't know how that poor man ever got any peace of mind, for I wasn't the only admirer. Mr. Woodward got a steady stream of visitors throughout the day, but he never seemed to grow tired of us. He was always ready with a kind word and a peppermint or two. He amazed me.

In the months that followed, I became accustomed to my new schedule. We all rose at 6:30 every morning, dressed, and ate breakfast. First we assembled in the big room next to the living room where Mr. Woodward read a chapter from the Bible. After that, we sang a few hymns, recited verses from Scripture, and prayed. Then we were off to classes until lunch time. After lunch, we finished our assignments, tidied our rooms, and the rest of the afternoon we were allowed to play outside or do whatever we pleased, within reason.

At first, I didn't like to be outside that much because I wasn't used to it. But I wasn't used to being around so many people either so sometimes I slipped outside just to escape the noise. The house and out buildings were surrounded on three sides by farmland and on the fourth side was a great clump of trees. I wandered about quite a bit just thinking, and before long, I came to enjoy being outdoors. Sometimes, when it was bitter cold out, I stepped inside the barn to visit with Walter, the Woodwards hired help, while he tended the horses and finished chores. When he was too busy, I played with the kittens that tumbled around in the hay.

Walter thought that I was a funny specimen. He was always laughing at the things I'd say.

"Landsakes, Missie! You's just a little woman!" was his most characteristic expression.

By Christmas time, I'd spent a month at Woodward's School for Girls. How well I remember the day Mother's first letter arrived. We were busy with preparations for the Christmas program and I was helping Genie hang glass bulbs on the Christmas tree when Mr. Woodward called me into his office. He was even more kind with me than usual. When he asked if I was enjoying the Christmas season, I replied, "Of course." I wondered for a moment if that was the only reason he'd pulled me away from all the fun. Then he asked how I'd like to spend Christmas vacation with him and Mrs. Woodward.

"Mother doesn't want me to come home, does she?" I asked knowingly.

He looked a little startled. "Yes," he answered, 'she'd like you to stay at school this time."

"Then I must stay," I said. "May I go back and help Genie now?"

That night after Genie was asleep, I crept out of bed to look out the window. I heard Mr. and Mrs. Woodward talking downstairs.

"Did you tell Elizabeth that she's staying here for the holidays?"

"Yes," Mr. Woodward said.

"How did she take it?"

I heard Mr. Woodward sigh and then reply, "Who's to know? I wish I could read her mind. For the faintest moment, I thought she might cry. But the next minute, she looked like she always does. Maybe I was imagining things."

"Poor dear," Mrs. Woodward said.

I got back in bed and pulled the covers over my head. I squeezed my eyes shut, but a few tears managed to slip through anyway. The truth was I did care. I'd hoped that if I studied hard and made good grades, Mother would be proud of me and let me go home even if I wasn't very pretty. But it didn't seem to matter that I was at the top of my class in every subject or that I was ahead of girls two or three years older than me. Nothing I ever did pleased Mother.

I clenched my fists and whispered to myself, "One day, I'm going to be famous and rich, and then Mother will be sorry!"

I cried myself to sleep that night with this unwholesome thought in my mind. The next morning, I presented my usual placid face at the breakfast table. I doubt if anyone ever suspected that my heart was breaking.

On Saturday, all the girls except me were packed and ready to leave. In the afternoon the sleighs began to arrive filled with parents who'd come to see the Christmas program. Soon the parlor was packed. My parents weren't there, even though they'd been invited.

The program wasn't long. I was chosen to recite a poem at the beginning, and we all sang several Christmas carols. Then Mr. Woodward read the Christmas story as a troop of giggling girls wrapped in dressing gowns and wearing towels on their heads acted out the parts of the shepherds and wise men and Mary and Joseph. We sang one more carol, and then it was over. The guests milled around, sipping hot chocolate and eating cookies while the girls laughed and admired each other's dresses. But I slipped upstairs and went to my room. I knelt beside the window and watched as one by one, the sleighs began to leave.

A few minutes later, Genie ran in and smothered me with a hug.

"Here, Elizabeth," she said, putting a small package into my hands, "Merry Christmas!"

"I didn't get anything for you, Genie," I said slowly.

"I don't mind," Genie said, as the wrapping fell away and a little hand-stitched doll smiled crookedly at me. "Now you won't get lonely. You'll think of me every time you look at her."

"Thank you," I said. "Goodbye."

I felt desolate after she'd gone. The house was getting quieter, and soon I'd have to go to bed. I looked at Genie's doll by the light of the moon, and it was beautiful to me, crooked face and all, and I hugged it close.

I heard footsteps on the stairs, and Mrs. Woodward came in carrying a candle and a tray with hot chocolate and cookies on it.

"What are you doing up here in the dark, Elizabeth?!" she exclaimed, setting the tray down on the stand by the bed. She wagged her finger at me and said, "You'd better put on your warm nightgown and get into bed before you catch a cold."

Suddenly, the night seemed just a little brighter, and my heart was almost light as I snuggled under the covers. We drank hot chocolate and ate cookies together, and then she sat by the lamp and knitted until I fell asleep. I remember thinking drowsily that it would've been nice if Mrs. Woodward were my mother.

The holidays passed quite pleasantly for me. I spent a lot of time in Mr. Woodward's study eating more than my fair share of peppermints. Mrs. Woodward and I made a gingerbread house, and I read to my heart's content.

On Christmas morning, we all gathered around the Christmas tree, and Mr. Woodward solemnly presented me with my first journal. He told me that if I wrote in it every day about things that happened that day, when I was very old, I could read it and remember what had happened on December 25, 1906. It sounded like a grand idea to me, and I sat right down and wrote in it.

Mr. and Mrs. Woodward and I spent a quiet two weeks together, and then the other scholars returned. I was almost sad to see them arrive. I'd come to enjoy having the Woodwards all to myself. But with the arrival of Genie, all such thoughts flew out the window. She bounced in like a sunbeam, bringing happiness to everyone.

The girls had a day to get settled, and then we began work in earnest. I worked harder than anyone because I was determined to be the best. I would prove to my mother that she couldn't ignore me for long. I'd learn everything that I could possibly learn. I would do something great.

I was so driven by these goals that I was oblivious to everything else. The others began calling me "Elizabeth the Bore" because all I did was study. I didn't talk to the girls much because I didn't have time, and frankly, I liked being left alone. I never thought I was very unusual for a seven-year-old. Even now, when I look at other young children, I find myself thinking that they all act rather childishly. And then I realize that it's how children are supposed to act, and I wonder what I would've been like if I'd been born into different circumstances.

The only person that I had time for besides the Woodwards was Genie. She was the one who stood up for me when the other girls complained about my sour disposition. Genie was rather in awe of me because she wasn't a very good student. She had dreadful times with arithmetic, and she couldn't spell worth two cents. She could never remember what a noun was, and she didn't even know the year that Columbus discovered America. But for some reason, it didn't matter to me. Genie was someone I could tell my secrets to and know that she wouldn't think they were silly.

She could come up with some pretty silly things herself though. She told me the most interesting fairy tales at night in a low whisper. They generally began with a fair maiden in distress and ended up with a daring rescue by a knight in shining armor. But she always added little twists and turns that made me laugh out loud. She kept this up until Mrs. Woodward knocked on the floor from downstairs with her broom and admonished us to go to sleep.

When spring came, Genie and I played outdoors. Genie made up all of the games, of course. Sometimes we'd just walk beside the big field that belonged to the farmer next door, talking about grown up things such as what kind of men we were going to marry and how many children we'd have. Genie proclaimed that she was going to have twenty. I wasn't sure if I wanted any, but I supposed I'd have to have some.

On one of these walks in late spring, we stopped to watch the farmer and his son plow the fields. It was warm enough to go without coats, and the sun was shining brightly and the birds were chirping. Genie called it a cheerful day. She took time to be unladylike by whistling through her thumbs with a blade of grass.

Maybe it was because the day was so beautiful and happy that I was filled with a longing to be a part of it all. Maybe, I don't know. I saw the farmer and his son working in the field. The boy looked so carefree and happy, like he didn't have one single thing to worry about. I just felt like I had to tell Genie about what I wanted to be and do, only I didn't know what I wanted to be and do. I just wanted to be anything but average. I wanted people to take notice when they heard of me. But because I couldn't put everything I felt into words, I just stared at Genie in desperation, wishing she could read my mind.

"What's wrong, Elizabeth?" she asked.

"I want to do something important someday, Genie," I said, "something that no one has ever done before!"

Genie looked at me soberly for a little while and asked, "Do you think you'll be happy then?"

"I don't know," I quickly answered.

The question took me by surprise, and I just stared at the dirt. Then I turned to look across the field at the farmer and his son with their overalls rolled up around their ankles. The boy glanced up, flashed us a big smile, and waved. Genie waved back, but I was too preoccupied with my confusing thoughts. *What if it didn't make me happy to be important? But it has to,* I thought. *That's how life is. Mother and Father are important because they have lots of money. Mother has admirers because she is beautiful. Father has business associates that respect him and ask him for advice. But are Mother and Father happy?* I wondered.

"Well," Genie said with a laugh, "when you get famous, don't forget me."

Then she smiled at me and we went back to the house. It was almost time for supper.

Chapter 3

When I was nine, I received a package in the mail that changed my life. I found it on my bed after Genie and I had run in from outside, our cheeks rosy with exercise and sunshine. Mrs. Woodward didn't often hand out mail this way. Usually we received mail during opening exercises before classes began, but she must have overlooked this package. I never got letters. The only word I heard from home came through the Woodwards when Mother would write to them. So I stood and stared at this package. The sender was someone I didn't recognize, a certain Jane Poleson. But my name was written there in a familiar hand so I sat down and tore the wrapping off. It was a little book, like a copy book, and there was a message written inside the front cover.

Dear Elizabeth,
    I've thought of you so much since you went away to school. I hope you're strong and well. I take care of another little girl now, and she's full of questions like you were. She's a dear girl, but she's not as smart as you are!
    I remember your questions about God and my inability to answer them. I feel like I failed you somehow. I've believed in God since I was very small, but I didn't know how to explain Him. I still don't know how to explain Him, but I know that we must believe in Him. He's all we have for life. If you take Him away, there's nothing left. I still pray for answers.
    Do you remember asking me if God is really everywhere? I read this poem recently and copied it into this book for you. It's very long and sometimes hard to understand, but you're such an intelligent girl I know you can manage it. God bless you!
    Love,
    Nanny

I was happy to hear from Nanny again, although she sounded a little confused. I opened the book and my eyes went to the title, *The Hound of Heaven* by Francis Thompson. It was written in a very neat, meticulous hand, and I smiled thinking how like Nanny the handwriting was. I almost considered closing the book up and putting it in my drawer. I didn't care much for poetry, and this was such a long poem. But then I felt a little guilty about that, considering how long it must have taken her to copy it out, and she had such faith in my ability to understand it. I decided I should read at least part of it. And it wasn't long before I hadn't the slightest intention of stopping. The words seemed to jump off the page and burn into my heart.

> I fled Him, down the nights and down the days,
>   I fled Him down the arches of the years;
> I fled Him, down the labyrinthine ways
>   Of my own mind; and in the mist of tears
> I hid from Him, and under running laughter.
>   Up vistaed hopes I sped;
>   And shot, precipitated,
> Adown Titanic glooms of chasmed fears,
> From those strong Feet that followed, followed after.
>   But with unhurrying chase,
>   And unperturbed pace,
> Deliberate speed, majestic instancy,
>   They beat—and a Voice beat
>   More instant than the Feet—
> "All things betray thee, who betray Me."

I couldn't put it down until I'd read all one hundred and eighty lines. And then I started over again. Many parts in the poem made no sense at all to me, and I didn't understand some of the words. But I did understand that the author was running away from a hound that was God, and that God kept stripping things away, sniffing him out, and tracking him down until he was cornered like Jonah and the whale. *But why?* I wondered. *Was God chasing me like that?* The old fear began to return. I wished Nanny hadn't sent the poem.

I remembered recently watching a stray dog loping across the farmer's field, his nose to the ground. He was tracking a rabbit. Genie and I saw the poor creature scrambling to get away, but the dog eventually caught up with it. He had it by the throat and shook it. Soon, the rabbit hung limp from the dog's jaws. I was trembling inside when the dog finally trotted away, the rabbit swinging from side to side in time to the dog's steps.

As I lay in bed that night, questions tumbled around in my mind. *Does God see me right now?* I thought. *Is He chasing me? What does He want with me? God is supposed to love, so how can He hunt me down and love me at* the same time? Maybe He only loves people like the Woodwards. They're so good. But I'm not, I hate my Mother. He must want to punish me.

The last few lines from the poem were repeating themselves in my mind as I fell asleep.

Ah, fondest, blindest, weakest,
I am He whom thou seekest!
Thou dravest love from thee, who dravest Me!

But I couldn't understand it. I just couldn't…

AT NINE YEARS OLD, time seems to stretch out indefinitely. It was no different for me. By the time the summer holidays rolled around, it seemed like I'd been at school for years. And once again, Mother sent word that I was to stay at school.

The day before the students all left, I sat on my bed upstairs, watching Genie pack her clothes. Genie's usually bright face was drooping that day. She'd been crying earlier. She told me that she was "school sick" already, even though she wasn't gone yet.

"I'm going to miss you, Elizabeth," she said.

I nodded but I didn't say anything because I had a funny feeling in my throat, and I thought I might cry. Three months without Genie seemed like an eternity.

Mrs. Woodward called me to help her wrap up some sandwiches she was sending with the girls that were leaving. When I came back, I found Genie on her knees in front of her bed, praying.

"…and please help Elizabeth not to be sad and lonely," she prayed. "And help her to have a good time while all of us are gone. Amen."

I tiptoed out of the room before she saw me. I thought that God couldn't help but love Genie. I hoped He would answer her prayer.

I felt just as lonely as I had at Christmas time when the last girls left. I clutched Genie's doll close to me that night as the shadows deepened. The room seemed too quiet, and I wished morning would come.

But soon the loneliness dissipated. I was always a little melancholy, but I still managed to enjoy the summer. When Mrs. Woodward could pull me away from my books long enough to send me outside, I often went for long walks. Sometimes, I'd sneak a book out with me, and I'd hunker down under one of the trees that lined the farmer's field and read to my heart's content. Other times, I took my sketch book and pencil and improved my talent for drawing. From my vantage point, I could watch the farmer and his son as they planted and cultivated. They always waved when they spotted me. But as the crop grew, I said goodbye to my two friends and watched the golden wheat swishing back and forth in the breeze until harvest time, just listening to the sounds of summer.

But I had a disappointment in store. About three weeks before summer vacation ended, I found out that Genie wouldn't be coming back. It seemed her parents finally recognized that academics were not Genie's strong point and decided to hire a tutor to work with her at home. Just like that, Genie left my life, and the only evidence that she'd ever been there to begin with was the doll with the crooked face. I put her in a box, dragged a stool to the wardrobe, and stuck it on the top shelf. I didn't want to be reminded of what I had lost.

Chapter 4

That winter, shortly before the New Year, Mr. Woodward called me into his office. I felt that something was not quite right. I'd never been called to the office in this way to hear good news, so I braced myself for whatever he might tell me. He was holding a letter in his hands that I could tell was from Mother, judging from the handwriting on the envelope.

"Elizabeth," he began, "your mother is sending for you. Your father is very sick, and she thinks you should come home for a little while. She wants you to leave as soon as possible."

"Travel on a train all by myself?" I asked in alarm.

"I'd be glad to take you, if you'd like," he assured me.

I did like actually, so Mrs. Woodward soon had me packed and ready to go, and we boarded the train at noon. Mr. Woodward had brought a book to read to me as we went along, but I couldn't keep my mind on it. My thoughts wandered off to that imposing mansion called home and to the sick man that lay dying there. I stared out the window at the drifting snow, my heart as chilled as the landscape. As my hometown came into view and the train gradually slowed down, Mr. Woodward turned to me.

"Pray to God about your trouble, Elizabeth," he said. "He loves you."

"Does He?" I asked.

"Yes," he assured me with a smile.

But then I looked out the window and caught a glimpse of Mother as she waited for me, standing straight, head turned to the side showing a perfect profile, looking hard as flint.

"No," I quietly said in response. "No, I don't think He does."

I didn't see Father right away. Mother sent me to my room for several hours to rest and unpack. In the evening she brought me to his room. The doctor was just leaving and told Mother not to let me stay very long. The curtains were drawn over the windows and I smelled medicine and smoke from the fireplace. The air felt heavy and old. Father's face was drawn and white and the blankets swallowed up his body. But when he saw me, he sat up and held out a thin, wasted hand.

"Come here, Elizabeth," he said the way Mr. Woodward would have said it. His eyes were bright and he looked happy to see me.

I felt a smile coming to my own face as I went to him. Mother shut the door behind me and we were alone. I sat on the bed holding his hand, wondering at the change that had come over him. The distracted man with the newspaper was gone and in his place was a frail and thoughtful one.

"I think the country agrees with you," he said. "You look pretty and healthy."

I smiled again, my heart leaping inside me. Had he really just said that?

"Thank you, sir."

"How do you like school?" he asked.

"I like it, sir. The Woodwards are nice. Mr. Woodward gives me candy sometimes, but not too much. It doesn't make me sick. I'm ahead of my class."

"Are you? And do you miss home?"

I thought a moment and then said, "No sir, not much."

As soon as the words were out of my mouth, I wished I could take them back again. My father's eyes glistened with tears, and he turned his face to the wall.

"I'm sorry, sir," I said fearfully, "I didn't mean to say anything wrong."

"Don't call me sir anymore, Elizabeth." His voice was muffled. "Call me Papa."

"Yes, Papa," I whispered.

He stared at the wall for a long time and then looked back, and the pain in his eyes was too great for me. I stared at the blankets instead of looking at him.

"I should never have let her send you away," he said. "I should've been a better father. Look at me, Elizabeth," he said. When I did, he made me a promise. "I will be a better father. I'll begin now."

Then Mother opened the door and said it was time to leave.

"I'd better go," I told him.

"Yes," he said, squeezing my hand. "But you must come back tomorrow. Come back tomorrow morning, as soon as you wake up."

"I will, Papa. I promise."

"Goodnight, my dear."

"Goodnight, Papa. I'll see you in the morning."

When I woke up the next morning, the sun was shining and I thought of Papa. I dressed quickly and tiptoed down the stairs. I opened the door and saw Papa sitting up in bed. He looked so much improved. There was color in his face and his breathing was stronger.

"Good morning, Papa!"

"Come sit with me," he said. So I rushed over and I sat on the bed and held his hand.

"It's too dark in here, Papa. We should let in the sun."

"Well, then. Go open the curtains." I pushed the heavy curtains aside with great effort, standing on a chair to tie them back.

"Do you mind sitting with me, Elizabeth?" he asked. "You'd rather be playing, I suppose."

"No," I assured him. I thought a minute and an idea came to me. "Mr. Woodward let me borrow Robinson Crusoe. I could read it to you!"

"I'd like that," he responded.

I ran up the stairs to my room, two steps at a time, grabbed the book and began to run back down the stairs. But I saw Mother and quickly slowed down and walked properly.

"Where are you going, Elizabeth?"

"I'm going to read to Papa," I replied.

"He must be improved," she said to herself. "Well, go along then. I'll come with you."

Mother stopped at the door while I went in ahead of her. She looked at my father's happy face strangely, hesitantly.

"The light doesn't hurt your eyes?" she asked.

"Not today," he answered.

"Very well, then. Don't keep him up too long, Elizabeth."

She left, shutting the door behind her.

I spent two hours reading and talking to my father until the doctor came and spoiled the fun. I had to go upstairs again and pass the time in my room. Father had looked so much better that I began to think he couldn't possibly die. He'd get well, he had to get well. I couldn't lose him now. Maybe I could live at home and see him every day. I would miss the Woodwards, but they'd come and visit I felt sure. I'd go to school like other girls and walk home in the afternoon and wait for Father to arrive in the evening. We'd talk together at supper time and sit together after supper with Mother in the drawing room, but I wouldn't let him read the newspaper. Then he wouldn't get angry.

But what if he doesn't get well? I wondered. *What then?*

It was too hard to think about, so for a week I didn't think about it. Father seemed to improve so much in that week. He even stood up and walked a few unsteady steps with the nurse's help. But then on Sunday evening, he began to have more trouble breathing. He tried to sit up when I came to say goodnight, but the effort was too much, and he lay back in bed gasping for air.

"Goodnight Papa," I whispered.

"I...love...you," he struggled to say. It seemed like my heart stopped beating. It was the first time anyone had said that to me.

"I love you too," I answered. "I'll see you in the morning."

I bent down and kissed his cheek and went to the door. I turned to look back at him, and he smiled but his eyes were sad again. I went to my room and knelt down beside my bed to say my prayers, but I couldn't chant my usual, "Now I lay me down to sleep..."

Then I remembered what Mr. Woodward had said to me, "Talk to God about your trouble, Elizabeth. He loves you."

"Dear God," I began. My heart was too full, and I didn't know what to pray. So I simply said, "Dear God, please let Papa get well. Please don't let him die."

I fell sound asleep that night, almost as soon as my head touched the pillow. But I dreamed I heard footsteps coming and going down the hallways and up the stairs of our house. I heard smothered whispers. I felt my father's hand in mine and heard him say, "Goodnight, my dear."

Sometime in the early morning, I woke up suddenly. The house was still. I went downstairs in my nightgown, and I opened the door to Papa's room. It was dark so I opened the curtains, and the sun's rays fell on Papa's face. It was white and set like marble, and when I bent to kiss him, he was so cold. I took his stiff hand between both of mine to warm it, but he didn't wake up.

"Elizabeth." Mother put her hand on my shoulder. "He's gone now," she said. "There's a black dress laid out on your bed. Go put it on." I simply obeyed.

It seemed a very hard thing to me, as I sat gazing at the white face of my father, to think of what could have been. Mother sat beside me, rigid, white-faced, and impassive, while the minister read the usual portions of Scripture on death and dying. He told of my father's life, his membership in church, his many gifts to charity, his goodness, and his brave death in the midst of pain. At the cemetery, I threw a flower into that gaping hole in the ground and watched as the clods of dirt bruised its petals. Then we went home, and Mother shut herself in her room.

I climbed the stairs to my own room, my feet dragging. I looked at myself in the mirror contemplating my black dress.

"Is that all?" I asked the mirror.

Tears came to my eyes, but I dashed them away. Words from the poem sprang unbidden to my mind.

I pleaded, outlaw-wise,
By many a hearted casement, curtained red,
Trellised with intertwining charities...
But, if one little casement parted wide,
The gust of His approach would clash it to.
Fear wist not to evade, as Love wist to pursue.

"I hate You," I whispered then to God. "I hate You."

After a month had passed, Mother sent me back to school. When I got to my old room, the first thing I did was pull the box down from the wardrobe shelf. I took the poem out of its place in my drawer and put it in the box with Genie's doll. Then I closed the box and put it back on the shelf, and that's where it would stay for the next eight years. I stopped praying to God. I stopped thinking about Him. I tried my best to daydream during opening exercises when Mr. Woodward would read from the Bible or when we had to read aloud as a group. The day after I returned, we stood together and read these words, "Thou shalt love the Lord thy God with all thy heart, and with all thy soul, and with all thy mind. This is the first and great commandment. And the second is like unto it, Thou shalt love thy neighbour as thyself."

Thou shalt, thou shalt, I thought. But then I decided, *I won't!* I determined to live my life without Him from then on.

Chapter 5

For the next eight years, only a handful of events stick out in my memory. The rest is a blur. I grew from a little girl into a tall young woman. I went home only once a year to have clothes made and visit Mother. But we were perfect strangers to one another. And so, Mrs. Woodward played the part of mother to me when my body began to change and reshape itself. All the talks that I should have had with my mother, I had to have with Mrs. Woodward instead.

After my father died, I became reconciled with the fact that I'd never find the love and acceptance that I craved from my mother. So I gave up trying to please her academically and began to study for myself, mostly to discover what level of excellence I could achieve. I still had such a longing to do something important, something that would bring me fame and admiration. But what that something was, I still didn't know. In the meantime, I studied as if my life depended upon it. Other than the Woodwards, my books were all I had and were all I cared for.

The habit of journaling that Mr. Woodward had instilled in me so long before grew stronger as I got older. Hardly a day went by that I didn't write something. Sometimes I illustrated my journals with drawings of birds, the old cat in the stable, Mr. Woodward and his wild hair, or anything that went along with what I happened to be writing about.

One journal entry that deserves notice is the one marked May 21, 1913:

Dear Journal,

I'm afraid the farmer has died. I saw him and his son several weeks ago when they began plowing, but he looked very ill that day. He stopped quite a bit to catch his breath, and the boy would stop and look at him. He finally went back to the house, and his son finished the plowing alone. I haven't seen him since that time. I'm sitting beside the field now as I write, and the farmer's son is planting alone. He doesn't wave to me anymore. I don't think he even sees me.

I think he's going to leave soon. Last week, I saw a "For Sale" sign by the field close to the road. Walter says it's been sold already. I'll miss him and the farmer. It won't be the same without them.

Two weeks later, he did leave. I stood looking out my bedroom window as he trudged up the road, a bag slung over his shoulder and his eyes to the ground. He stopped a moment to look back at the farm, and in turning, he saw me in the window. He lifted his cap and smiled, a sad phantom of the old one, and he waved with his free hand. I waved back and wished him well in my heart.

The following year, all the news was of the assassination of some important man I'd never heard of before—Archduke Ferdinand. Powerful people are always and forever killing each other. So why that particular incident sparked a chain of events that put the world at war, I didn't understand then nor do I to this day. Always cursed with a vivid imagination, I tried my best to keep away from the newspapers. Otherwise, I thought horrible thoughts of muddy trenches, explosions, and dead bodies.

Perhaps because of all the talk of war, periods of gloom would settle down on me like a thick, black cloud. They came and went without any warning. Suddenly, life would seem worthless and futile and dark. When these moods were upon me, I could scarcely drag myself out of bed in the morning. And then, without warning, they'd be gone without a trace. Mrs. Woodward tried to convince me to seek God and read the Bible when I felt the gloom coming on, but I wouldn't hear of it. Hadn't God allowed this war?

It was three years after the assasination when my life changed again. Shortly after my eighteenth birthday, Mother wrote me. It was the first letter I'd ever received from her. She said:

I've been watching your progress and now feel that you've learned all that you can from the Woodward establishment. You'll return home next week. Your ticket is enclosed. We'll discuss your future when you arrive.
—*Mother*

Different emotions raged inside of me as I read it. I was sad, confused, hopeful, and angry all at once. I'd always known that this day would have to come. I knew that I wouldn't be able to live at school the rest of my life. But it was so sudden, and I felt like the floor had collapsed under me. I was angry at the cool way in which Mother had ordered me home, as if I were not a living, breathing human with feelings and emotions.

My only hope lay in the last line of the letter, "We'll discuss your future when you arrive." Maybe she meant to send me to college. I'd entertained hopes of going to college for about a year now. Then after I hoped, I worried.

I wondered if she'd be ashamed of my looks. I thought I was quite ugly, after all. I had blond hair like mother's, but my eyes were brown while her and father's had been blue. She was tall and so was I, but I tended to slouch, while she stood ramrod straight. My nose was too long, my teeth were too crooked, and my hair was too straight. It was torture for me to look in a mirror, thinking the contrast between me and my mother was so great.

Then memories of that mansion called home came back to haunt me, and as I remembered, every ounce of fortitude seemed to drain out of me until I felt as limp as a rag doll. The isolated and lonely childhood was in the forefront of my mind. I tried to convince myself that things would be different now that I was older and didn't mind being alone. I lay down on my bed, trying not to think too much.

Mrs. Woodward found me there a few hours later. She read Mother's letter and shed some tears herself. "God knows best, Elizabeth," she said as she stroked my hair. "I knew we couldn't keep you here forever, but I'll miss you so much."

I spent the next few days packing my things and saying my last goodbyes. I'm sure most of the girls were glad I was leaving. But I was on speaking terms with a few of them. I had to visit my favorite spot by the field for the last time. It was misting, and the field looked barren and sad. I could see a little wisp of smoke coming from the chimney of the house where the new farmer lived with his wife and baby. I stopped by the stable to chat with Walter and pat all of the horses and hold the new batch of kittens. There were no kittens in Mother's mansion, and she certainly wouldn't allow me to fraternize with the stable boys.

"You sure has growed up, Missie," Walter told me. "I be right sorry to see you leave."

I was sorry too. He was a dear heart.

I'll never forget the tears that welled up in Mr. and Mrs. Woodward's eyes as they stood with me at the train station. Mrs. Woodward hugged me. Mr. Woodward squeezed my hand as he said, "Goodbye, Elizabeth. God bless you."

He slipped something into my bag and helped me up onto the train. I put a hand on my hat as I made my way along the isle to my seat. The young man in the seat opposite mine stood up and hoisted my suitcase to the shelf overhead. I sat down and looked into my bag to see what Mr. Woodward had given me. The train began to move as the scent of peppermint reached my nose and red and white candies spilled into my lap. That was the last straw. I jumped to my feet, mints spilling everywhere, and waved frantically out the window at the Woodwards. I waved and waved until I couldn't see them anymore.

When I turned around, the young man was kneeling on the floor, picking up all the mints I'd dropped.

"Oh, dear, I'm so sorry!" I apologized, bending down to help.

"That's quite alright," he replied with a smile.

He pulled out his handkerchief and handed it to me. I hadn't even known I was crying. I took the handkerchief, my face turning hot with embarrassment. He quietly picked up every last peppermint and put them back in the bag and then handed them to me.

"You must be a student at the Woodward's school," he said.

"I am...or was," I replied. "I'm finished now."

"I see." He sat down and leaned towards me. "And now you're returning home?"

"Yes," I answered, hoping my eyes weren't too red.

He kept staring at me and then grinned sheepishly, "Pardon me for being so rude, but you look familiar to me. I used to live at the farm by the Woodward's school. I remember there was a little girl that lived at the school who used to come out by the field and watch us when my father and I were working. You look like her."

Suddenly, I knew who he was and wondered why I hadn't seen it before. "I'm that girl!" I said with surprise.

"Are you really? I didn't know for sure. You're all grown up now. " He laughed and I joined in. "Where are you heading?" he asked.

I named my hometown, and he laughed again, "I live there too. What a coincidence!"

"And what do you do?"

"I'm a reporter for the Gazette."

"I'm so glad that you've been successful. I hoped you would be."

"Well, I'm not living high on the hog, but I'm not playing an accordion in the streets either. I have a place of my own now." We smiled delightedly at each other, but we didn't say anything for the next few minutes.

"Oh, my name is Christian Brown," he suddenly added.

"Pleased to meet you. I'm Elizabeth Millhouse."

There were so many things I would've liked to ask him. I wanted to know how his father died, how he'd faired until he got a job, and how he became a reporter. But I didn't want to be impolite, and besides that, it was much more pleasant to look at him while he asked the questions. He'd turned into a handsome young man. His eyes caught my attention first. I'd never seen them up close before. They were a mixture of blue and gray and green—I couldn't tell what exactly to call them. They changed with the light. His face was angular and pointed. One minute, he looked stern and serious, and then he smiled and turned into a happy-go-lucky boy again. He rested his hat on his knee and his shirt sleeves were rolled up to his elbows so I could see his arms. They were strong and brown.

"Are you excited to be going home?" he asked.

It was a hard question to answer. If I said no, then he would ask me why, and I didn't know how to explain. I felt awkward, sitting there saying nothing. But when I looked at him again, I instinctively knew he wouldn't criticize my answer or think badly of me. His face was open and kind like Mr. Woodward's, and so I disregarded the question and gave him the explanation for it instead.

"I don't know my mother," I said. "Not well, that is. I've been away at school for nine years."

"Surely, you've been home to visit. Summer vacation…holidays…"

His voice trailed off as I shook my head.

"The days I've spent at home from school would amount to maybe a month or two if you added them all together. Mother didn't like me to come home for holidays. So I stayed at school. And when I did come home, Mother and I didn't see much of each other."

At his incredulous stare, I added, "It's a very large house."

"I see." He thought a moment and then asked, "Do you have any plans then? Things you'd like to do now that you're finished with school?"

"I don't really know. Mother said we'd talk about it when I get back home. I've thought that I'd like to go on learning, go to college perhaps."

"Ah," he nodded. "And what would you study?"

"I don't know that either." I stared down at my lap and then glanced up at him. "You must think I'm foolish."

"Not at all," he assured me. "No one could think that."

A lull descended on the conversation with both of us lost in our own thoughts.

"Would you like a peppermint?" I asked. "The least I can do is to offer you one after all your help."

"I believe I would," he responded.

The way he smiled set my heart to thumping in a way it never had before.

I found I couldn't look at him anymore without blushing to the roots of my hair, so I sucked my mint and stared out the window. The effect he had on me took me by surprise. I felt happy, shy, and confident all at once, and the combination was enough to make me dizzy. We spent the hour on the train alternating between conversation and a comfortable and happy silence. But when the train approached our destination, my heart sank, knowing I would have to say goodbye soon. As the train slowed to a stop, Christian stood up, got my bags down for me, and insisted upon carrying them down the steps to the platform.

I gave him my hand and thanked him.

"Well, goodbye then," I said. "I'm so glad we ran into one another."

"I wouldn't say goodbye yet," he smiled. "This isn't such a large town. We may run into each other again."

"Yes, I suppose you're right." I smiled up at him and then cleared my throat. "Well, until then."

He lifted his hat and went on his way. I watched him as he disappeared into the crowd, his coat slung over an arm. I wondered if I really would see him again. I knew that I wanted to, that was for sure.

Chapter 6

A few minutes after I parted with Christian, I stood in front of my home, my hand resting on the wrought iron fence that surrounded the property. It rose above me in the meticulous splendor that I remembered so well. There wasn't a stray branch on the green lawn, and the shrubs were perfectly sculpted.

"I'll take your luggage up to your room, miss," the chauffer told me.

I nodded and followed him to the door. When I stepped inside the house, Mother wasn't there to greet me. Instead she'd sent the maid to inform me that she was busy and that we would talk tomorrow after I'd had a good night's rest. Instant gloom settled over me as I stood in the hall looking up once again at the tall ceilings and elegant furnishings.

"Thank you, Rachel," I said, removing my hat and handing it to her.

"Would you like a bath before supper, miss?"

"Yes. I'll be up in a while."

"Very good, miss. And if I may be so bold, you've grown into a lovely young lady."

"Thank you," I smiled.

I went into the drawing roomm but there was no blaze this time in the enormous fireplace at the far end of the room. It gaped at me as if trying to remember where it had seen me before. Father's chair was on one side and Mother's chair on the other. Against the wall was the little stool I had sat on many years ago while Father read his newspaper and Mother stared into the flames.

I walked through the house, stopping beside my Father's bedroom. I wanted to go inside but the door was locked.

"Oh, Rachel," I said as she bustled past me. "Do you have the key to this room?"

"Well, yes, miss. But are you sure you want to go in there?"

"Yes," I assured her.

She unlocked it and went away, and I closed the door behind me. The curtains were closed to keep the bed linens from fading, I suppose, but I opened them anyway. I sat on the bed, and then I curled up on it. I could almost see Mother looking in through the door with that strange expression on her face. I could almost hear my father's rasping voice.

"I...love...you," I remembered vividly.

After a few minutes, I got up and left and went into the bathroom where Rachel had drawn the water for me. I was sore and tired from travel and the warm water soothed my aching muscles. I listened to the silence, but it was too quiet. I missed the sounds of young girls talking and laughing. I missed the bustle and business of school. There was too much time to think here. I got out of the bathtub and wrapped myself in my robe.

I walked into my old room, the room that had been my nursery so many years ago. I pulled some clothes out of my trunk and dressed. Then I began to put my things away. The room had changed since I'd last been here. Mother had seen to it that every childhood vestige was taken away in deference to my age. But even then, a whole flood of memories washed over me as I moved in it. I pictured Nanny frowning in her rocking chair, squinting at the enormous Bible in her lap. I remembered the nights I lay awake in bed, staring at the ceiling or listening to guests talking downstairs. What I remembered most, however, was the loneliness and isolation.

Then I stopped. I looked at myself in the mirror, my wet hair dangling past my shoulders. Almost unconsciously, I held a conversation with myself. I understood that I was a woman now, not a helpless child. I determined that I'd no longer allow the house of my childhood to dominate and oppress me. Marching to the window, I threw the curtains open. A few rays of sun left over from the day found their way in. I finished my unpacking with Rachel's help and ate some supper. I got into my nightgown when the evening passed and lay down in bed. My eyes closed with fatigue as sleep overtook me. But in those few seconds before unconscious rest, I saw Christian's face, his eyes dancing and his hair rustling in the breeze as he waved to me from the field.

"You've done exceptionally well in school, Elizabeth," was the first thing Mother said when I saw her the next day.

She removed a pair of spectacles and put them on top of a stack of papers she'd been paging through when I came into her room. I think they were my school records. Besides the spectacles, Mother hadn't changed. She seemed ageless. Her complexion was perfect with hardly a wrinkle in sight. I stood up straighter as she turned her eye upon me.

"Very well, indeed," she remarked, studying me. "I'm somewhat at a loss as to what to do with you. I could continue charting out your life, but I feel you're a grown woman now and should begin taking responsibility for your own affairs. Do you have any ambitions, any goals? What would you like to do?"

I didn't know quite how to answer. She'd just ordered me home a week ago and now, suddenly I could do whatever I liked.

"Further education?" she continued, "teaching?" Then smiling wryly to herself she said, "Marriage? Surely, there must be something you'd like to do."

Still, I made no answer. My mind was working frantically to come up with something that sounded half-way intelligent.

"I can't carry on in a one-sided conversation, Elizabeth. Either you reciprocate or I'll go back to my writing."

"I'm sorry," I rushed in. "I think I'd like to continue my education."

She'd turned back to her manuscript on the desk. But now she smiled and removed her spectacles again to look at me.

"I've thought for a while now that I'd like to attend college," I explained.

She tapped the desk with her pen a few times and then said, "You'd be outnumbered, you know. You might be criticized. Women generally don't go to college, and men don't appreciate the ones that do. Did you know that?"

"I hadn't given it much thought."

She stared thoughtfully at the pen and then roused herself to say, "It's a good plan. However, you must understand that I'll be putting forth a good deal of money for this. I'm not concerned about the expense, but I wouldn't like it to be wasted. So, I'd ask you to take this step seriously."

"I will," I answered. "I'm always serious."

"Yes, well…" she paused. "You've never been exposed to the company of young men before. But you will be if you go to college. You may find that young men will begin to pay attention to you. You mustn't let their attentions distract you from your goal."

"Why should they pay attention to me?" I asked, truly confused. I was nothing to look at, I believed.

Mother snorted but didn't answer.

"You can attend the college here and live in this house, of course. But I warn you things have changed considerably since my husband died, and I don't entertain anymore. I have very few visitors, and I keep to this room and work. I doubt that we'll see one another more than once or twice a day. I'm sure that would be to your satisfaction. You wouldn't enjoy my dull company."

She put her spectacles back on and turned back to her desk.

"Dinner is at six o'clock. I'll see you in the dining room."

I was dismissed. I took my journal out to the garden and settled myself on a bench. With trembling hands, I wrote about college. I drew my mother, bent over her desk, her spectacles resting on her finely sculpted nose, writing and writing. She was always writing. She wrote when I was little, before I went to school. She shut herself up in that room when I came home to visit, always writing. It was there in the garden that the question finally presented itself. *What did Mother write?* She never spoke about it, and I'd never thought to ask. After turning the question over in my mind a few times, I dismissed it and went inside to get ready for dinner.

As I dressed, I pondered the events of the last few days. Things changed so quickly. I wondered at this new-found freedom I'd come into. One day, I was a school girl and the next, the keys of my life were handed to me on a silver platter. Mother and I would live our separate lives but not entirely. There were unspoken terms that I understood by instinct. I remembered the way Mother's lip had curled when she uttered the word "marriage," and I remembered how seriously she had warned me about young men.

I hated to confess it to myself, but I'd been thinking about Christian frequently. I'd never considered marriage before, but ever since talking with Christian on the train, the prospect had looked quite pleasing. It was silly of me, I told myself while I brushed my hair. It was entirely possible that I'd never see him again, anyway. And even if I did, he'd only be a distraction to me. Mother was right, of course. I would focus on my education.

I was excited about this new change in my life. I couldn't wait for the summer months to pass so I could begin. But beneath it all ran an undercurrent of vague disappointment. I felt it as I sat alone in my room, knowing that Mother was glad I was grown up, out of the way, and self-sufficient. I knew Mother would never be affectionate the way mothers usually are. I did hope we might be friends, but it was not to be. She was content to stay cloistered in her sanctuary apart from me. I was on my own now.

When school started in the fall, I didn't have time to think about my disappointments. A few weeks into the term, I was thoroughly embroiled in my studies, trying to juggle philosophy, mathematics, literature, history, and Latin. The college was not more than fifteen minutes walking distance from my home, so I walked to school every day, swinging my books back and forth. All the venerable old trees in my neighborhood were just beginning to put on their fall colors, and the air had a pleasant nip to it. I took deep breaths, reveling in the season.

I was at school every day of the week except for Saturdays and Sundays. I attended classes until lunch, at which time I went to a secluded part of the campus full of trees and shrubs and chattering squirrels to eat the lunch I'd brought along. Sometimes I studied while I ate. Sometimes I just watched the squirrels and an occasional rabbit as they went about their business. Then I went off to the library to study some more. At four o'clock, I walked home and ate a silent meal with my mother an hour later. In the evenings, I went to an occasional symphony concert or lecture by myself. The rest of the time, I studied or wrote in my journal until it was time to go to bed. Then I got up in the morning and started the whole routine over again.

To some, such a life would seem dull and dreary, but it kept me from brooding. It gave me something to focus my energies on. I looked at my studies like a duel to be fought, the outcome already determined in my mind. By focusing wholeheartedly on my studies, I had a purpose in life that forsook me when I didn't have anything to learn. Then one day Christian came.

It was a windy day in October around two o'clock in the afternoon. I was in the auditorium listening to a speech by a visiting professor. I don't remember his name or even what he was talking about. I do remember that his speech was a publicized event and that a few reporters from the *Gazette* were there taking down notes. I didn't pay them much attention at first because there was a photographer to my right, fiddling around with his camera and making a terrible amount of noise. After a bright flash, he seemed satisfied and finally stopped. I looked toward the podium just as one of the reporters turned to his neighbor and whispered something. It was Christian.

To my dismay, he looked behind him right then and caught me staring at him. He smiled slightly and nodded his head. Then he turned back around and continued his work. My heart pounded wildly, and I could feel the heat rushing to my face. I bit my lip, angry at how foolish I was acting but feeling powerless to stop it.

I should leave, I thought. *This is ridiculous.* But I didn't leave. The last thing I wanted to do was leave. *Did he remember me? Did he think I was being rude? Would he talk to me? Did I have my mouth open when he saw me?* That was a dreadful thought. It was closed now, anyway.

Oh, if Mother could've seen me then. I was in such a flutter, I neither heard the speech nor saw the man who was speaking. When it was over, I stood up and gathered my things, determined to leave before I embarrassed myself any further. Christian turned around and began moving in my direction. I wanted to bolt, but I wanted to stay at the same time.

"Miss Millhouse!" he said, holding out his hand. "How good it is to see you again. Didn't I tell you we'd run into each other?" He paused for a moment studying me and then asked, "What's wrong? You do remember me, don't you?"

"Of course," I stammered shaking his hand. "How are you?"

"I'm well," he began, then darted a look behind him. "Listen, I have to go interview the speaker, Mr. What's-his-name. You won't leave yet, will you?"

"No, I'll stay," was my only reply.

"Good," he smiled delightedly. "I'll try to hurry."

"No hurry. Nothing's pressing."

I sat down, heart pounding, as I watched him talk and scribble efficiently in his notebook. As soon as he finished, he came back to me.

"I hope I haven't kept you from anything," he apologized.

"No," I replied. "I was only going to walk home."

"May I walk with you?"

At my nod, we set out. He insisted on carrying my books for me. I didn't know quite what to do with my hands, and after some awkward fumbling, I finally folded them in back of me as we walked along.

"How are you and your mother getting on, if I may ask?" he said after we had exchanged pleasantries.

"Well," I answered curtly. Then I added, "That is, we don't see much of one another. It's a very large house."

"I see. But she does approve of you going to college?"

"Oh, yes. She was very much in favor of it."

"And how does college treat you?"

"I don't know," I shrugged. "I'm used to studying, I suppose."

He glanced sideways at me and then looked ahead, then back at me again. We walked on quietly.

"How did you get the name of Christian?" I asked.

"Well, my parents were very devout Christians, and I suppose that's why they chose the name. It's not a common one. "

"And are you a devout Christian?"

"I'm sorry to say that since my father died, I haven't set foot in church. I'm even sorrier to say that I haven't regretted it, either. You must think I'm very wicked. "

I laughed at the matter-of-fact way he put it. "No indeed! If you are, then so am I. Mother hasn't gone to church since my father died, and so I haven't since I've been home.

"Even as a boy, it never did anything for me," he said. "I suppose I wouldn't have gone, even then, if I hadn't known how much it meant to my parents."

Then all too soon, we reached my neighborhood.

"Well," I said reluctantly, as I stopped in front of my home. "Here we are."

Christian stopped and stared. "You live here?" he commented as he gawked at the house.

"Yes," I answered quizzically.

He whistled and shoved his hat back to look all the way up to the fourth story.

"It's a very..." I began.

"...large house," he finished. "It certainly is."

He handed my books back and smiled down at me. His eyes looked blue today.

"May I walk you home tomorrow?" he inquired.

I gasped. Suddenly, I remembered Mother and her warnings about young men.

"Well...I don't know," I mumbled hesitantly.

"I'm sorry, I shouldn't have asked. It was impertinent of me."

"Oh, no!" I protested. "It's just that Mother has notions and doesn't seem to like young men very much..." My voice trailed off, but he waited without responding. "But I'd like it if you would," I finally said.

"I won't get you into a scrape with your mother?"

I shook my head, hoping I was telling the truth.

"Til tomorrow, then," he declared with a smile. Then he lifted his hat to me and was gone.

I ran all the way up the stairs to my room and pounced on the bed. I lay there on my back, smiling at the ceiling. *What on earth was happening to me?* I didn't know, but it had to be wonderful.

Chapter 7

Christian was true to his word. The next afternoon, I came out of my last class of the day to find him waiting for me in front of the building. Because of his work, he couldn't always meet me. But there were certain days, Mondays and Wednesdays mostly, when I always saw him. Sometimes he walked me home. Other times, he went to the library with me and wrote in his notebook while I studied. Most of the time, we talked, and it was then that I was the happiest. After hours spent alone with no companionship, it felt so good to talk to someone again the way I could with the Woodwards. There was something about Christian that drew me out of myself and made me tell him things I'd never told anyone else before.

I told him about how I'd dreaded going away to school when I was little and then dreaded going home after I'd spent so many years away. I told him about life at the Woodwards and about Genie and how I wondered where she was and what she was doing. I told him about my father's death. I told him how much I wished there was just one thing I could do that would earn my mother's approval. He just listened quietly. He didn't bother to give advice or criticism. And after a long, serious talk, he'd flash that grin of his and say something so funny that I couldn't help but laugh.

I didn't do all the talking, though. I remember one day in late October, we were sitting on the grass, enjoying one of the last days of Indian summer before the cold set in for good. Christian was sprawled out on the grass, his shirt sleeves rolled up around his elbows, reading Sunday's edition of the *Gazette*. I was sitting with my Latin balanced on my lap, memorizing parts of speech. Suddenly, Christian swore and smashed up the paper.

"What's wrong?" I reacted. I'd never seen him angry before.

"Alexander Stonely!" was his only reply.

He glared at the name printed underneath the article he'd been reading. I covered my mouth with my hand so he wouldn't see me laughing. He looked up at me and cringed.

"Oh, I beg your pardon," he apologized. "I try not to swear around ladies, but I couldn't stop myself."

"You make me think of my father," I said. "He used to do the same thing when he read Alexander Stonely's column. But he said much worse things, I'm afraid."

"Have you ever read this claptrap?" he asked, shaking the paper.

"I've only heard about it."

"Look at this!" he said, smacking the paper with the back of his hand. "This is such outrageous nonsense. He blames all the problems of the world on the male gender. He makes it sound as though all men are wife-beating, immoral drunkards. That's all but him, of course. Read it."

I took the paper from him and began to read. My eyebrows went up after the first paragraph or two and I looked at Christian over the paper in surprise. "It does seem a trifle radical," I remarked.

"A trifle?" he shouted. "I've never heard a man refer to his own gender with such disdain and contempt," he said, pulling out grass by the hand full. "I tell you one thing. If Alexander Stonely is a man, the first time I meet him in the street, I'll punch him in the nose."

"What? You think he's a woman?" I asked in disbelief. "How silly you are!"

He was grumpy all day after that, and it was all I could do to restore his good temper.

THE FALL TURNED TO WINTER and soon the Christmas season was upon us. Exams descended on me before Christmas vacation. I still spent time with Christian but, as I suppose must happen, doubts were beginning to prey on my mind. I was terribly attached to him, but I didn't know what he was thinking about the two of us. Did he feel the same way about me as I did about him? Was I just a friend or something more? I couldn't bring myself to talk to him about it. I was too shy, and it felt improper. So I just went on as before, glad to find him waiting for me when I got out of class.

One day he didn't wait for me to walk down the steps before blurting out some news.

"I've been promoted!" he shouted, running up the steps.

"Well done!" I shouted as I laughed at his exuberance. "What does that mean exactly?"

"It means I have a higher salary and a lot more work to do, but it also means that my little house should be paid for in its entirety in the next three or four months!"

"That's wonderful!" I smiled, even as my heart sank. "I suppose that means I won't be seeing you as often…you being so busy and all."

"That is one of the drawbacks," he admitted sadly. He peered down at me, noticing how quiet I'd become. "Don't look so sad, Elizabeth. I'll find a way to see you. I promise."

He straightened his shoulders and announced, "And now, in celebration of this momentous occasion, I propose that we go down to the ice rink and skate this afternoon. What do you say?"

"Well...I should study for my exam tomorrow..."

"I'll take that as a yes. Let's go!"

I couldn't resist that grin. We skated for an hour with the cold nipping our noses. We laughed and talked as the snow dusted the ice. Finally, I insisted on going home to study.

"All right then, you little bookworm," he said mocking me. "Go home and study your life away." Just then his chuckle turned into a cough, and I looked at him in alarm.

"What's wrong? Are you ill?"

"No worries," he assured me. "It's just a little cold. I'll be fine in a few days."

I smiled in relief.

"Your last day is Friday?" he asked.

I nodded to confirm his thought.

"Then I'll be there to walk you home."

"Will you have time?" I asked with concern.

"I'll make time." He smiled at me, and we lost ourselves in one another's gaze until he finally spoke up. "All right," he assured me, "Till then."

Before I went inside, I turned around and waved. He was still at the gate watching, and he waved back. I went up to my room and watched him walk down the street. His lips were pursed in a whistle, and he looked back and waved to me in the window. I sat down at my desk, fully intending to study, but my mind perversely wandered off at every opportunity. Finally, I scolded myself and got down to business.

It snowed and snowed and over the next couple of days, more candles appeared in window panes up and down my street. Men dragged huge pine trees on sleds, children chasing behind, to set up in houses and cover with Christmas finery. I began to think of getting a Christmas present for Christian. In my spare time, I went to several shops and looked at handkerchiefs and scarves and mittens. But I really didn't know what he'd want. Feeling perplexed and frustrated, I turned to leave the last shop when something caught my eye. Perched on a shelf in the window display was a beautiful gold pocket watch. I picked it up and stared in wonder at the country scene engraved on the cover. A barefoot boy stood in the middle of a field of wheat, swinging a scythe. It reminded me so much of Christian as a boy that I knew I'd found the right gift.

The store clerk was a cheeky fellow. He smiled knowingly as he wrapped my purchase. I pretended to ignore him. I trudged home happily through the snow, thinking of what Christian would say when he opened it. I'd give it to him on Friday. But until then, I was in a flutter of excitement, and it was all I could do to settle down and study for my last final.

The last day finally arrived. I fidgeted through the entire exam, checking to make sure Christian's gift hadn't grown legs and walked away. My professor frowned dourly at me and tapped his wristwatch. Chastened, I ducked my head and concentrated on my work.

When I finally burst through the door, my eager glance didn't find Christian in his usual spot at the end of the stairs. That was strange because he'd never been late before. But then I remembered he'd said he would make time. He was probably trying to finish up his work. My classmates surged past me laughing and smiling, wishing each other a Merry Christmas. Not being daunted, I went along with the rest to stand outside and wait for Christian. I tried to contain the smile that hovered around my lips, but it would break loose from time to time.

The temperature was frigid. My nose and hands began to feel numb, and I clapped them together to warm them. I walked briskly back and forth in front of the building to keep my blood circulating. I stopped every so often to look and see if Christian were anywhere about.

Soon, I began to worry. This wasn't like him at all. It was an hour later when I finally gave up and began the walk home, feeling bewildered and frightened. The brightly-wrapped gift hung limp from my hand. *Why hadn't he come? He promised he would. Was he sick? Suppose he was lying in bed with a fever. Was anyone looking after him?*

But the worst possibility was lurking in the back of my mind. Had he grown tired of me, after all? I walked home, my worries and fears tumbling over one another in my mind. My head began to hurt, and I went directly to bed when I returned home. I couldn't sleep. I tossed and turned for hours, my head aching, my thoughts consumed with Christian. I lit a lamp and tried to read, but I couldn't concentrate. In the wee hours of the morning, I finally fell asleep, only to wake suddenly a few hours later with an idea. I'd go to the office of the *Gazette*. Surely, someone there would know where he was. I had to have some news of him.

As soon as I could get out of the house without awaking suspicion, I was gone. I made it all the way up to the door, when it occurred to me how embarrassing it would be if I walked in and Christian was there and not sick at all. I put my hand on the door but couldn't open it. *What if he really didn't want to see me anymore?* It would be embarrassing for him if I appeared at his place of work. I slowly turned around and went back home.

The next two weeks were sheer torture. I thought of him every minute of the day. Visions of him lying in bed burning up with fever haunted me. But the thoughts of him going about his life, oblivious and indifferent to me, were even worse. I didn't want to eat, and I couldn't sleep for more than two or three hours a night. *What would I have left if he were taken away from me—school?*

Mother and I ate Christmas dinner together. Mother actually attempted a conversation with me, but I was so preoccupied I could only answer in monosyllables as I pushed the food around on my plate. In honor of the day, we sat in the drawing room together trying to be festive. But I was too miserable and Mother too bored. She went back to her room, and I sat alone in mine as the shadows of Christmas day deepened. There was nothing to be done but wait and worry.

When classes resumed, I'd all but given up ever seeing him again. He could have come to visit me. He knew where I lived. But he didn't come. I went back to school although I had no desire to. Life had become a lonely chore. I studied because it was my duty, but I didn't care whether I passed or not.

Two weeks after classes had begun, I walked out of my philosophy lecture on a cold Thursday afternoon. I was hunched up inside my coat, not really paying attention to my surroundings, when I heard my name.

"Elizabeth."

I looked in front of me and at the bottom of the steps was a very pale, thin, exhausted-looking Christian. The cheek bones stood out in his face and his beautiful eyes had dark circles around them. I drew in a sharp breath. The shock of seeing him again made my legs go weak, and they buckled beneath me. I sat down hard on the top step and covered my face with my hands. Silent, wrenching sobs shook my whole body and tears poured down my face. I felt Christian's arms go around me.

"I'm sorry. I was too sick to send word. Please don't cry, Elizabeth," he begged me.

I couldn't stop the tears. As hard as I tried, they just kept coming. I wanted to tell him that I was afraid he'd died. I wanted to tell him that I was afraid he'd left me. But I couldn't say anything.

He pried my fingers away from my face and wiped my tears. He kissed me, and I thought my heart stopped beating. I smiled up at him through my tears, loving him more than ever.

"Don't cry. I love you. I'm going to marry you," he declared to me.

I buried my head in his coat, and now I sobbed because I was happy. It would've made a funny picture. There we were in the middle of the campus, students passing on either side looking out of the corners of their eyes, with me sobbing and Christian embracing me. It was most improper, and I suppose I could've gotten into trouble for it. But at that moment I could've cared less if my entire academic career went up in smoke. Christian was alive and he loved me.

Chapter 8

When my eyes opened the next morning, I stared at the ceiling feeling wonderful without knowing why. And then I remembered. Christian loves me! I repeated that over and over to myself as I got ready for school and ate my breakfast. I sat at the table, pushing my food around on the plate once again. But this time it was because I was too busy with happy thoughts to eat. I was beginning to annoy my mother.

"What are you smiling about, Elizabeth?" she asked in exasperation, jolting me out of my reverie.

"Oh, nothing much," I mumbled.

"Then please refrain from smiling at the wall. It's very disconcerting."

After I had melted into a puddle of tears at the sight of him, Christian and I went inside, out of the cold, and talked for hours. He told me that after he left me at my house that day before Christmas vacation, he went straight home. As the evening progressed, he began to feel ill and had to put more effort into breathing. But he shrugged it off and went to bed. When he woke up the next morning, he didn't feel any better and his chest was hurting. He went to work anyway and soldiered through until his editor noticed the way he looked and sent him home to rest. Christian tossed and turned with fever that night and struggled to breathe. After that, he didn't remember anything.

"When I came to," Christian told me, "Warren, that's my editor, was there with a doctor and a nurse. He told me that he'd been concerned about me and stopped by my house the morning after he sent me home. He pounded on the door for a long time, and no one came. So he just broke it down and found me in my room, rasping. He's the one that called the doctor."

I sat and listened to him in awe, holding his hand and amazed that I was looking at him. I was acutely aware of the fact that he could have died. He really should have died, except for Warren's intervention. I squeezed his hand in both of mine, and the tears came to my eyes again.

"You shouldn't be out in this cold," I said.

"I know," he smiled. "But I had to let you know what happened. I didn't want you to think I'd forgotten about you." Then he chuckled and paused a minute. "You know, I wasn't going to ask you to marry me today. I was going to ask you when the house was all paid off. I've wanted to ask you for a long time though. "

"How long have you wanted to ask me?" I responded in shock.

"Since you were a little girl at the Woodwards, the prettiest little girl I ever saw. From the first day I saw you by the field with your little friend."

"That long?" I stared at him in wonder.

"That long," he stated firmly. "I was so afraid I'd never see you again when I had to go away from the farm. But I just kept hoping."

It was amazing. It was almost as if some unseen hand had planned it all. Was it just coincidence that we should happen to meet on the train and then happen to meet again at college a few months later? Could it be just random luck that Christian's friend had come by at the point when Christian was nearer to death than he'd ever been in his life? *Was it God?* I began to wonder. But my mind recoiled at the thought. God had never brought me anything good. I decided that it must have been coincidence.

Christian improved every time I saw him. He gained back the weight he'd lost, and the circles under his eyes began to fade. The doctor said his lungs would probably always be weak and advised him to take extra precautions from now on to prevent pneumonia when he was out in cold weather.

In one way, his weakness gave me peace of mind because he was not healthy enough to fight overseas when the United States joined the Great War in April. Many of the young men from college were signing up and leaving amid great fanfare and cheering friends. Marching bands played while the soldiers waved and smiled from the train windows. I shuddered inside when I thought of how many would probably never come back. I tried my best to keep the war out of my thoughts and centered on my love.

Christian and I were full of bright hopes for the future. We both thought I should finish out the school year before we were married. By that time, the house would be paid for, and Christian felt he would have enough income. That was a sore spot for him. He'd seen my house and had guessed at the way in which I'd been brought up.

"Elizabeth, I promise to take care of you the best I can. But I'll never have as much money as your mother has right now. I'm afraid you don't know what it means to go without something because you can't afford it."

I told him over and over again that I didn't care. I was too happy to care. I wanted to tell the whole world how happy I was. But the one person I hated to tell about us was the person I was required to tell—Mother. She would care about Christian's money or lack of it. She'd be angry that I'd become involved with a man while I was attending college at her expense. She wouldn't like the fact that he didn't come from a fine old family and that he was a farmer's son.

Christian and I talked about this problem. He was determined to do things the right and proper way.

"I'll talk to your mother when you've finished this school year. I'll ask permission to marry you."

"She won't like it," I warned.

"Yes, but I doubt she's as unreasonable as you think."

"We could just elope," I offered.

"I won't have it," he said firmly. "I'm going to talk to your mother as I should. It's only right."

"And if she refuses to let me marry you?" I asked with concern. He didn't have an answer for that.

The day of reckoning was a long way off, several months at least, and so I put it out of my mind. I basked in the knowledge that Christian loved me.

"...and I love him," I wrote in a letter to the Woodwards. I surveyed the words I'd just written, marveling at how beautiful they looked. I continued, "You'll be surprised to know that the man I'm going to marry lived next door to you while I went to school there. He's the son of Mr. Brown, the man who farmed the land by the school. His name is Christian. I'm so happy!"

Spring came and every day as I walked to school, I saw the snow melt a little more as crocuses pushed up out of the ground. Finals were upon me again, and it was only two more months until Christian talked to Mother. Even though I was happy, it was terrible anticipating that day. But every time I saw Christian waiting for me when I finished class, I knew I could endure the talk that Mother would surely have with me when she was done with Christian.

Christian came to my house the last week of May, after I'd just successfully completed my exams. Christian told me the day he would come but instructed me not to go downstairs and meet him at the door. He would just ring the bell and let Rachel call Mother. That morning, I was up in my room watching for him out the window. When he arrived, he saw me and smiled, his head up and shoulders back as always. I wondered if he would leave feeling as confident as he did now. I listened to the bell ring and Rachel scurrying to the door. I could hear their muffled voices, and then Rachel scurrying away. A few moments later, I heard Mother's voice and receding footsteps as Christian and Mother went deeper into the house.

It was hard staying in my room. I opened the door and sat down at the top of the stairs, my head leaning against the banister. Sooner than I thought possible, I heard a door open and footsteps coming towards me. I sat forward anxiously as Christian reached the foot of the stairs. He looked up at me and then back towards where he'd come.

"Well?" I asked.

He came up the stairs, sat down beside me, and scratched his chin. I noticed he'd missed a few hairs when he shaved that morning but that didn't matter now.

"Your mother is a frightening woman," he said, looking at me with new understanding in his eyes.

"Yes, but what did she say?"

"She said. . ." he began and then paused, "she said it was your life to do with as you please. But she said she wants to talk to you first."

"Right now?" I asked fearfully.

"I don't think right now but sometime soon."

The knot tightened in the pit of my stomach. Christian agitatedly ran his fingers through his hair, making it stand on end. Then he coughed.

"Elizabeth, you don't have to go through with this," he said earnestly. "Maybe I shouldn't have asked you to marry me. I don't have anything to offer you, nothing like all this anyway." He looked around at the house and its perfection. "She may say she'll let you do what you like, but she'll persuade you against it."

"She won't!" I whispered violently. "I've been miserable in this house. I hate it! Please believe me, Christian. I've never wanted anything more than I've wanted to marry you." I threw my arms around his neck.

"All right, you win," he said. I could hear the smile in his voice. "You'll do fine. You might just be the match for her. I certainly wasn't. As soon as she looked at me, I stammered and stuttered with the best of them. And me a reporter!"

I steeled myself for the ordeal I would soon face. That evening, I went down to supper, expecting the worst. But Mother didn't say a word all through the meal. Her face was calm and controlled as usual. It was all I could do to eat, but I remembered Christian's words and did the same as my mother. I went up to my room after supper, half expecting to hear her call me downstairs. But there was nothing. I lay awake for a long time, wondering what she was thinking.

Three days passed exactly as they had before. It was if she was purposely trying to wear me down with suspense. On the fourth day, my nerves were wearing thin. Then that evening, as I left the dinner table and said goodnight, Mother stopped me.

"I'd like to speak to you in the library for a few minutes, Elizabeth."

My heart pounded wildly, but I straightened my shoulders and put my head up. I followed her into the library, and she shut the door behind us. Mother turned and faced me with her hands folded in front of her. Her left eyebrow lifted and the side of her mouth turned up in a scornful smile as she surveyed my defiance. I stared her in the eye, my lips tight.

"I had occasion to meet your young man a few days ago, a certain Christian..." she waved her hand as if his name was of little importance.

"Brown," I finished.

"Yes, that's it—a reporter, I believe."

She waited for me to say something and when I didn't, she went on.

"He asked my permission to marry you. I suppose he's spoken to you about this?"

I gave her a short nod of my head.

"And have you agreed to marry him?"

"Yes."

"I see," she said, tapping her fingers on the back of the chair beside her. She sighed. "Well, beside the fact that you've deliberately gone against the advice I gave you at the beginning of the school year, your complete lack of due consideration in this matter is disappointing to me. If you feel you must marry, then by all means marry someone. But who is this Christian Brown? Do you really want to marry a reporter?"

Mother shook her head in disbelief as she continued. "His family is utterly unknown. He has no money or prospects of making any; of all the people to choose!"

I refused to say anything.

"Elizabeth," Mother reasoned, "You're a bright girl. You have a future ahead of you. You have the opportunity to do whatever you want. I can give you that future. Do you know how many girls would sacrifice the clothes on their backs for such an opportunity?"

I shook my head.

"If you marry this man, what will you have? Your education will end. Your opportunities will be lost. You'll be nothing more than his personal slave to cook and clean and wash and have child after child and wear your life away raising them. Is that what you want?"

I clenched my hands together, anger rising in me. Mother tried again.

"Elizabeth, as your mother, I insist that you listen to me. I gave birth to you. I provided for you. I gave you an education..."

"You starved me!" I burst out, unable to contain my rage.

"Whatever do you mean?" Mother asked, her voice rising.

"I feel no obligation to listen to you or heed your advice," I continued. "You gave me a roof over my head and food to eat and clothes to wear, but you didn't love me."

Mother slowly turned her back to me as I poured out the anger and bitterness and hurt that had built up in me for eighteen years.

"When I was little, you never bothered with me for more than ten minutes at a time. Then you sent me away to school so you wouldn't have to be bothered with me at all. You never wrote. You hardly ever let me come home. You never held me in your arms and told me that you loved me, and that day when I woke up with blood on my bed sheets, it was Mrs. Woodward and not you who explained what was happening to me. If it hadn't been for the Woodwards, I would've withered up and died for lack of love. And now, after all these years of your neglect, you expect me to listen to what you have to say?"

I looked around at all the fine books, the fine furniture, at Mother's fine figure. It was a wasteland and I loathed it. Mother still wouldn't look at me.

"I will marry Christian Brown. I will. He loves me and I love him."

"Love!" she shouted at me.

Mother's fist came down on the chair. She whirled around and stepped towards me. I had never heard her shout in my life. Her face shook, and the look in her eyes made me gasp and take a step backwards.

"What do you know about love? But you think you know all about it, don't you? You think because this boy makes your heart skip a beat and glow inside that you've seen it all. Well I know about love, and it's nothing but an empty dream, shattered after you've given all of yourself to it. Love never did anything for me."

I stared at her, feeling something akin to horror. She shook her fists in front of her.

"Everything I have in life—this house, the money—I took with my own two hands, and love had nothing to do with it. I have a man's possessions, I have a man's power, a man's influence, and I took all that with a man's name. Every week, I reshape minds with a man's pen."

Instantly, my mind flashed to my childhood days. I remembered standing in front of my mother's desk strewn with letters addressed to a radical—the radical my father swore at.

In sudden understanding, I breathed out, "You're Alexander Stonely."

"Yes, I'm Alexander Stonely," Mother affirmed. She sat wearily in the chair, hands shaking.

So this was the one who said that men were just slightly higher than apes in intelligence, that they were little tyrants who viewed women as nothing more than avenues for their own pleasure, reproductive machines at best. But I knew Mr. Woodward. I knew Christian. They weren't such men. Had my father been a man like the ones my mother condemned?

"What did Father do to you that you should hate men so?" I whispered.

"Your father..." Mother started to say, but stopped herself. Her eyes darted up at me and away again. "We won't speak of this anymore.

She stared down at the floor, her head resting on her hand. When she spoke again, her tone of voice was flat and tired.

"I won't prevent you from marrying this man. But I warn you that if do you marry him, you're no longer my daughter. I'll never see you again. I'll cut you off from your inheritance, and I'll never aid you financially. You have two weeks to think it over."

"I'm going to marry him," I repeated.

"Two weeks," she stated forcefully.

I went quietly out and shut the door behind me. The parting glimpse of my mother was telling. She still sat in the chair, shoulders slumped, head in hands. I was the winner. But I couldn't feel happy.

Chapter 9

Dear Journal,

    I've finally done it. I won the fight I knew was coming. But I didn't know it would be like this. I'm shaking all over. My head aches, trying to fathom what I've done, what I've learned tonight. I've learned what I should have guessed a long time ago. My mother is Alexander Stonely. How could this have happened?

    I sit here at my desk, perplexed and angry all at once. I can't understand why she's chosen this dual existence. Why must she always be a mystery? With this new revelation, I realize that I know even less about my own mother than I thought I did.

    I will never tell Christian. Alexander Stonely's identity has always been a secret and it will remain a secret. Oh, what would Christian think of me if he knew I was Alexander Stonely's daughter? I hardly know what to think of it myself.

    Mother has given me an ultimatum. Either I give up Christian, or I give up her. The choice is obvious. I'll leave this house for ever. I'll never willingly see her again. She can stay in this miserable place and brood on her self-imposed bitterness, writing her railing accusations. I'll be the happier one.

I wrote all these things, but I couldn't erase the memory of my proud mother, slumped in a chair, trembling. It cut me to the heart. She was not impenetrable after all.

Excluding Alexander Stonely, I told Christian about what had happened. Relief seemed to wash over me, just being with him. I needed the reassurance I found in his quiet strength. He shook his head thoughtfully, as I told him what had happened. When I finished, he looked at me sadly.

"We tried our best," he reassured me.

"Yes, we tried," my voice shook a little.

Christian pulled me to him, comforting me. "I have the license," he said. "Whenever you're ready, we can get married."

"I think I can be packed by Saturday."

"Then Saturday it is. Elizabeth, are you sure?"

"I'm sure."

It was hard knowing what to take and what to leave behind. In the end, I just packed the clothes in my closet and my small collection of books and the box with Genie's doll and the poem inside. Even so, those things filled three trunks. On Saturday morning, Christian came driving a wagon. He hoisted the trunks one by one and loaded them. Mother kept herself scarce. But there was light coming out from under her door, and I knew she was there hearing us.

"Ready to go?" asked Christian, taking my hand.

I nodded but had nothing to say.

I looked back at the house once as we drove away. The curtain in my bedroom window rustled. Someone was there watching, but it was impossible to tell who it was from the distance. I turned back around in my seat and refused to look back anymore. The farther we went, the more the weight seemed to lift from my spirits. When we reached the Justice of the Peace, I could not stop smiling. We walked into the office hand in hand, smiling from ear to ear. The judge was bored, but it didn't bother us. We promised faithfulness to each other from the bottom of our hearts. The cleaning lady, who we recruited to act as our witness, beamed at us when the ceremony was over. She insisted on kissing us both and wishing us the best in life.

As we drove to our home, Christian was very quiet. My excitement mounted with each mile of road we covered. *What would it be like, having a home of my own?*

"What does it look like, Christian?" I asked.

He smiled and said, "You'll see."

I pouted but he laughed.

"Well, at least tell me a little about it!" I insisted.

"You'll see," he repeated. After a few minutes, he instructed me to close my eyes and not to peek.

"Are we almost there?" I asked.

Christian called out to the horses to stop. He lifted me out and steadied me. "Now you can look," he whispered.

I opened my eyes, and the first thing I saw was a little picket fence surrounding a small white house with two gables in the front and green shutters. There was a rose bush by the porch. Christian watched me closely.

"Do you want to go in?" he asked.

"Of course!" was my gleeful answer.

I shrieked as he picked me up, he was so quick about it. He just laughed at my joy.

"We mustn't forsake tradition, you know," he explained.

Then he carried me up the steps and set me down inside. My breath caught with delight. It was so bright and happy and small inside. There were two armchairs in the sitting room, one blue and one yellow. The fireplace crackled, and there was a braided rug on the floor. I felt something warm and fuzzy swishing around my ankles and heard a cat meowing.

"Hello," I said, bending down to pet it.

"This is George," Christian said. "I forgot to tell you about him. I hope you don't mind. He's good company."

I picked up George and rubbed under his chin. He kneaded my shoulder with his paws, purring contentedly. Now delighted with everything, I roamed into the kitchen. Christian followed me and leaned against the door frame. I scanned around the room and took it all in. There was the iron stove in the corner, the little round table, the charming cupboards, and the red and white checked curtains in the windows.

"What's upstairs?" I asked.

"Let's go look," he teased me.

I followed him up, and there were two rooms—one was empty, but the other room was Christian's bedroom. The bed had a homemade quilt spread over it that Christian said his mother had made. A desk and chair stood beside it with a few papers stacked neatly on top. I sat on the bed and looked out the window over the pleasant street. I couldn't express in words how happy I was that all this belonged to me. I set George down and walked to the window.

From the doorway, Christian finally spoke.

"Do you like it?"

I nodded at him with a big smile.

He cleared his throat and softly assured me, "I know it's nothing spectacular, but I think it'll do for now. In a few years, after I've saved some more, we can get something bigger if you like…new furniture perhaps…"

He was so anxious to please me, so afraid that I wouldn't be happy. "I'd rather stay right here," I reassured him. "It feels like home. I think it's adorable."

"You're adorable," he said, his eyes so soft they made me blush.

I twisted the edge of the curtain between my fingers, feeling the need to do something with my hands.

He crossed the room and put his arms around me, kissing me on the nose.

"And you're my girl, now."

I wrapped my arms around him and smiled to myself. *Christian's girl*. It had a nice sound.

The change was enormous for me. Marriage is a life-altering change for any girl, but it was especially so for me. Me, the girl who'd never had to cook anything, clean anything, sew anything, share a bed with anyone, or arrange my life around one person. Suddenly, I had to learn to do all of those things and more.

That first morning, I woke up to the sun shining through the window. George hopped up on the bed, meowing and purring. Christian was still asleep so I stroked George's furry head, thinking he must be hungry. Then it occurred to me that I was hungry, and Christian would be hungry when he woke up. And that was when reality dealt me the first blow. *Who was going to make breakfast?*

"Christian!" I called out.

He stirred and stretched.

"I don't know how to cook!"

"I know," he yawned. "You'll learn."

"But what'll we do in the meantime?"

"I'll cook."

"You know how to cook?"

"Well, bachelors eat too."

"Oh," I finally answered.

"I'll show you how to fry eggs as soon as you say good morning properly."

I smiled and gave him a kiss. He scratched his head thoughtfully. "That'll do in a pinch, I guess," he said, full of teasing and playfulness. "Let me brush your hair," he said as I tried to arrange it.

"Certainly not," I reacted. "You'll have it in a mess of tangles."

"No I won't. Please?"

"No. I didn't ask to shave your mustache, did I?"

"That's different. Let me try!"

"Stop it!" I smacked his hand as he tickled me.

George looked stoically on from the bed. Eventually, we went downstairs to the kitchen where Christian showed me how to light a fire in the stove. It looked complicated, and I began to feel discouraged.

"It's not as hard as it looks," Christian assured me. "You'll catch on."

He showed me how to crack eggs. I kept getting eggshells in the pan, but I finally cracked one successfully.

"See, you're a natural."

Christian made it look so easy, keeping the fire from getting too cold or too hot. We sliced bread and toasted it on the stove. He showed me where all the plates and cups and forks and knives were, and I set the table. Christian pulled some strawberry jam out of the cupboard and placed that on the table, and finally we sat down to eat. It was such a comfortable meal as we talked about all sorts of things. Christian promised to buy me a cookbook the next day.

I spent the day getting acquainted with the house, discovering the wash tub, the irons, and the clothesline in the backyard. Christian brought down an old bookshelf from the attic to put all my books in, and we arranged them together. Then I put all my clothes in the wardrobe. I thought it might burst at the seams after I'd crammed the last dress in. Poor Christian, his trousers were plastered against the side.

Nighttime fell after our first day together, and Christian fired up the stove again. I soon realized that Christian's cooking was a theme with variations on eggs and toast. He made very good eggs and toast. His industrious efforts made me smile into my hand. But the sooner I learned to cook, I decided, the better.

That evening, Christian took a notebook downstairs and did some work for the next day while I dangled a string for George to chase. Christian didn't get much accomplished. He kept looking up and smiling. I was very happy. My only worry was that I wouldn't be a good enough wife. There was so much to learn, and how would I learn it all?

"Little by little," Christian told me, after we'd gone to bed. "You'll do fine."

"Oh, Christian," I sighed. "When I think of all the girls in this town who can cook and sew circles around me, I wonder why you even looked at me twice."

He laughed at my concern.

"You made me look twice. Stop worrying."

"I suppose if I can learn Latin, I can learn to keep house."

"That's the spirit."

I fell asleep to the sounds of Christian's even breathing, his arms around me. Tomorrow, Christian would go to work, leaving me in the house by myself. My domestic education would begin in earnest. I was thinking how different life was. It was safe and frightening, happy and worrisome all at once. But it was good. I knew I'd never regret leaving wealth behind to marry

Christian Brown. We would have a good life together. The troubles and sadness of my past were behind me now. I would meet the challenges of marriage head on, and I would win that battle too.

Chapter 10

Christian was as good as his word and brought me a cookbook the next evening. I set to work as soon as possible, trying to make sense of the recipes. It was like learning a new language. What did sautéing or basting or broiling mean? And how was sautéing different than frying? What was the difference between simmering and boiling? Poor Christian came home to more burnt meals than I can remember. But he was so good-natured about it. He was probably glad for anything besides eggs and toast.

I wrote more than a few letters to Mrs. Woodward about my conundrums, and she answered them for me, promising to come and visit me when she could to help make things clear. As a rule, trial and error were my best teachers.

My life was very full and pleasant with all this learning. But there were times when all the work was done and Christian was gone and the house was quiet and still. It was then that I thought about my old life. I missed the structure and the deadlines. I missed excelling in the classroom. The kind of learning I was doing right now didn't give me a grade at the end of the term. But all the same, to see Christian's tired eyes light up when he saw me at the end of the day was more than enough reward. And then to hear his, "Hey, good-lookin', whatcha' got cookin'?" seemed like more reward than I could hope for and even better than an A+.

And I found ways to satisfy my craving for learning. I often walked to the library in town and took books home with me by the armful to read during the quiet times when Christian was gone. I read some novels, but I was more often intrigued by anything to do with the natural world. I liked to find out the habits of animals, to recognize the birds that sang outside my kitchen window by their calls, and to look at the delicate structure of a leaf. I loved to brush the tips of George's sensitive whiskers as he whipped his pointed ears back and forth and twitched his tail in annoyance. On sunny, pleasant days, I took my journal outdoors and sat on the back porch while the sun warmed my bent head, drawing the little robins and sparrows that gathered to peck for worms and bugs.

There were many things to think about, but I couldn't seem to put my mother out of my mind entirely. Though physically cut off from her, the intruding, long arm she had, reached out to me through the newspaper every week. In disgust, Christian had given up Alexander Stonely as a bad lot, and I wanted to as well. But every Sunday the paper was like a magnet to me. I waited until Christian dozed off for a nap, and then I read it. Her article was always the same sort of thing—men were all monsters, striving to keep women chained in ignorance and subordination. Women, as nurturers of mankind, were superior to men in morality and intelligence. Men were simply subject to their own passions so they kept their wives at home to satisfy their every whim.

I looked at my unsuspecting husband, exhausted from a week's work, trying to find this horrible creature in him that my mother described. But there was no comparison between the two. He found me quite the opposite of ignorant and loved me still. He didn't bark orders at me or make me wait on him hand and foot when he arrived home from the office. In fact, he was full of encouragement when I was discouraged. And his passions, though strong, were not more voracious than my own. We were young. We loved each other, and it was natural.

I began to wish for the burdensome children that my mother declared were the causes of ill health in women. I found myself wandering upstairs to that empty room once or twice a week, wondering if there would ever be a rocking chair and a crib with a baby in it. I looked down at my very slim waist, asking myself how it could possibly stretch so far. I had no experience with babies at all. I scarcely knew how to go about holding one. But there was something that stirred inside of me every time I saw a young mother pushing a buggy through the park in town. It was something that was almost like pain.

Inevitably, after reading the week's article, I concluded that there must be some of these horrible men in the world, although I didn't know any. I wondered who the man could have been in my mother's life. It couldn't have been my father. He was flawed, I knew, but he wasn't the man she described. Gloom settled over me when I thought about it too long.

The months ran quickly by, and I began to notice a few things about George.

"Christian," I finally announced, "I think we'll have to change George's name to Georgette." I was sitting on the floor with my head resting on Christian's knee as I stroked the cat's sleek fur.

"Georgette?" he asked. Christian looked bewildered.

"Yes, I believe George is a female."

"Whatever made you think that?" he responded.

"Well, look at his round tummy. It's become very fat lately."

"Oh, you're just feeding him too much."

"No more than I usually do. And look at that," I pointed at George's chest. There were teats visible, swollen for the first time.

"George is going to be a mother," I confidently announced.

Christian whistled. "Well, I'll be!" he said with surprise.

Georgette became her name, and each day she got wider and wider. When the time came to have her kittens, I watched. The experience made me feel a little sick to my stomach, but I was fascinated with the process. Georgette gave birth very early one morning. Christian found me next to her basket on the floor a few hours later, leaning up against the kitchen cupboard, fast asleep. When he woke me up, I smiled and pointed to the three little balls of fur nestled close to their mother. They were so sweet, and I loved seeing them change a little each day. They stumbled around weakly with their eyes shut at first and then they finally opened them. Curiously, the kittens took in everything around them, straying away from the basket without hesitation. Often, my hand would go instinctively to my abdomen as I observed Georgette with her kittens.

I thought to myself, *If Georgette can manage three, certainly I can manage one.*

That's because, about the same time I noticed Georgette's swollen belly, I began to experience strange sensations of my own. I was so sick in the morning now, and my waist wasn't as flat as it used to be. But I wasn't sure, and I didn't want to bring it up to Christian just yet. If it wasn't a baby, then something else was wrong and he'd be worried. How I wished I could talk to Mrs. Woodward!

And then one day, she came as she promised, bringing an old friend with her. Christian had just left, and I was cleaning up the kitchen, when I heard a knock at the door.

"Mrs. Woodward. How are—" I stopped and gasped, for behind her was a young woman with a baby in her arms. She had a sweet, happy face that I recognized. "Genie!" I screamed with excitement.

Laughter bubbled up out of her, and she sprang forward to hug me. I was so happy, I couldn't think of a single thing to say. I stood looking from one to the other in surprise until we all burst out laughing at once. I took them both by the hand and brought them into the house.

"Come in, come in. Do sit down," I scurried around to make them comfortable. "Oh, dear me, you have a baby."

"Yes," Genie replied, "and the other one stayed with his father."

"You have two already? Well, you always said you wanted twenty."

"Yes," Genie laughed, "But on careful consideration, I think five or six will suffice."

Genie's baby was named Rebekah. She was a happy, good-natured little thing like her mother. Genie could see that I ached to hold her and handed her over to me directly. She drifted off to sleep on my lap as Mrs. Woodward and Genie and I talked about old times. Genie had married at the ripe old age of sixteen. Her husband was a seminary graduate and already had a small church in the country.

"You should come and visit us, Elizabeth," Genie told me. "It's not very far, and you'd like it. You and your husband could come to church some Sunday and stay the day with us."

"Yes, well…perhaps we can."

There was a long pause in the conversation.

"Elizabeth, are you feeling well?" Mrs. Woodward asked. "You look very tired, and you have such circles under your eyes."

"Oh, I'm not very tired. But I have been feeling a little ill lately. It does hang on, and I think that's why I may look tired."

There was another long pause as I looked from Genie to Mrs. Woodward.

"Well, you both know about these things better than I do," I began. "So, I'll tell you. I think I may be expecting a baby, but I'm not sure."

Genie and Mrs. Woodward looked at each other knowingly. Mrs. Woodward asked a few probing questions about other symptoms I'd had and then smiled.

"Yes, Elizabeth, I think you're right."

"Have you told Christian about it, yet?" Genie asked me.

"No, I wanted to be sure." Then I smiled. "Now I can't wait to tell him."

I wanted them to stay so badly until Christian came home so he could meet Genie, but they had to leave.

"Oh, I am so thrilled for you," Genie said, as she kissed me goodbye. "I'm so delighted to find you married and happy. I can't tell you how sad I was when I found out I wouldn't be coming back to school to see you again all those years ago. And I've prayed for you every night since then, hoping that everything would go well with you."

"You really prayed for me every night?" I asked with surprise.

"Yes," she answered, almost surprised by my question.

"You know, I still have the doll you made for me." I had to run up the stairs and pull it out of the box to show her. Genie was shocked to see that I still had it.

"Really, Elizabeth, you must come and visit," Genie insisted. "I know. You should come and celebrate Christmas with us. Please do."

"I'll talk to Christian about it," I promised. "But I'd love to."

When Christian came home that evening, I told him the news. He picked me up and whirled me around in circles.

"It's grand!" he said, kissing me. "What will we name him?"

"What if it's a girl?" I laughed.

"We'll name her after you, of course."

I was so happy but a little frightened at the same time. Would I be a good mother? Would I be strong enough for the pain of child labor? Any number of things could go wrong. Girls died giving birth. I hoped I would love my baby better than my mother loved me. I suppose I was afraid of being like her.

"You won't be like her," Christian assured me when I talked to him about it. "You're not like her now. You'll see."

The news of the baby had a dramatic effect on Christian. He was the same man fundamentally, but gradually, he became quieter and more sober. He was very thoughtful, and I often found him staring into space with his brow furrowed, looking almost worried. When I asked him what was wrong, he wouldn't tell me, so I didn't bother him about it, trusting that he would tell me when he was ready.

It was mid-December when I discovered that I was going to be a mother, and soon I began to think about Christmas. I'd never given Christian the watch I bought him the Christmas before. Somehow it got lost during the time Christian lay in the balance between life and death. But I discovered it again in a box in one of my trunks, and I was so happy to see it. Although we had enough money, we didn't have much left over for luxuries like Christmas presents. I decided I'd give the watch to him this Christmas.

Shortly after Genie's visit, we received a letter from her begging us to share Christmas dinner with her and her husband. Christian remembered seeing Genie with me at the Woodwards so many years ago, and he was anxious to meet her. So we decided to go. When Christmas day arrived, the morning sickness had the consideration to leave off for the day and give me a rest. I was very pleased. Christian borrowed Warren's automobile to drive into the country, but I was a trifle nervous about that.

"Are you sure you can manage it?" I asked him, looking dubiously at the mechanical contraption.

"Of course, silly, it's no trouble at all. Just get in and I'll fire it up."

He twisted the crank in front, and it jumped to life with a bang. I squealed and Christian laughed heartily at my surprise. He hopped in the driver's seat, grandly pulled out his new watch to check the time, and off we went. It was a beautiful Christmas day. The fresh, cold air felt so good after nearly a month of being cooped up in the house and feeling ill. I reached across the seat and held Christian's hand. It was like going back in time as we drove past snow-covered pastures, watching smoke float up out of farmhouse chimneys. These were the things that Christian and I grew up seeing.

We left early enough in the morning so we could go to church at Genie's request. I didn't relish the idea of stepping inside of a church once more, but I liked to make Genie happy. When we arrived at the white church house, she met us at the door, holding the baby in one hand and steering her little boy with the other.

"I am so glad you came!" she beamed, her breath making little clouds around her face in the cold air. "You'll sit with us, won't you? Some of the children are going to sing Christmas carols, and my husband is giving the sermon. It's going to be lovely!"

Genie had changed a little, but in essentials, she was exactly the same Genie I'd loved as a little girl. If anything, she was more happy and radiant, and it was a pleasure to see her talk to the congregants and look after her children. She seemed to light up the room with her smile.

There was something about that church service that was different than anything I'd ever experienced in church before. Maybe it was me that was different. Some of that old fear was with me when I thought about God, but as I listened to the little row of fresh-faced, singing children dressed in their Sunday best, I began to remember Christmas at the Woodwards. I could almost hear my own childish voice singing, "Away in a manger, no crib for a bed. The little Lord Jesus lay down his sweet head. The stars in the bright sky look down where he lay. But little Lord Jesus, asleep on the hay." I could hear Mr. Woodward's voice reading the Christmas story, and my hand went to my belly as I thought of young Mary giving birth in a cold stable like the song said, "in the bleak midwinter, long, long ago…"

I turned my head to look at Christian and was surprised to find a tear on his cheek. He caught my eye and smiled, squeezing my hand.

"I'd forgotten how beautiful these carols are," he whispered in my ear. "It's been a long time."

We had such a pleasant Christmas dinner. I held the baby while Genie bustled around in the kitchen, putting food on the table. Christian sat and talked to Lawrence, Genie's quiet and sober husband. He held his little boy on his lap. The contrast between Genie's personality and Lawrence's was striking, but they suited each other to perfection. Genie made him smile and put a twinkle in his eye, and he made her thoughtful when she could naturally be a little too giddy. We all held hands around the table while Lawrence gave the blessing on the meal, and then we ate. It was the first big meal I'd eaten since the morning sickness set in, and it tasted wonderful.

I helped Genie clear the table and wash the dishes afterwards. The children were taking naps, and Christian and Lawrence were conversing again.

"You look very well, Elizabeth. Much better than the last time I saw you," Genie remarked.

"I am much better, thank you."

"You must be getting excited!"

"Yes," I smiled and then shrugged my shoulders. "I suppose I'm a little afraid, too."

"Well, that's natural," Genie reassured me. "It's quite a responsibility raising children. It's always worried me. It still does, in fact. So I pray about it, asking God to help me be a good mother to mine."

"Yes, well…I don't pray that much anymore. At all, for that matter," I admitted.

"But why?" Genie asked in surprise.

"I don't know. Well yes, I do know," I confessed, wondering what she must be thinking of me. "I'm a little angry with God. He's been hard with me. I often wonder why He seems to love people like you, but either hates or doesn't care about me."

"Elizabeth, dear," Genie took both of my hands, speaking earnestly, "I don't know all the details of your life, but I know God loves you. He came to die for the sins of the whole world, not just mine. He came to offer us forgiveness. How could His love be any greater?"

I stared at her, the wheels of my mind turning inside. I'd never once in my life thought of Jesus as God. It was something entirely new to me, even though I'm sure I'd heard it multitudes of times and even agreed with it in a clinical, knowledgeable sort of way. Was that innocent, helpless baby born so long ago, the same God who seemed to lay in wait for me at every turn? It was something to think about. In fact, I thought about it all the way home, with my head resting on Christian's shoulder. And I would think about it for many days to come.

Chapter 11

After Christmas, Christian and I set our focus on getting the baby's room ready. Christian brought home a sweet little bassinet one evening to surprise me. Diapers and clothing began to come in from all quarters—from the neighbors, from the wives of men that Christian worked with, and from Mrs. Woodward and Genie.

I wished sometimes that I could tell my mother about the baby. It seemed so wrong that my baby would never know his grandmother. But I knew that Mother wouldn't care to know him. Even if she did care, she could never admit it after all that had passed between us. I just accepted the fact that my baby would have no grandparents.

"Don't let that bother you, little one," Christian would say, patting my belly. "We love you."

Christian chuckled when the baby kicked the palm of his hand. It was good to see him laugh. He'd become so serious and thoughtful during those days, he'd almost seemed gloomy. Still, he didn't talk to me about it.

Then one night he gave me a scare. He didn't come home on time one Saturday evening. He always came home around six o'clock and that night, supper was hot and on the table at the usual time. Still no Christian. I ate by myself at seven-thirty and cleaned up the kitchen. However there was still no Christian. I sat down by the fire with a book, but I couldn't concentrate and I jumped at every noise. *Oh, where is he?* I wondered.

Finally, I drifted off to sleep in my chair. I woke up at midnight to a loud pounding on the door. Startled, I tensed and sat straight up. I couldn't imagine who it would be.

"Mrs. Brown!" a man's voice yelled. "Mrs. Brown, don't worry. This is Warren. I've got Christian with me."

I hurried to the door and unlocked it, remembering that Warren had a reputation for breaking down doors. He stumbled in with Christian leaning heavily on his shoulder, wearing a silly grin on his face and his clothes all disheveled. My hand went to my mouth, and I stared at him in shock.

"What's wrong with him?" I blurted out. "What happened? Was there an accident? And what's that awful smell?"

"He'll be all right in the morning, ma'am. He just had one too many. I'll get him upstairs to bed," he said, staggering up the stairs.

"One too many what?" I demanded.

Warren tipped his head back and gestured as though he'd tossed the contents of an imaginary glass down his throat.

"He's drunk?" I responded in shock.

"I'm afraid so."

Slowly, I followed Warren upstairs and helped him get Christian beneath the covers. He was asleep before his head hit the pillow. I walked back downstairs and stood silently by the door. Warren had his hat in his hands and stood there looking ashamed.

"I'm sorry about this, ma'am. It's my fault, really. I was trying to cheer him up."

But I didn't say anything.

"Just get him a good, strong cup of coffee tomorrow morning. He'll be as good as new in no time."

I waited with my arms crossed, feeling very tired and very pregnant.

"Is there anything I can do for you before I leave?" he asked me, fiddling with his hat.

"No. I think you've done quite enough already," I sighed. "Thank you for bringing him home."

I closed the door and locked it behind him. Then I went upstairs to check on Christian. He was sound asleep so I went back downstairs and settled myself with a blanket on one of the easy chairs. I was angry and confused. All sorts of wild thoughts flew into my mind. *Had I made Christian unhappy? Why had Warren wanted to cheer him up? Was this the misery of marriage that Mother was always writing about? Was this the start of it? What had I gotten myself into?*

Georgette came meandering up and rubbed against the chair, purring. I picked her up and stroked her soft fur. She settled down on my ever shrinking lap, and I slept fitfully.

As I made breakfast the next morning, I could hear Christian bumping around upstairs so I made a strong pot of coffee as Warren had suggested. When Christian came downstairs he was washed and dressed and shaven, but his eyes were red and tired. He looked penitently in my direction, but my lips tightened as I whirled around and busied myself with pouring the coffee. He sat down heavily at the table, and I put his cup of coffee in front of him a little harder than necessary. He groaned and rested his head in his hands. I filled his plate with food, hating the silence between us. Finally, there was nothing left to do, so I sat down opposite from him and waited.

He slowly lifted his head and looked at me.

"You're not really mad at me, are you girl?" he asked.

I crossed my arms and bit my lower lip, trying not to cry.

"You weren't too very worried, were you?"

In frustration, I threw up my hands and let them fall down on the table hard. The blow hurt my hands, and Christian took both of them and rubbed them for me and then I did cry.

"I waited and waited but you didn't come, and I didn't know what to do because you didn't tell me you'd be out late, and your supper got all cold, and I've never seen anyone drunk before, and I was scared," I finished, unsuccessfully trying to take my hands away and cover my face.

Christian knelt by my chair to put his arms around me, stroking my hair while I cried.

"I'm sorry," he whispered. "It was wrong of me. I promise you this—it'll never happen again, never!"

"Christian, what's wrong?" I pleaded. "Why did Warren want to cheer you up? Did I do something wrong? Is it something about the baby? I thought you were excited."

"No, Elizabeth!" he stopped me. "You've done nothing wrong."

"Then what is it? What are you worried about?"

He sighed and looked sadly at me for a long time.

"I keep thinking," he said very quietly, "about our baby. I keep thinking about how much I want to be a good father. I want to be a good example. I want to teach our children how they ought to live, what should be important to them, and shape them into good people."

"That's wonderful. I'm glad you want to do that."

"But, Elizabeth, how can I do all that when I don't even know why I'm here?"

"What do you mean?" I was alarmed by the anguish in his eyes.

"I don't understand what the purpose of my life is; what the purpose of anyone's life is. We're born, we live for a while, and then we die. Our friends bury us, and no one remembers us a generation later. Is that where it all ends, in a cold, dark hole in the ground? Right now, I have you and the baby coming, and I love you both. But how long will I be able to stay with you with my lungs the way they are? Do I just stop existing when my body starts turning back into dirt?"

I didn't know what to say. What can you say to questions like those?

"I'm sorry," Christian smiled. "I shouldn't worry you with my dark thoughts."

I put my arms around him and held him close to me.

"You've got to stop thinking about things like that," I told him. I didn't know what else to say.

After that, Christian didn't talk to me about those things anymore. He never came home drunk again and, in many ways, he returned to the old Christian I knew. But for the first time, I recognized what had been there all along. I could see the pain beneath his cheery mannerisms and his twinkling eyes. I shoved his questions to the back of my mind, refusing to think about them. Questions like that could wither a person's hope in time unless there was something more, something better, after everything in life was gone. Genie and Mr. and Mrs. Woodward would say that God was something more and something better. But I could hardly encourage Christian to pursue what my own mind rebelled against.

Besides, he was already thinking in that direction. I came upon him a few times reading an old family Bible that belonged to his mother. It made me uneasy, even though I berated myself for thinking that way. Why should it bother me if religion comforted him? Just because I didn't want it didn't mean he couldn't have it. Even after reasoning with myself, though, I instinctively knew that if God became as important to Christian as He was to Genie and the Woodwards, an invisible wall would grow between Christian and me. We wouldn't think the same things anymore and be perfectly contented with each other. I became frightened the more I thought about it. Why could I never leave God behind?

I hoped that Christian would soon forget all his dark wonderings and be happy. I didn't want anything to change.

SPRING TURNED INTO SUMMER, and I felt heavier and heavier as the days went by. The extra weight I carried around every day made me tired and listless. Christian urged me to get plenty of rest, but getting comfortable enough to sleep in the summer heat was a difficult task. Sometimes both of us lay awake at night, hoping for a cool breeze to wander in through the bedroom window. It rarely came.

One night, after I thought he'd gone to sleep, my throat was dry and I quietly got up to get a drink.

"Where are you going, girl?" he whispered loudly.

"Did I wake you up?"

"No, I've been laying here awake for a long time."

"I was just going to get a drink. Are you thirsty?"

"I'll get it for you," he said, steering me back to bed. "You might trip on the stairs."

He got the water for me and came back. He lay back down with his arm under his head, staring out the window. I put the palm of my hand on his chest as my habit was, and he put his hand over it. For some reason, it comforted me to feel the beat of his heart.

"I wish I hadn't done that," he whispered so quietly that I barely heard him.

"Done what?" I asked thinking he was speaking to me.

"Oh," he sighed, "I was just laying here thinking about something I did when I was a boy."

Now I was curious so I propped myself up on my elbow and looked down at him.

"Well, tell me about it."

"My father and I used to go to town on Saturday afternoons," he began softly. "We'd go to Mr. Johnson's store. Papa would get the things my mother put on her list, and I would wander around looking at all the things that fill a boy's heart with delight. I always ended up in front of that harmonica. It was under the glass at the front counter. I wanted that harmonica, but Papa told me a nickel was too much, and I'd have to do without."

"Did you ever get it?" I asked.

He shook his head.

"But eventually I had an idea on how to get it. I knew Mama kept some extra money in a jar on the shelf in the kitchen. She saved it for a rainy day, you know. Well, I convinced myself that it would be all right for me to take a nickel out of the jar without asking permission. They'd never know it was missing, I decided, so I took it. Then I convinced my Mama to let me go to town by myself one day. I carried that nickel with me even though I was miserable with guilt. But I was determined to have that harmonica so I kept going.

"Just before I reached the store, I took my nickel out of my pocket, and while I was taking it out, it slipped out of my fingers and fell in the road. Just then a cart went by and a horse hoof kicked it farther away from me. It got kicked again and just like that, the nickel was gone. I felt miserable all the way home. I wanted more than anything to have that nickel back so I could put it away in Mama's jar. Every time I went to town with Papa after that, I couldn't bear to look at that harmonica. It made me sick."

Christian looked at me and gave a short laugh but didn't smile.

"I wanted to tell my parents what I'd done but I was so ashamed. Now they're dead and it's too late."

"It was just a little thing, Christian. You were just a little boy."

"But it was still wrong, all the same, and I knew it was wrong. And that isn't the only wrong thing I've done." He paused a minute, then asked, "How do you make things right that you've done wrong?"

"I suppose you really can't. I guess you just try to make up for them by doing good things now. That shouldn't be hard for you. You're such a good man."

I leaned over and kissed his cheek as he sighed again. He was still staring out the window as I drifted off to sleep.

Chapter 12

August came and my anticipation mounted with each day that passed. I was due to have the baby somewhere near the end of August. The baby's room was ready with all the diapers neatly stacked on the shelf, the curtains hung just so, and a rocking chair in one corner with a teddy bear perched on the seat. During the day, I would come upstairs and sit in the rocking chair while I held the bear, staring out the window and thinking. Even though I was excited to see my baby, I was afraid too. It was the labor that I dreaded the most. I'd never experienced severe pain and I knew that this would be painful beyond anything I could imagine. I hoped it wouldn't take a very long time. I hoped I would be able to withstand it.

I was relieved to find Christian becoming less gloomy and preoccupied. It was a gradual and almost imperceptible change over several weeks, but he slept better at night and seemed relaxed and happier. Unfortunately he'd also decided he wanted to go to church on Sunday mornings. He asked me to go with him, but I didn't want to and he didn't press me. It was lonely spending the morning alone, but he seemed to look forward to going to church so much that I swallowed my disappointment and didn't complain. He was always home before lunch, looking rested and thoughtful. He'd greet me with his old smile and a kiss, then get the old Bible down from the shelf and pull a notebook out of his coat pocket. He'd sit at the table until lunch time, pouring over the scribbled notebook and the Bible, sometimes smiling and reading a few lines for me.

"What is all that you've written down in there?" I asked him one day, peering over his shoulder.

"Just some notes I took from things the minister said in his sermon this morning."

"What kinds of things do you write down?" I inquired.

"They're mostly things that strike me or make me think."

"Well, what struck you today?"

He smiled at me and then looked down at his notebook, flipping a few pages and following the writing with his finger.

"And the scripture was fulfilled which saith, 'Abraham believed God, and it was imputed unto him for righteousness: and he was called the friend of God.' That's quite a thought," he said softly, "that the God who created the universe is my friend."

"That seems a bit much," I responded, "don't you think?. After all, Abraham was Abraham and you are, as much as I love you, just Christian."

"I thought that at first, but the whole chapter that verse comes from was about believing God and then acting as if you believed Him, and how the acting proves your faith. Abraham was the example that James used to show people how they should act. It's quite amazing that I can be a friend of God like Abraham was. I'd hate to be His enemy."

"I'd hardly think of you as God's enemy, dear," I tried to reassure him.

"I suppose. But as I understand it, you must either be His friend or His enemy. There seems to be no middle ground."

His friend or His enemy. It was rather irritating to hear him say such things. If what he said was truly the case, there could be no doubt about my status with God.

Christian started praying for and about everything. He prayed before each meal, thanking God for the food. I didn't mind that so much. "Giving grace," was something I had grown up with. It was the "everything" that became wearisome. Georgette developed a limp and favored her right paw. Christian prayed for Georgette's paw to get better. When I mentioned my apprehensions about childbirth, he would say, "I'll pray for you, girl," or "Let's pray about that together." And he would proceed to do just that. Sometimes early in the morning, I would wake up feeling Christian's absence in bed only to see him kneeling by the window, praying as the sun came up. How he could run on so long to an invisible entity was beyond my comprehension.

One of the common themes I heard while listening quietly in the dark was His thankfulness to God for saving him from his sins. That bothered me the most because Christian was not my idea of a sinner. He had his rough spots, but overall, he was a kind, loving husband and as generous as a man could be on a limited income. I believed that he was honest and patient to a fault. He was a far better person than me. So if my Christian was a sinner, then what was I? Besides all that, I didn't think God really listened anyway. He'd never listened to me. *Why did Christian think God would even care?* Still, I held my peace and let him be.

September came and still there was no baby. I was more than ready to have my waist back such as it would be. It was such a chore to drag myself out of bed in the morning, feeling ugly and ungainly. I'd never thought the day would come when I'd waddle about like a duck.

"You're as pretty to me as you were the first day I saw you," Christian consoled me one night when he chanced to notice me talking to him and took his nose out of that Bible of his. He read it almost every spare minute, and some evenings, I would find myself staring quietly at the wall while he was engrossed with it.

"Christian, I haven't seen you all day. Couldn't you just put that away for a while and talk to me?" I begged him.

Immediately, he closed it, looking a bit ashamed.

"I'm sorry, Elizabeth. It was very thoughtless of me. Was there something you wanted to talk to me about?"

"Oh, I don't know," I sighed, feeling irritable, "nothing in particular."

We sat awkwardly in our chairs, on my part trying to think of something comfortable to say that would break the silence. But I had some awkward and uncomfortable questions to ask that had been lurking beneath the surface of my mind for several weeks. I was quite sure they wouldn't go away until I asked them.

"Christian, you've changed so much lately. I wonder why you needed to. We used to be so happy together. We'd talk for hours and hours… Now it seems that all you want to do is read and pray and talk about God. Have I become boring to you? Are you still in love with me?"

"Of course I am," he assured me. "I'm sorry you've felt that way. I didn't mean to give you that impression. Truly, I didn't." His eyes spoke sincerity and I liked that look. "It's just that I feel as if I've discovered something recently that was always missing before; missing all my life, in fact. When I married you, I thought you were the thing I was missing."

"I wasn't?" I asked, feeling a sinking in my stomach.

"No, but don't look so downcast," he said, patting my cheek. "I love you dearly."

"What do you mean then?"

"It's hard for me to explain." He sat down beside me, holding my hand. "As a little boy in church, I wanted God to think well of me. And I knew that I must be very good if He was going to let me go to heaven. I understood that if I tried hard to be good and do right all my life, perhaps God would overlook my bad points and let me into heaven."

"I'm sure you were quite a good little fellow," I interrupted.

"Ah, but there's the rub," he quickly countered. "I wasn't, and I knew it. I told you about the time I stole some money from my mother. It seemed that no matter how hard I tried, I was always sinning. I disobeyed my parents, I told lies, and when I got a bit older and started noticing young ladies, I would find myself thinking about them in ways I knew wasn't right."

"You didn't have to mention that," I said, blushing for him.

"Well, it's the truth. I wasn't a good little fellow as much as I'd like you to believe. What's worse, I often resolved never to repeat my mistakes, only to go right back to them a day or two later. It seemed a hopeless task. To my chagrin, I found myself thinking it would be quite all right to do something wrong because I could always just confess it later on and be rid of it. But that attitude began to weigh heavily on my conscience, and I became more discouraged. I lost interest in church because it didn't seem to work, and all the time, I was afraid when I thought of God and how unhappy He must be with me. And so, to end the charade and the constant reminding of my own glaring imperfections, I stopped going to church as soon as I possibly could."

"Yes, you told me that," I remembered. "You said you didn't care."

"And I was afraid because I didn't care. I felt it was a sign of my hardness of heart.

"You're not hard-hearted," I answered forcefully.

"Then I saw you on the train," he said as he smiled at me, eyes soft like I remembered them. "You were lovely and sweet and self-possessed, and I determined once again that I would marry you. For the time being, I forgot all about my troubles. It's only been the last nine months that they've come back to haunt me. It was when I thought about being a father and raising children. But since I've been going back to the church in town and reading my Bible, some things have begun to make sense."

"Like what?" I asked, now genuinely curious.

"That I can't keep myself out of hell by doing good things or send myself to heaven by not doing wrong things. That phrase Jesus uttered, 'It is finished,' truly means it's finished. It means that Jesus did everything to make my salvation complete, and all I have to do is believe in Him. It's a great load off my mind." When he finished, he sat thoughtfully for a minute.

"And the best thing is," he continued, "I belong to God and He belongs to me, like I've never belonged to anyone in the world or anyone has ever belonged to me. You and I will have to part some day when one of us dies, but death will never separate me from God. Isn't that wonderful?"

"Yes," I said, half-heartedly, "wonderful."

My mind had begun to run far ahead of Christian. Those last words of his shook me to the core. This was not a phase Christian was passing through. It was here to stay, and things would never be the same again. I was being gradually shut out from this new love of Christian's, simply because I could not bring myself to want to love God. *What am I to do?* I didn't sleep well that night as I wrestled with all my thoughts.

I held a grudge against God for a jumbled mess of reasons that were hard for me to sort out. But that night, the main crux of the matter began to take shape—God was all-powerful, everywhere-present, and all-knowing. If I could've convinced myself that God was just a wizened, doddering old man in the sky with a long, white beard, who got the world started and then minded His own business, I wouldn't have hated Him so much. I even believe that I could've felt something like affection towards a God like that.

But I'd been too carefully taught to believe any such thing. It made me angry that God in his perfect omniscience knew that I would be born to unloving and indifferent parents, yet allowed my mother to conceive me anyway. An omnipotent God could have changed my mother's hard heart, or kept my father from dying before his time, or given me a happier childhood, or prevented the estrangement between my mother and me, but He didn't. He let all of that happen, seemingly without lifting a finger to help me. And now He was taking away my most treasured source of happiness for Himself. He was taking Christian from me, and I was frightened.

My troubles were compounded as several days passed without any signs of impending labor. My back hurt and the baby kicked so hard at times it was almost painful. I was worried about Christian and worried about the birth. The combination of thoughts and emotions was making me jumpy, and I snapped at Christian over the silliest things. His patience and kindness made me feel guilty which, in turn, increased my irritation.

It all came to a head on Sunday morning. Christian had wanted to go to church, but I wasn't feeling well for obvious reasons, and he wouldn't leave me at home alone. So he got me settled in a chair downstairs and then reached for his Bible.

"I thought that we could read a few verses together since it's Sunday," he explained.

I listened passively, my head resting on my hand. I'm sure his choice of reading material was meant to comfort me. But it didn't.

"Come unto me, all ye that labor and are heavy laden, and I will give you rest. Take my yoke upon you, and learn of me; for I am meek and lowly in heart: and ye shall find rest unto your souls. For my yoke is easy, and my burden is light."

I was bristling inside when he laid the book down, but I didn't say anything.

"I know you're worried, Elizabeth," he put his hand on mine. "I'm sure everything is going to be fine."

But I reacted and pulled my hand away. "You're not the one that has to do the work," I curtly answered him.

"Let's pray about it together," he urged.

"Christian, I wish you'd stop saying that!"

He drew back like I'd slapped him in the face, but I was angry enough that it didn't stop me.

"I don't want you to pray for me, I don't want you to read that Bible to me, and I don't want you to talk to me about it anymore. I'm tired of hearing about it."

"But why?" he asked intently.

"Do I have to tell you why? I just don't want to hear about it anymore."

He surveyed me quietly but sadly. "Well, I certainly don't want to force anything on you, girl. I'll just pray for you by myself."

"I said I don't want you to pray for me. In fact, I wish you'd leave your religion out of our marriage altogether."

"But Elizabeth, I might as well cut off my right arm," he pleaded. "How can I pretend to be something other than what I am? How can I keep something a secret that has made me so happy? It's a hard thing you're asking me to do."

"I'm not good enough for you then. I don't make you happy?"

"You're not being fair, Elizabeth. I've told you so many times how much I love you. Don't you believe me?"

"I understand that you love something else better than me."

"No, Elizabeth. I love you just as much as I ever did," he ran his fingers through his hair and paced around the room. "How can I make you understand? I hardly understand it myself. It's new to me. I know that somehow I'm a different man now, but I feel that I have an even greater capacity to love you than I did before."

"If you really love me, you'll forget about this nonsense," I said deliberately. I folded my hands and put them in my lap. I was desperate, but I composed myself, knowing I had to be calm if I was to get anywhere with him. I sat up straight in my chair and in doing so, caught a glimpse of my face in the mirror hanging on the wall. To my shock, it was as if I was staring into my mother's steely gaze. I could tell by the pained expression in Christian's eyes that he saw the resemblance.

"I can't, Elizabeth. I love you, but I can't."

"Very well then, I'll sleep downstairs tonight."

Christian knelt in front of me squeezing my shoulders.

"Elizabeth, be reasonable. This doesn't have to ruin our marriage. It can make it stronger. Please listen to me."

I stared at my hands, refusing to speak.

Christian dropped his arms, his shoulders sagging.

"All right," he sighed, "if you insist. But I'll sleep down here. You're in no condition to be sleeping in a chair."

Again, I didn't sleep at all. I was being unutterably cruel to him. But I knew he loved me, and I was sure that he'd break if I stood firm long enough. I smothered my tears in my pillow. But in the night, words came back to me that I thought I'd forgotten.

> I tempted all His servitors, but to find
> My own betrayal in their constancy,
> In faith to Him their fickleness to me,
> Their traitorous trueness, and their loyal deceit….
> Still with unhurrying chase,
> And unperturbed pace,
> Deliberate speed, majestic instancy,
> Came on the following Feet,
> And a Voice above their beat—
> "Naught shelters thee, who wilt not shelter Me."

As those words echoed in my mind, I remembered the Hound of Heaven. He never rested, but He wouldn't have me. I would make sure of that.

Chapter 13

It was a horrible time to have a quarrel. The next morning, I began to have occasional mild, painless contractions, and Christian began to cough. He had episodes like this from time to time that were simple to resolve if he took proper precautions. He'd be fine if he did things like not over working himself, breathing deeply, and getting enough sleep. I stopped myself a dozen times a day from urging him to do all those things because I remembered I wasn't speaking to him. I couldn't risk it. It was hard enough seeing the pained expression on his face and the longing in his eyes whenever his glance met mine. If I let down my guard for a moment, I'd give in and I was determined not to let that happen.

For five days, Christian went to work, instructing me to telephone the office from the neighbor's house if anything happened or if I felt anything unusual. I maintained a stony silence until he walked out the door. Each of those days, I dissolved into tears as soon as he was safely down the road. For five days in a row, he came home to dinner, asking the same question.

"How are you feeling, girl?"

"Fine," I would tersely reply.

At the end of each of those five days, he stood at the bottom of the stairs, kissing me and telling me he loved me. I just stood there with my neck stiff and rigid and my arms at my sides, allowing him to do it but not returning his affection. More than anything, I wanted to throw myself in his arms and tell him how sorry I was and how much I loved him. But I was too proud and too stubborn, too intent upon having my own way.

By the end of the week, I was exhausted emotionally and physically. I awoke that Saturday morning to Christian moving quietly about in the bedroom, buttoning his shirt and putting on his tie. I watched him as he collected a few papers off the desk and put them in his briefcase. Before leaving the room, he walked to the bed and leaned over to kiss me on the forehead, but stopped, seeing that I was awake.

"I'm sorry, Elizabeth. I was trying to be quiet and not wake you."

"Christian," I whispered, my eyes filling with tears.

"What is it?" he asked, sitting on the side of the bed.

"Oh, Christian!" I sobbed as I sat up and threw my arms around his neck. "I do love you. I do!"

"I know you do," he assured me.

"Please, Christian, can't you give up this idea for my sake? I don't want things to change. We were so happy."

"Elizabeth," he protested, looking as worn out as I felt. "I can't."

My shoulders slumped as he stared at me, perplexed.

"I truly don't understand why my faith terrifies you so much."

And I couldn't tell him why, for fear he'd think much worse of me than he must already.

"Now listen to me," he said, laying me back down on the pillow. "You're upset and tired, and you need to sleep. I don't want you to get out of bed for at least another hour. We'll talk about this more tonight, alright?"

"All right," I said through my tears.

Before he closed the door, I called him again.

"Are you angry with me, Christian?"

"No," he said smiling, his beautiful eyes heavy and tired. "Now go to sleep. I love you."

I heard his footsteps as he passed under my window, coughing as he walked.

I was so relieved. Everything was right between us, and we would talk again tonight. Surely there was still time to change his mind. It couldn't possibly be as bad as I thought.

I woke up at noon, feeling vaguely uneasy. Maybe it was the weather. It had been fitfully stormy all week, and the sky was already clouding over. I got up and dressed slowly, every movement taking twice as long as it would have six months ago.

After I'd eaten, the rain began a steady descent that didn't show any sign of letting up. I tried to keep busy doing small tasks around the house, but it was hard for me to settle down to anything. As evening came on and the skies darkened, I made a simple dinner and sat down to wait for Christian. The fatigue of the last five days caught up with me again, and my eyelids drooped. I woke up four hours later, and it was pitch black in the house. Sleepily, I lit the lamp in the kitchen and looked at the clock. It said ten o'clock. I turned around and saw the food still sitting on the table, untouched.

"Christian!" I called, but he didn't answer. I took the lamp with me and looked upstairs, but there was no sign of him. Panic washed over me.

"I have to be calm," I said aloud, lowering myself to a chair. There was really only one thing I could do. I had to go look for him. I stood up as quickly as I could and threw a scarf over my head. The rain stung my face as I left the house. Small rivers of water coursed down the street, soaking my feet to the ankles. I hardly noticed how wet and cold I was or even the gradually increasing pain in my back. I headed straight for the church. I thought perhaps Christian had stopped to see the minister and been carried away in conversation, not noticing how late it had become.

But the church was dark and the door locked when I reached it. The parsonage had an equally empty and vacant look, and no one answered my knock. I walked the streets for hours, looking for any sign of him, but nothing turned up. Tears of desperation mingled with the rain and streamed down my face as I took refuge in a doorway. I had no idea what to do short of going to the police. But then I looked up and realized I was standing directly across the street from the *Gazette*. A faint glow of light coming from one of the windows shone through the rain, and I saw a familiar automobile parked outside.

I crossed the street and pounded on the door. "Warren!" I called. "Please come quickly!"

"Mrs. Brown?" he asked incredulously when he opened the door. "It's one o'clock in the morning. What on earth are you doing out at this time of night in this weather? Come in out of that rain and sit down."

"No, I can't," I protested. "I…"

"Sit down before you fall down," he ordered.

"Is Christian here?" I probed.

"No, of course not. He left hours ago."

"But he never came home."

Warren grunted as he turned away, "I don't blame him. I would've been gone long before this if I were him. He's gone through hell on earth with you this week. I hope you're satisfied." I hung my head, feeling the truth of his words. "Now I'm not a religious man," he continued, lighting a cigarette, "but it didn't bother me when he talked about his faith. Why couldn't you have just let him have his religion? It wasn't hurting you. And anyway, nine times out of ten, these conversions are just passing fancies. He'll probably forget all about it in a year."

I lifted my head and wiped my tears away. "I know. I know I've been awful to him, and I haven't been the wife he deserves. But I do love him, and I'll do anything to find him. Please help me, Warren," I begged him. "I don't know what else to do."

He sighed and ground out his cigarette in an ashtray on the desk. "Where have you looked?" he asked me.

"Everywhere," I said, wincing and rubbing my belly.

"What's wrong?"

"Nothing," I answered defensively.

"Are you in pain?"

"A little, but that doesn't matter. I've got to find Christian."

He stood there, looking perturbed and concerned all at once.

"Have you checked the hospital?" he asked.

"No." I responded in fear.

"Okay, I'll take you. I suspect that whether he's at the hospital or not, you'll need to make a trip there soon." With that, he helped me up, and we headed down to his car. As we rode along, I sat silently in Warren's automobile, clenching and unclenching my fists.

"Oh God," I whispered, staring blindly out the window, "if I find Christian safe and well, I promise I'll never make him unhappy again. I'll even be a Christian if that's what he wants. I swear it."

At that moment, I was willing to do anything to have him back again, even if it meant going to church every Sunday for the rest of my life, praying with him, listening to him read the Bible for hours at a time, and pretending that I liked it.

"We should've stopped at your house so you could change into dry clothes. You're soaked through," Warren said, glancing in my direction as we approached the hospital.

"I'll be fine," I said, my hand on the door handle.

"Just slow down now, Mrs. Brown. I'm going to hold on to your arm. The last thing you need is a fall."

My eyes squinted as we walked through the door of the hospital. There was an attractive young nurse about my age at the desk along with an old grim one. As we walked closer, I could see the young one's eyes were puffy and red, and she sniffled as she wrote something on a piece of paper.

Warren cleared his throat, "Excuse me."

The old nurse looked up while the young one ducked her head down.

"We're here looking for this young woman's husband."

"Name, please?" she asked coldly.

"I'm Elizabeth Brown," I responded, "and my husband's name is Christian."

At my words the young girl's head shot up. "Where have you been?" she demanded of me, crying again. "He's been calling your name for the past three hours!"

"Get a hold of yourself, Becky!" The old one glared sternly at her.

"Where is he?" I asked my panic rising. She came around the desk and put a kind hand on my arm.

"I'll take you to him right now, but you must understand he's very ill."

"I didn't know," I said looking from her to Warren. "Warren, was he sick when he left the office?"

"He was coughing and a little flushed," Warren admitted.

"How did he get here?" I asked.

"A stranger found him around eight o'clock this evening and brought him in. He was lying on the ground very weak and feverish,"

"Is he going to be all right? He's not going to die, is he?"

"I'll be honest with you. If he pulls through the night, it'll be a miracle. I'm very sorry."

My legs were suddenly weak, and I reached out and steadied myself with a hand on the desk. Warren tightened his grip on my arm.

"You'd better sit down," he said, trying to steer me to a chair. But I pulled my arm away.

"No, I think you're wrong," I told the nurse.

Slowly, she shook her head to indicate her doubt.

"Please take me to him. I'll help take care of him. He'll get well."

The halls were stark and cold, and our shoes made a harsh clatter on the immaculately clean floor. The new electric bulbs hanging from the ceiling glared into my eyes. Through the haze of my mind, I saw a group of weeping people gathered around a young man in a bed. His face was still and lifeless. From somewhere farther away I heard a rasping, labored breathing that became louder as we went on. My heart pounded in my ears. I could scarcely hear the nurse as she directed me to one bed in the ward. The man lying there was struggling to breathe, his mouth wide open with a blue color to his skin.

"Elizabeth," he whispered, turning his head with great difficulty.

My hand went to my mouth as I recognized my husband. His chest heaved in the struggle to get air into his lungs. I knelt by the bed and took his hand. He clutched it with all the strength he had left in his body.

"I'm here, Christian," I said, putting my hand on his forehead. There were flecks of blood on the white sheets.

"Elizabeth, I...," he tried to tell me something, but began to cough. His whole body shook with the coughing, and I thought it would never end.

"Can't you do anything for him?" I begged the nurse. "There must be something!"

She simply shook her head.

"I'm sorry, Christian," I sobbed. "I didn't know."

"Elizabeth," Christian tried again. With his other hand, he held out his Bible to me. "He…loves you."

Shaking, I took it from him. Then he gave up. The light went out of his eyes, and he was gone. My hand was still locked in his, but he was gone.

It's my fault was all I could think.

"But I didn't know he was so sick," I said to no one in particular. "If I'd known, I would've taken better care of him." I stared at the flecks of dried blood on his still face. "I didn't know, or I would've come," I mumbled. I tried to stand up, but I couldn't loosen my hand.

Then the grief overwhelmed me. "I didn't know!" I sobbed more deeply. Then I screamed, the pain I'd been ignoring all night intruding on Christian's quiet rest. "I didn't know. I didn't know!" I kept crying.

I heard the old nurse calling for help, and Warren was kneeling beside me trying to pry Christian's fingers away. People were lifting me up and carrying me away, and I screamed and screamed.

It's a strange thing. When my labor began, the pain of my grief far outstripped the physical pain I'd dreaded and feared for so many months. During those long hours before daylight, I remembered every harsh and cruel thing I'd ever said to him. I saw him slowly turn his head, chest heaving, looking so anxious. His eyes pleaded with me.

At day break, my baby came into the world. It was a little boy. I stared down into his tiny red face as I kissed his cheek. He opened his eyes after I nursed him and looked solemnly at me.

"I'm sorry," I whispered, my tears falling on his face. What a sad world I had welcomed him into. He was a poor, fatherless little boy. "I love you," I whispered through my tears.

"What will you call him?" the nurse asked.

"I'll name him after his father, Christian. Does Chris suit you, little one? It's a little name for a little boy." When they took him away, I fell into a fitful sleep, hearing bits of a whispered conversation.

"We've had two deaths since Mr. Brown's… similar symptoms… too dangerous for her to stay… leave right away…"

"I understand. As soon as you can get her ready, I'll drive her home."

I was too exhausted for the news to alarm me. I did what I was told and found myself riding home, holding little Chris.

"I'm very sorry, Mrs. Brown," Warren said.

"Thank you, Warren."

"I'd like to take care of funeral arrangements for Christian if you'll let me. He was a good friend."

"Yes, of course."

"Please don't hold what I said against me. You know, at the office last night."

"No, you were right to say it. He might be alive now if it weren't for me."

"Please don't say that," he urged.

I rested my head on one hand, and we said no more to each other as we traveled home. When we arrived, Warren helped me to bed and asked the neighbor to look in on me once or twice a day. He assured me that everything would be taken care of. But I just wanted him to leave. I wanted to be alone. I held Chris close to me and watched him fall asleep. In a twenty-four hour period, I'd lost my husband and gained a son. I grieved, I rejoiced, and I feared. I saw Christian's contorted face as he held out his Bible to me.

"He...loves you," were his last words to me.

I turned my face to the wall and wept.

Chapter 14

Dear Journal,

    I buried my Christian in a cold, dark hole in the ground. Little Chris lay in my arms so quietly, gazing in infant wonderment at this new world he'd come into, unaware of all the people dressed in black around us. I dread the day when he'll understand that the world isn't new—that it's old and ugly and full of misery and heartache. Even as we buried his father, we were but two of the seven people in the graveyard, staring into dark holes in the ground.

I fell into bed every night, fatigued in mind and body, only to wake up every hour because of my dream. It wasn't a nightmare. It was always the same beautiful dream. I dreamt of bright skies and heads of wheat waving around me. There, ahead of me, was a young barefoot boy in overalls, with his head thrown back, whistling. He smiled when he saw me and we ran to each other. I laid my head on his shoulder and I felt his arms around me.

"You're my girl now," I heard him say. Christian's girl. I loved that thought.

That's when I always woke up and saw the empty side of the bed. His pillow lying undisturbed next to me was a harsh reminder of what had happened. For a couple of days, I could smell the scent of him on the pillow, but even that was beginning to dissipate. I was alone, and I didn't belong to anyone now.

    My world was upside down, changing from a life of security and happiness with Christian, to an existence of crushing responsibility and ever-present fear. After I buried Christian, I finally awoke to the situation around me. The papers spoke of influenza, the worst seen in possibly centuries. People were dying; strong, vibrant young people in excellent health were taking ill and dying one or two days later. Cruelly, many of them were soldiers. Warren told me that the dead young man I saw at the hospital was a soldier recently wounded at the front and sent back to the States to recover. He'd survived mortar, grenades, and mustard gas, only to return home and die of influenza.

    Fear was almost tangible. I could feel it as I looked through my window at people walking quickly by on the street, avoiding their friends and acquaintances to get to the safety of their homes. I saw it in my neighbor's eyes as she set a meal on my table and scuttled back out the door as soon as she discovered what Christian had died of. She never came back.

I thought of my mother all alone, and I hoped she was well. I watched the newspaper and was relieved to find her voice still there. I wondered if she thought of me. Each night, I held Chris close to me in the dark, expecting influenza to take hold of us in the morning. In my braver moments, I prayed that it would, but it didn't. As He'd refused me in my father's case and Christian's, God would not even give me this. He seemed just as determined to keep me in the world as He was to take Christian out of it, and every morning I woke to the questions. They endlessly circled in my mind. *How will I live? I have to have money. How can I get money? I have to work. What can I do?* Nothing, was my realization; it always stopped there. My privileged life hadn't taught me any working skills, and the ones I'd learned since marriage were feeble, nothing someone would pay for. *So, how will I live? How will I provide for my child?*

If it hadn't been for Warren, I don't know what would have happened to us. He came every day, out of a sense of responsibility I suppose. The first few days, he came to make sure I was recovering, lumbering up the stairs like a bull in a china shop. He stepped on poor Georgette's tail often enough that she finally took to hiding under the bed when she heard him coming. When it was certain that we were in the midst of an epidemic, he continued to come, checking for fevers or coughs. He brought groceries and tried to cheer me up. He had a way with little Chris, loud bear of a man though he was. When Chris fussed and cried, Warren could calm him down almost immediately. In Warren's arms, Chris looked like he weighed no more than a teaspoon. He was also the one that came with the unexpected answer to my questions.

"Mrs. Brown," he said, as he was getting ready to leave one day. "The boys at the office have been thinking about your situation for quite a while. We've set up a fund for you. We're all pitching in. We've done some figuring, and we can send you seventy-five dollars a month."

"Oh, it's too kind," I protested. "They all have families to care for."

"It's only until you're back on your feet and can provide for yourself, you understand." Warren seemed firm in his plan. "Please let us do it for Christian's sake at least."

My shoulders slumped and I stared at a crack in the wood floor. I nodded my head finally. "Please thank them for me," I responded.

"I will," he assured me as he turned to leave. Then he stopped. "I wish you wouldn't blame yourself for what happened. Even if you'd waited on him hand and foot, he wouldn't have had a chance. Not against this influenza, the way his lungs were.

"I suppose you're right," I mumbled soberly.

He shuffled his feet and said, "Well, I'll be going now."

I tried to believe that it wasn't my fault, but the memories of those five days before Christian's death were too fresh. There was no doubt in my mind that I was guilty in some small degree.

Christian's pastor came to visit me, offering his condolences. I said as little as possible in the hopes he would go away soon. I couldn't bear to have him there, thinking horrible things about me. He asked if I needed anything, and I told him I didn't. He invited me to church, and I declined. He left after telling me to contact him if ever I needed anything. After he'd gone, I wished I hadn't behaved so rudely. Christian would have wanted me to be kind to his pastor. It seemed I was bound to fail Christian in every way.

But I mustn't fail little Chris, I thought.

I wanted to be a good mother. I resolved that he'd grow up feeling my love for him. He wouldn't be lonely and cast off as I was. Even in my grief, I loved to hold him in my arms, rocking him back and forth. He stared up at me with those solemn eyes. It made me feel calm to look into them. He was so innocent and curious and trusting. I talked and sang to him. I sang the songs I learned at school from the Woodwards, songs about God's love. It didn't seem hypocritical to sing of God's love to Chris, even though I didn't love God. I reasoned that though God didn't seem to love me, it was only natural that He must love Chris who'd done nothing wrong. And Chris liked the singing so much. He opened his little eyes wide and cooed along with me. It was as close to happiness as I could feel.

A month passed and the influenza finally left my hometown, although it continued to travel throughout the country. I received a letter from Genie and one from Mrs. Woodward. Both were worried about me and anxious to hear how I'd faired. Genie's husband had been very sick but was recovering, and the Woodwards had lost one student to the disease. I was glad they were all well, but it was a few days before I could bring myself to reply and tell them about Christian. All I said was that he'd died of influenza. I kept my shameful behavior before his death to myself. I'd decided that I would never tell anyone. It would stay between me, Warren, and my journal.

Chris was healthy and growing. He was beginning to sleep more at night, which made me feel much more rested. When I put him on the floor on a blanket, his eyes followed Georgette as she prowled around the house. I remember the first time he smiled at me. It was on the day a fierce wind blew all the leaves from the trees. I carried him with me everywhere I went in the house. I talked to him while I worked, smiling at his concentrated attention to every word I said.

I sketched pictures of him in my journal while he napped, stopping to watch his chest rise and fall in a peaceful, even pattern. I was fascinated by such perfect rest, wondering when the serenity of babyhood would end and the fears of life would enter. I hoped it would be a long time before that happened. I smiled for him when he was awake, even through my worries about money matters. I wanted him to feel safe and secure whether I did or not.

I WAS SITTING IN MY CHAIR reading a book one evening in early November when change arrived again. Warren had just left after starting a fire in the stove, and I'd already put Chris to bed. The wind was blowing wildly outside, and I threw a blanket over my legs. I thought I heard footsteps outside but couldn't tell for certain because of the blowing. Suddenly, there was a smart rat-a-tat on the door. I got up and looked through the keyhole. There was an old woman standing on the steps with a suitcase, holding her hat on her head with both hands. Her face looked vaguely familiar.

I opened the door and nodded her in, struggling to keep the doorknob from flying out of my hands.

"Good evening," I said. "How can I help you?"

"Don't you remember me, Elizabeth?"

"Not quite," I answered quizzically. I stared at her for a moment and then it dawned on me. "Nanny?" was my tentative reply.

"Yes, but as you're a grown woman now, I think it would be permissible to call me Jane."

At that we both laughed. She looked the same but different too. Somehow she wasn't quite so grim and stern as I remembered her looking. There was a quiet patience about her, the kind of patience that comes from living a hard life and living it well. Perhaps it was my perception of her that had changed.

"How did you manage to find me?" I asked. "The last I heard from you was...oh, at least ten years ago or more. You were taking care of a little girl."

"Yes, I was still with that family until September, but she died then."

"I'm sorry," I said, my eyes filling with tears.

"By this time, she would have been married. I could've stayed on with them, but it was too hard. She was like my own child, and I wanted to get away for a while."

"Of course," I replied.

"Life brings its share of sorrow, does it not?" she asked, giving my hand a squeeze.

"Come and sit down, Jane. You must be tired," I urged her, taking her hat and coat and hanging them up. "It seems so strange for you to be here, talking to me after so many years. You look well."

"For an old woman, you mean!"

"Indeed, I thought no such thing!"

"Well, it's the truth. I feel the years. My back aches in weather like this. But I can work just as hard as I ever did, I'll have you know."

"I believe it." I chuckled as she thumped her fist on the arm of the chair.

"My, how the time speeds by." She smiled, shaking her head as she looked at me. "I can remember as clear as day, sitting by your bed with my knitting, trying to get you to eat something, anything. You were so thin and pale and quiet. How I worried about you. And now here you are, a lovely young lady, the picture of your mother."

"Thank you."

"It's quite remarkable how young she looks."

"You've seen her?" I asked quickly.

"Well, naturally. She told me where to find you."

She knows where I live? I thought to myself. *What else does she know?*

"Did she say anything about me? Or send any message?" I asked.

"No, she didn't."

I nodded once again, looking past her at the fire. Of course she wouldn't send a message. It was silly of me to ask. Jane cleared her throat, turning her piercing gaze upon me.

"You must tell me all that has happened these past years. Perhaps you should begin with why you live here in a house by yourself and your mother lives across the same town in a house by herself, yet neither of you seems to know much about the other."

"She didn't…tell you anything?" I asked hesitantly.

"Nothing at all, I'm afraid."

"I got married."

"How lovely," she commented with a smile. "I must meet him."

"No, you can't. He died in September."

"I see," she paused. Her eyes were sad with understanding. "Are there any children?"

"One," I smiled. "Little Chris. I put him to bed a while ago. Would you like to come and see him?"

"Oh, I would love to see him," she answered.

So we tiptoed up the stairs together. I opened the door and we walked in softly. The light from the hall lit up his little face. Jane smiled as she peered down at him, arranging his blanket.

"He's a beautiful child," she whispered. "And it's no wonder."

She reached up and patted my cheek.

"Mother didn't want me to marry Christian," I said, once we'd left the room and shut the door. "She wanted me to marry someone of means. Ultimately, I think she would've been happier if I hadn't married at all, and when I insisted upon marrying him, she disowned me. I haven't seen or spoken to her since."

I wondered if Jane knew about Alexander Stonely. I almost asked and then thought better of it. I hadn't even told Christian, so there was no need to tell anyone else.

"Do you have any money?" she was asking.

"No," I answered as I hung my head, "just charity. Warren King, Christian's boss, has very graciously been sending me money for the past month, but it makes me uneasy to live off what I haven't earned. I don't know what else to do, though. I've wracked my brain for ways I could earn some money, but I can't think of a thing."

Jane sat quietly for a few minutes, pondering. Then she straightened and tapped her foot on the ground.

"Well, I have some savings. I think if we pooled our resources, we could make a go of it."

"What?" I was stunned at her statement.

"That is, between the two of us, I'm sure we could find some way to keep ourselves. For now, we can use my savings."

"Jane, I couldn't ask you to do such a thing!"

"You didn't ask me. I offered. And what's more, I won't be turned down."

"But Jane—"

"Now, Elizabeth," she stopped me. "I don't have anyone, and you don't have anyone. I must make myself useful. You need the help so let me help you."

I just smiled, not knowing what I could say. Finally I admitted, "You seem to have come at just the right time."

"God arranged it, and I'm sure He'll show us the way. There must be something you can do to earn your keep."

I didn't contradict her. I would never try to change a Christian's mind again. It was better to leave well enough alone. Besides, her determination filled me with hope. Of course there was something I could do. There had to be. I wasn't stupid, after all.

I piled blankets on the floor in Chris' room and let Jane have the bed. There would be time enough later to rearrange the furniture and get another bed for me. I curled up on the floor that night, listening to her snore from the other room, but I didn't mind at all.

Chapter 15

I was inclined to ignore the circles under my eyes that appeared after Chris' birth. All I wanted to do was roll up my sleeves and find some way to earn a living right away, but Jane wisely urged me to wait and rest a while. Jane took charge of the house as she cooked, cleaned, and fussed over me and Chris, and scolded me when I didn't eat enough. In a way, handing over the reins to her and letting someone else do the worrying was a great relief. After a few months had passed, though, her bossing began to wear on me.

She was strong-willed, and she had black and white ideas of how a household should be run. She had a routine and a formula for any task, whether it happened to be the ironing or washing the dishes. Naturally, I never did things the way she thought they ought to be done. I didn't put quite enough starch on the collars or scrub the dishes long enough to make them sparkle. When I remarked that I wasn't overly conscientious about a strict schedule for Chris' feeding and napping, Jane was scandalized.

But most of her huffing and puffing I could overlook. If I thought about it long enough, I could see that her mode of operation was truly the best way. She had so much more experience than I did. When it came to Warren, however, I wasn't willing to bend. Upon meeting him for the first time, Jane took an instant disliking to him.

"I don't approve of that man," she told me, her knitting needles clicking furiously. "He's loud and profane."

"He has a kind heart, Jane," I returned mildly.

"Kind heart or not, he ought not to hang about. It's indecent."

My head shot up when I heard that. "How?" I demanded.

She shifted uncomfortably and replied, "You're only newly widowed, Elizabeth."

"Why Jane, I'm surprised at you!" I sputtered. "He's fond of Chris, that's all."

"Hmm, well I think you ought to discourage him."

I realized then, that if I didn't put my foot down and put it down as gently as possible, there would be trouble down the road between us.

"Listen, Jane," I said quietly. "As much as I love having you here with me and appreciate all you've done, you've got to understand something. I'm not a little girl anymore, and if we're going to get on well together, we have to decide right now who's going to be in charge. Since this is my house, I think it ought to be me."

She looked at me over her spectacles, frowning.

"And as for Warren," I continued to inform her, "he will always be welcome in this house. He was a friend of Christian's, and I owe him a tremendous debt. Had it not been for him, Chris and I would be on the street."

I put my hand on her arm as I appealed to her, "Don't be angry, Jane."

She patted my hand and coughed.

"I'm a nosy old woman, and I apologize."

"Accepted," I said with a smile. "To put your mind at ease, I truly doubt Warren has any intentions towards me besides that of a man trying to look out for his friend's widow. But if I'm mistaken, you're right to object. It would be indecent. But don't worry. I don't believe I'll ever marry again. I could never love anyone as much as I loved Christian."

Jane was wrong this time, much to my relief. Warren quickly determined that Jane was a permanent fixture, and his visits decreased to once or twice a month, instead of once or twice a week. In spite of Jane's disapproval, Warren took to asking where the "old mother hen" was whenever he did come by, and he teased her as she worked in the kitchen. Bit by bit, he wore away at her until she was rushing about to get him a snack if she saw him coming.

"Incorrigible man!" she'd sputter as soon as he left, shaking her head. "Such a quantity of mud he tracks all over my clean floor." But I knew better and I smiled to myself.

It was good to smile on occasion. Even though life had taken a turn upwards, I still felt the empty void where Christian had been. The dream didn't wake me up anymore, but sometimes my mind played tricks on me. If I was upstairs at suppertime and Jane chanced to open the door downstairs, I thought it was Christian. Some days, I even had to stop myself from running down the stairs to greet him, my heart pounding. When Chris rolled over by himself for the first time, I had it in my mind to tell Christian all about it when he came home. Then I remembered.

I didn't tell Jane about my struggle. But somehow she knew exactly what I was thinking, anyway.

"Take your time, Elizabeth. It'll pass," she told me. "Do the things you enjoy. Play with the baby. Write about what happened. I think that would help you."

I shuddered inside. She didn't know the half of it. She prayed all the time, just like Christian. Sometimes, I heard her praying for me. *Would she keep praying if she knew everything?* I wondered.

She was worried about me. The circles weren't going away and my clothes were beginning to hang loose about my already slender body. I was still losing sleep at night, worrying about the future, and I had no appetite. I forced myself to eat anyway since Chris depended upon me. I'd lost interest in reading, and I sat and stared out the window, feeling restless and ill at ease when Chris was down for his nap.

"I'd like you to write your friend, Genie," Jane announced abruptly one evening.

Her voice jolted me out of my reverie. I'd lost track of time, sitting with my hands folded in my lap, staring into the fire.

"Hmm?" was my only response.

"Yes. I'd like you to ask her if you can come and stay with her for a few days, maybe a week or more. Warren and I agree that you need a change of scenery."

"Is that so? And who prescribed Genie?" I couldn't help but smile a little.

"Well, at least consider it, Elizabeth," she answered firmly.

"It does sound nice," I admitted, staring back into the fire. "I'd hate to impose upon her though."

"From what you tell me, she's not one to feel imposed upon. Why don't you write her tomorrow morning?"

I knew it would do me good to see her again so I wrote the letter, and a few weeks later, on a bright but frigid day in January, I received her answer. "Of course, you must come!" she wrote. "Bring Jane with you and stay as long as you like. We have plenty of room. I can't wait to see your little man."

So we went. It was still very cold the day we left, as we locked the door behind us. I'd bundled Chris up in a few blankets. His bright eyes and little nose peeped out at me and I laughed. Warren was kind enough to drive us there. I'd thought about taking the train, but I wasn't sure if I could handle the memories just then.

As we pulled up to the house after an hour of driving, Warren honked the horn. The door opened, and there was Genie waving with one hand and desperately trying to prevent her little boy with the other hand from running out in the snow without his coat and shoes. Lawrence appeared behind her and scooped the little fellow up in his arms. There was a catch in my throat to see them standing there together, a complete family. I forced a smile as I stepped out of the automobile. I didn't have to force it for long though, with the welcome I received. Genie wrapped her arms around me with tears in her eyes.

"Oh, I'm so glad you're here," she whispered.

"Welcome, Elizabeth." Lawrence smiled. His eye quickly moved to Jane, loaded down with blankets and bags. "Let me get that for you, Jane."

After I'd introduced Warren, he took his leave. "No need to worry about the house," he told me. "I'll keep an eye on it. And I'll make sure to feed Georgette. Just get rested up."

"Thank you, Warren," I said, pressing his big hand. "Travel safely."

Genie had arranged everything so that Jane had her own room and Chris and I had another.

"The children will sleep in our room for now," she explained. "I wanted you to have a place you could go to have some quiet. Things can be a bit rowdy with these two." She nodded her head at a mischievous Jimmy, peeking in through the door, and Rebekah, just taking her first few shaky steps on the rug.

It was a simple room, but pleasant with a nice view of the church and the snow-covered hills behind. "It's lovely," I said. "Thank you, Genie."

"Well, I'll let you get settled. We'll have dinner in a few hours," she told me.

I unwrapped a sleepy Chris from all his blankets and laid him down on the bed for a nap. Then I unpacked my clothes, hanging them up as I went. At the bottom of the trunk was my journal and sketch book. I sat down on the bed and curled up under a blanket, careful not to awaken the baby. I stared out the window at the snowflakes falling softly down and began sketching the landscape while the clock ticked on the wall. Chris sighed and smiled in his sleep.

A few minutes later, I was aware of little Jimmy watching me from the door, hanging back bashfully. "Come see my picture, Jimmy," I whispered, "but quietly."

He climbed up on the bed and peered down at it with interest. "What do you think?" I asked. "Is it any good?"

"That's where I play," he said pointing at my landscape, hopping up and down.

"Shhhh," I warned. "See, the baby's sleeping."

"I hold the baby?" he asked, holding out his arms.

"Not now, sweetie. When he wakes up you may." He nodded soberly, showing how serious he took this job.

"Perhaps tomorrow I'll draw a picture for you. Would you like that?"

He smiled and nodded.

"What kind of picture would you like?"

"I want fox."

"A fox, is it? You know your mind, don't you?" I chuckled. "Well, I'll give it a try."

"I go now," he said, jumping off the bed and running out of the room like a man with places to go and people to see.

IT WAS GOOD TO GET CAUGHT UP with Genie again. I spent time in the kitchen with her, talking about old times as I chopped vegetables and dried dishes. Lawrence was usually holed up in his study, working on Sunday's sermon. But often he would get cold over there and come to the kitchen to warm up, and we would talk. The more I knew of Lawrence, the more I liked him. I didn't understand how so much goodness could reside in one person. He was quiet but not morose, thoughtful but not brooding, and calm but not cold. He was firm with the children but not harsh. He was serious about his duties as husband and father, but he wasn't so serious that he couldn't laugh and wrestle with Jimmy. He was kind all of the time with no exceptions. He said very little compared to most people, but when he opened his mouth, everyone listened.

As I already mentioned, he was serious about his duties as husband and father, and I was introduced to one of those duties soon after I arrived. If asked, I doubt he would call what he did with the family every evening a duty. After dinner that first day, Lawrence got up and took his Bible down while Genie cleared the table. Jane's face brightened considerably when he did that. I hoped mine didn't fall, but something in my expression prompted Lawrence to explain.

"We read and pray after dinner every night," he said to me. "You're welcome to join us. Don't feel like you must though, if you're tired."

"Oh, I'll stay," I replied, shifting Chris in my lap. He was drifting off to sleep.

"We won't be long," Lawrence assured me.

"Yes, there are some sleepy ones among us," Genie smiled, nodding her head towards a heavy-eyed Jimmy.

"We've been reading through the Gospel of John the last few days," Lawrence said for Jane's and my benefit and then he began,

Jesus went unto the Mount of Olives. And early in the morning he came again into the temple, and all the people came unto him; and he sat down, and taught them. And the scribes and Pharisees brought unto him a woman taken in adultery; and when they had set her in the midst, they say unto him, 'Master, this woman was taken in adultery, in the very act. Now Moses in the law commanded us, that such should be stoned: but what sayest thou?'"

I was a bit surprised by the account. Of all the Bible stories I'd read, and I'd read a great deal, I'd never read this before. It didn't seem quite appropriate for children, but I forgot about that soon enough in my eagerness to hear the rest.

"This they said, tempting him, that they might have to accuse him. But Jesus stooped down, and with his finger wrote on the ground, as though he heard them not. So when they continued asking him, he lifted up himself, and said unto them, 'He that is without sin among you, let him first cast a stone at her.' And again he stooped down, and wrote on the ground. And when they heard it, being convicted in their own conscience, went out one by one, beginning at the eldest, even unto the last: and Jesus was left alone, and the woman standing in the midst. When Jesus had lifted up himself, and saw none but the woman, he said unto her, 'Woman, where are those thine accusers? Hath no man condemned thee?' She said, 'No man, Lord.' And Jesus said unto her, 'Neither do I condemn thee: go, and sin no more.' Then spake Jesus again unto them, saying, 'I am the light of the world: he that followeth me shall not walk in darkness, but shall have the light of life.'"

Then Lawrence closed the Bible and looked up.

"He that is without sin among you, let him first cast a stone at her. And they all dropped their stones and left. That's quite an indictment. To say that Jesus expected those men to be completely without sin before they threw stones is missing the point. That kind of logic could lead us to believe that a murderer should go unpunished for his crime because aren't we all sinners? That leaves us with only one other way to understand this passage. All those men couldn't bring themselves to throw stones at her because they knew in their hearts that they were guilty of adultery too. The only one qualified to throw stones was the one sitting on the ground, drawing in the dirt, the one who was God in the flesh. And he said, 'Neither do I condemn thee.' Then what did he say, Jimmy?"

Stifling a yawn, Jimmy said, "Don't sin anymore."

"That's right," Lawrence said, ruffling Jimmy's hair. "We're almost done. Don't fall asleep yet. 'Go thou and sin no more,'" he continued. "Jesus didn't come for self-righteous people because He resists the proud. He came for sinners, to heal the broken-hearted and give grace to humble people. Well, let's pray and get these children to bed."

As I went to sleep that night, I remember thinking how glad I was that I wasn't an adulterer. Then I wondered why so many bad things had happened to me. It wasn't as if I deserved it like the woman in the story did. Of course, I wasn't perfect, but I'd never done anything that wicked. Then the painful remembrance of what happened with me and Christian flashed into my mind. But I put it out of my mind as quickly as I could.

Dear Journal,

I've been here in Genie and Lawrence's home for a week now. I don't know what it is about being here with them, but I feel so restful and quiet in myself since I've come. It's not for lack of noise, I can tell you. The children keep things lively. Little Jimmy is a handful and Genie is forever pulling him out of one scrape or another. We caught him trying to climb out the window upstairs onto the roof the other day. He intended to use the roof as a springboard to jump into a pile of snow down below. I have to remind myself that I may be in Genie's position with Chris in a few more years. I must brace myself.

Now that I'm here, total inertia has set in. I sleep and sleep, like I haven't slept in weeks. It's a sound, dreamless sleep. Jane and Genie are pleased, but I feel so lazy. When I'm not sleeping or caring for Chris, I spend a good deal of time drawing. I use Chris, Jimmy, and Rebekah as my subjects mostly, but I've even tried my hand at sketching a fox. Jimmy found one with an injured paw outdoors the other day and brought it to the house.

How he managed to carry it in without being bit is beyond me. It seemed very weak, so that probably had something to do with it. Lawrence set it up in a crate by the fire, and we're nursing it back to health. Apparently, Jimmy meant it when he said he wanted a picture of a fox. I'm sketching them together. I make slow progress because it's hard for Jimmy to sit still for more than ten or fifteen minutes at a time. But I like the progress I see.

Jane had been right as always. It was good for me to get away from home with all of its memories and cares. I could never rid myself completely of my sadness. It lay just beneath the surface, even as I smiled at Jimmy's antics. But new scenery and fresh faces helped me to keep it where it was, below the surface where it couldn't overwhelm me. The children helped me the most. Besides Chris, I'd never been around children before, and they lifted my spirits. If I sat still for any length of time, Rebekah climbed into my lap and Jimmy begged for stories. Rebekah was just a little over a year old and only said a few words, but Jimmy and I carried on conversations. We were great friends now.

"You get on so well with the children, Elizabeth," Genie remarked. "They love you already. Thank you for entertaining them." But really, they entertained me more than anything.

After I'd stayed for a few weeks, I felt rested and almost as energetic as I had been before I became pregnant with Chris. And with my surge of energy came the old desire to do something to earn my keep. I talked to Genie and Lawrence about it, but they were at as much of a loss as I was.

"If only I could put my education to some good use by teaching or something," I sighed. "But who would hire a woman with a baby to teach at a school? At this point, he's too young for me to leave with Jane all day."

"I wonder if the Woodwards could use your help," Genie said.

"I wonder," I echoed, then frowned. "No, then I'd have to leave my home."

"There's no harm in considering it or even asking," Lawrence put in. "You wouldn't have to do it if you didn't want to."

"I should invite them to dinner while you're here," Genie said. "The students are all gone for the holidays, so this would be the best time for them. Even if they don't have a position for you, they might come up with some better ideas. And besides, I'd just like to see them again."

Genie contacted them, and it was decided that they'd come the next Sunday. I waited for the day with much anticipation. I was eager to show Chris to them and eager to hear what advice they might have for me. In times of trouble, it's only natural to look to parents for help, even as adults. And the Woodwards were the closest thing to parents I'd ever had.

While I waited, I worked. I perfected Jimmy's drawing just to keep busy, and I kept searching for ideas. Because, as Jane was always saying, "Idle hands are the devil's playground."

Chapter 16

The Woodwards arrived early Sunday morning, much to everyone's delight. After church and the noon meal, we sat together in the parlor, talking and enjoying one another's company. I smiled as I looked around at the gathering. There was Mrs. Woodward, fussing over Chris in the corner. Beside her sat Genie and Lawrence, arms entwined. Jane was in a rocker, knitting. Mr. Woodward, who looked a little older since I saw him last but not very, was being showered with Jimmy's attention. Little Rebekah was toddling from one chair to the next, putting some contraband item or another into her mouth and causing a general uproar every time it was discovered.

Jimmy ran up the stairs and came down a little later with my sketchbook in his hand.

"I show Mr. Woodward pictures?" he asked, flashing me his most winning smile.

"Oh, I suppose. They're nothing spectacular, Mr. Woodward," I explained. "But I enjoy creating them."

He took the book and began paging through it, stopping every so often to examine a drawing a little more closely. He took his time, and I became lost in conversation with Genie again. A little later, I vaguely became aware of the fact that he'd finished and was looking thoughtfully at me.

"How long have you been drawing, Elizabeth?" he asked.

"Oh, I don't know," I said, trying to remember. "I suppose I began when you gave me that first journal. Why?"

"For some reason, it never occurred to me that you did draw. I must have seen you at it occasionally. There were so many other things on my mind... But these drawings are really quite remarkable...quite remarkable. Have you seen the drawing of Jimmy with the fox?" he asked Lawrence and Genie.

"No," Genie said, moving closer to look over his shoulder, "I never had a chance. I've been so busy." She moved over to look at the sketchbook in Mr. Woodward's hands and said, "Why, Elizabeth, that's lovely. Somehow you really caught them both. Isn't it beautiful, Lawrence?"

He nodded in his quiet way.

"Elizabeth," Mr. Woodward said, "I have an idea for you. What if you were to write a little story, perhaps about something like this fox here, and illustrate it with your drawings? It could be quite educational. You've had time to observe the fox and its habits. You could include many of those details."

"You mean, put a book together?" I asked, leaning forward a bit.

"Yes, nothing very long, you know. It would be for children, after all."

I'd never thought of that before. A world of possibility seemed to be opening in front of me, and I couldn't help smiling at everyone.

"But how do you suppose I'd go about publishing it?"

"Surely Warren could help you, or at least know someone that could," Lawrence suggested.

"Yes, that might work," I said, slowly. "It just might."

I couldn't wait to get back home again, as anxious as I was to talk to Warren right away. I finished out my visit in a flurry of excitement. I did some tramping around in the woods through the snow with Jimmy, sketching little winter birds and enjoying myself immensely.

"Jimmy, how did you carry the fox home, and where did you find it?" I asked him on one of these jaunts.

He brought me right to the place he'd seen our friend the fox, and after a bit more searching, we found an entrance to its den. He told me how he'd come across it, and there was my story—Jimmy and the Fox. The same day that Warren came to take us home, all of us went to the woods to send the fox off. Lawrence carried the fox in its crate, and it poked its nose through the slats, looking quite well and energetic. Lawrence set the crate down, and we stood back to watch. Out it bounded, looking around at us with its keen little face, and then it scampered away.

"Goodbye, fox," Jimmy said, waving mournfully.

Poor fellow, he lost his fox and his new-found friends in one day, and he was inconsolable.

"Don't cry, Jimmy," I said, kneeling down beside Warren's automobile and looking him in the eye. "I'll come and visit again, or maybe you'll come and visit me. Now look here." Then I pulled out the picture of him and the fox. "Someday, this is going to be in a book. And when it is, I'll send my first copy to you because you brought it all about. All right, come give me a kiss."

There were hugs and handshakes all around and tears from Genie.

"God bless your endeavors, Elizabeth," Lawrence told me, shaking my hand. "Safe travels."

When we'd gotten a fair piece down the road, Warren turned to me and asked, "What's all this about books and endeavors?"

"Oh, Warren, I have such a plan, but I need you to help me!"

I tried to show him my pictures on the way, but Jane became so nervous with him swerving this way and that on the road that she put a stop to it. So when the supper dishes had been cleared away that evening and Chris put to bed, we sat down at the table and discussed my idea. Rather, I rattled on while Warren listened.

"You see, I have the story all written and most of the drawings finished. I'd put the text on the left side and the drawings on the other. I'm so glad Mr. Woodward suggested this to me. Only, I don't know how to go about publishing it. I was hoping you could help me with that."

I stopped for breath to find him looking at me curiously with a bit of a smile on his face.

"She looks very well, doesn't she Jane?" he asked.

"Very well," Jane responded.

"Oh, never mind that," I said, waving my hand. "What about the book? Can you help me, Warren?"

He cleared his throat and looked down at my pile of papers and sketches a little more studiously.

"They're very good," he said, "and the story is nice. I don't know much about this kind of publishing, children's books and all. But I could make a few calls and talk to some friends and see what they have to say."

I smiled broadly and pressed my hands together.

"But, Elizabeth, you have to understand. It's not always easy to get your foot in the door," he warned me. "It may take quite a long time. It may never happen at all."

"Yes, but I have to at least try," I pleaded. "I have to have something to work on. I hate living off other people's money!"

I quickly put my hand on his arm.

"That sounds so ungrateful, Warren, but I don't mean it to be. I'm thankful for all you and the boys at the office have done. But if I can't do anything to support myself and Chris, then she'll think…" I stopped, startled at what I'd almost said and bit my lip. *Mother will think she was right* was the thought that I'd prevented from coming out.

If I could do this, if I could just accomplish what I'd set out to do, Mother would have to take notice of me. She wouldn't be able to look down on me anymore for marrying Christian, or for anything else.

Warren waited for me to finish, but I didn't dare say anything more. Jane looked at me in a quiet but sad understanding.

"Well, then," Warren said, "I'll do my utmost for you."

"Oh, thank you, Warren!"

"With such determination as you have, I'd say you can do just about anything you put your mind to." He smiled at me and lit a cigarette until he saw Jane's displeasure and ground it out.

WARREN MADE SOME INQUIRIES, and while I waited, I perfected my story and the drawings. I wrote a cover letter and put my manuscript together in an orderly fashion, ready to send out at a moment's notice. When Warren gave me an address that a friend of his had given to him, I was ready and took it to the post office the same day. Then came the waiting, which was the hardest thing to do.

"I spend half my life waiting," I grumbled, "always waiting, never getting anywhere."

"Wash the dishes," Jane retorted, rather unsympathetically I thought. "That'll pass the time."

I did that, and then because the dishes were all done, I'd bake dozens and dozens of cookies so I'd have more dishes to wash. Warren and the boys at the office were always more than willing to eat the excess. Sometimes, though, even baking and dishes did nothing to calm my agitated mind. When Chris was taking his nap, the dullness and inactivity would become too much for me to bear, and I'd throw on my coat and walk as fast as I could. After a half hour of fierce exercise, the weight would lift from my mind and my head would be clear again.

"It will all end well," I'd tell myself. Then I'd go home and get Chris up from his nap and he'd bestowed smiles on me like the angelic child he was. He was truly the sun my world revolved around. Besides the fact that I wanted to prove my mother wrong, it was for Chris that I worked and worried so hard. If I failed, I felt I would fail him too. I couldn't let him grow up relying on the charity of friends to give him a chance at life. I had to get that book published. There were no two ways about it.

In March, I got my first rejection. I had just neared the house after one of my wild walks, when Jane came out to meet me with an envelope in her hand.

"I think this is your manuscript," she said, waving it around her head.

I snatched it from her, ran inside, and opened it. On top of Jimmy and the Fox was a letter. I read it under my breath.

"Mrs. Brown, Thank you for your interest…etc., etc.…work shows promise… However, we are unable to take any new manuscripts at this time… Sincerely… etc., etc." I finished, the letter slipping out of my hand.

I slumped in my chair, staring down at the letter.

"I'm sorry, dear," Jane said, rubbing my shoulders.

"Well, then," I sighed, "I'll find someone who will take new manuscripts, that's all. Warren has another address for me. I'll send it out again."

I collected my papers and went upstairs to absorb my disappointment and avoid displaying the tears that threatened to spill over. I sat down at my desk and stared at the wall. I opened my drawer and got a new envelope out.

"That's all," I said to myself, reaching for a pen. "I just have to send it out again."

So I did, four times, to be exact. And once every two months or so, I received the same answer. They were all in different wording, of course, but it was the same answer each time.

"We regret to inform you…"

"Due to an increased volume of submissions…"

"We cannot take your manuscript…"

"We sincerely regret…"

By September, I was thoroughly frustrated and out of sorts. Chris was a year old, beginning to toddle about and get into everything. Added to this, it was the anniversary of Christian's death, and there were so many things weighing on my mind.

"Well, Warren," I said one evening when he'd stopped over. "I don't know what to do. Truly, I don't. I can't stand the thought of giving the whole thing up. I've worked at it so long. If it's not this, then what am I to do?"

He had a thoughtful, but somewhat strange look on his face. He contemplated my face deliberately and then my manuscript.

"Don't give it up, quite yet," he finally said. "There's someone I still haven't talked to."

"Who?" I demanded.

"Just a friend," he said, evading my question. "Someone I've known a long time. Don't lose hope."

More waiting, I thought. To me, things looked very bleak indeed.

"Christian," I whispered in the dark at night. "I wish you were here. I wish I didn't have to be ambitious."

While I'd been waiting and hoping through the summer, I'd taken to bicycling out into the country with my sketchbook and a lunch packed. I didn't go every day or even every week, only here and there when Jane didn't mind watching Chris by herself. And now that I had more waiting to do, I continued my excursions. There was something so restful about lying out in the grass, quietly watching the deer and the field mice pass me by or geese flying overhead. I did a great deal of sketching, gathering ideas for later projects.

Sometimes, I just thought about things. I thought about how I would take Chris with me when he was old enough. What fun it would be, eating picnic lunches and exploring together. Above all, out in the fresh, clean air with the humming of insects and chirping of birds, I felt closest to Christian. When I closed my eyes, I could almost believe he was just a little ways away, ready to smile and wave.

September passed, then October. Warren hadn't heard anything about his latest inquiry, and I was beginning to lose hope. I even talked to Jane about contacting the Woodwards again to see if they needed any help at the school. I hated the thought of leaving the house where Christian and I had been so happy, but I didn't know what else could be done. Then one afternoon, as I had Chris on my lap reading him a story, I heard Warren's familiar footsteps pounding up the walk to the house. He didn't bother to knock but came straight in and handed me an envelope.

I swallowed hard and opened it, and there was a check. There's no need to repeat the amount, but suffice it to say that there was enough money represented in that check to keep Chris, Jane, and I in clothing, food, and shelter for at least a year. I put my hand to my mouth and the book I'd been reading to Chris slid off my lap and fell to the floor.

"You did it, Elizabeth," Warren said. "You sold a book!"

I was still in shock until Chris, who'd been squirming around trying to get the book, took a dive to the floor and bumped his head. Total chaos ensued. Chris set up a wail, and Warren roared up the stairs for Jane to come down and hear the good news, while I distractedly tried to comfort Chris and gaze in rapture at the check simultaneously. Such a small piece of paper, yet it meant so many good things for all of us.

"Warren, whoever this friend of yours is, you must thank him for me," I said, stowing the check away in a safe place.

"I'm going to feature you in an article next week," Warren said, not hearing me in his excitement. *"The Town's New Author* is what we'll call it."

"Thank you, Warren. It's hard to believe," I said quietly, stroking Chris' soft hair. "I'll have to set right to work on the next project. I'll strike while the iron's hot.

Warren laughed, "What a girl you are, Elizabeth!"

Jane set the latest batch of cookies I'd made on the table, and we all celebrated.

Chapter 17

I'll never forget the day the box arrived with a dozen copies of my book in it.

"Thank the good Lord!" Jane exclaimed when she saw them all neatly stacked on the table.

I sat down directly and opened the first book. Carefully, I wrote inside the cover:

> To my little friend and inspiration, Jimmy.
> With much love, Elizabeth Millhouse Brown.

I wondered if writing my full name wasn't a little bit much but then shrugged my shoulders and packaged it up. Jimmy wouldn't mind. Next I got one ready to send to the Woodwards, my heart full of gratitude. When I'd finished with that, I sat at the table, feeling a bit empty inside. Something was still wanting, but I couldn't quite put my finger on it until I lay in bed that night. I wished that I could send one to my mother. I would've so loved to see the approval in her eyes. Then I laughed at myself. She wouldn't want or care about such nonsense. I could envision her tossing it into the dust bin with the other rubbish in the house.

Warren followed through and featured a story about my trials and success in the Sunday edition. Jane was so proud to see me on the front page that she cut out the article and carefully pasted it into my sketch book. The fragments of newspaper she'd left behind framed Alexander Stonely's article.

"Imagine that," I mused, "mine in front of Mr. Stonely's."

Jane looked over at it and snorted. "Well, naturally," she stated. "Yours is worth reading."

I smiled sadly to myself as I read my mother's writing. It seemed as though Mr. Stonely had mellowed a little, but I couldn't be sure. Instead of the usual diatribe, he discussed the importance of women educating themselves and taking control of their destinies if they were to be on an equal footing with men. I supposed that this was what I'd done, except to finish college of course, which would've been more to Mr. Stonely's liking. I sighed and pushed the paper away. I never quite measured up, somehow.

Just then, Chris came toddling into the room on his chubby legs and held out his arms to me.

"Mama!" he called in his sweet baby voice.

I picked him up and held him close to me. Maybe I didn't measure up, but this was something Mother never had, not even from me.

"Mama loves you," I whispered as I hugged him.

A few days later, Warren came to the house. "Elizabeth," he said, without so much as a how do you do, "I think you should look into getting a telephone installed here."

"A telephone?" Jane and I said at once, in a rare fit of uniformity.

"Whatever would I want with one of those?" I asked incredulously. "I'd much prefer to talk to people face to face, thank you."

"Now don't dismiss it so quickly," he said in his most charming tone. "I'll tell you why. I received two phone calls for you today from people who wanted to get in touch with you about your book. I have a feeling they won't be the only ones. I don't always have the time to be your go-between, you know."

"Oh. What did they want?" I inquired.

"First, more about the telephone and electricity," he insisted.

"You didn't say a thing about electricity," Jane glowered at him.

"I think you ought to consider installing both," Warren told me. "Your livelihood depends on your eyesight now, and electric lighting is much better for your eyes than gas lamps."

"But think of how much it must cost, Warren!" I protested.

He sighed. "Elizabeth, you can afford it now. Remember?"

"Oh. I suppose so," I admitted.

Eventually, Warren convinced us both and soon there were workmen swarming all over the house, causing mayhem. Once it was all said and done, I had to admit that I enjoyed the new found convenience. But I decided quickly that a confidential conversation was not meant for the telephone. My neighbor, the mousy woman who'd been so frightened during the influenza epidemic, was constantly spying on my calls. I knew it because I could hear her children quarreling in the background.

I could think of nothing bad to say against the electricity, though. The light was so bright that there was no need for me to squint down at my drawings in the evenings or search for a match to light the lamp on overcast days. When it came to an indoor toilet, however, I put my foot down. How disgusting. It couldn't be sanitary, no matter what Warren said.

As it turned out, the two people who'd wanted to talk to me were a certain Miss Tuttle from the library and a Mr. Snyder, the principal of the primary school in town. Warren gave them my address, and they called on me in the midst of all the chaos of workmen pounding, banging, and tramping in and out. They came peering in the wide open front door at a most inopportune moment. I was hanging on to Chris with one arm to keep him out of the workmen's way and grabbing Georgette to keep her from running outdoors in a panic with the other arm.

"I beg your pardon," said Miss Tuttle, clearing her throat.

I looked up, red-faced with my exertion, gritting my teeth as Georgette dug her claws into my arm.

"Do come in," I gasped. "I'll be with you in a moment. Jane," I called out, hoping for some help. "Jane, please take the cat and put her in my room upstairs." Then turning to my guests I said, "I'm so sorry for the chaos. We're having a bit of work done on the house and my cat is at her wits end. Please sit down. Your names were?"

They sat in my only two chairs in front of the fireplace, and I stood with Chris in my arms. Strands of hair were hanging in my face, and I was feeling quite at a disadvantage. They introduced themselves, or rather, Mr. Snyder introduced both of them, while Miss Tuttle looked keenly around at my disorderly house.

"We read the article about your book in the paper, Mrs. Brown. I've just bought a copy of your book, myself, and I'm very much impressed. Miss Tuttle and I are both very much impressed."

Miss Tuttle inclined her head and favored me with her smile.

"I thank you," I said, wondering what they could want.

"Well, not to mince matters, I have a proposition for you. You see, I've long felt that instruction in the arts should be a routine part of every child's education. I wondered if you might consider undertaking an art class for the children in the fall. I haven't completely convinced the board of the necessity for such a class, yet. But they have conceded the funds to allow a class to meet once a week during the school year. My hope is that you'll teach it," he said, concluding this lengthy speech.

"It's a kind offer, sir, and I'm flattered," I responded after the first thrill of such a possibility passed through my body. "You understand, though, that I've had no formal teaching myself. I picked up drawing on my own."

"All the better," he replied. "Yours is a natural talent."

I smiled at his enthusiasm.

"I'll need a few days to think it over before I give you an answer, one way or the other," I told him.

He sat there beaming at me as if I'd agreed already, while Miss Tuttle cleared her throat at regular intervals and at last, quite violently.

"Oh, yes," he began again. "Miss Tuttle has a request for you too. She—"

"Perhaps, Miss Tuttle," I interrupted, "you would tell me yourself. I find it much more productive to communicate directly."

She was taken aback. I knew I shouldn't have said that, but she was beginning to annoy me with her simpering and throat-clearing. Instead of apologizing as I should have, I waited for her to speak. It finally came out that she wished me to come to the library and read my book to the children. There would be a small amount of pay involved but not much. This, I readily agreed to, and we settled on a day that I'd come.

"Mrs. Brown," she said pointedly, during a lull in the conversation, "your talent for story making and drawing must be such a help to your church."

"My church?" I asked with surprise. "What do you mean?"

"You'd be such a natural Sunday school teacher," she said, smiling sweetly at me.

"I'm sure my talents would be a help if I attended church," I replied.

Mr. Snyder's face fell, possibly contemplating the effect this piece of information would have upon the board.

"You don't attend church?" he asked.

I scrambled for a way to save the situation.

"I haven't for quite some time," was my calm response. "But, I intend to begin again, this next Sunday, in fact."

Jane's sharp ears picked up what I'd said even over the noise of the workmen, and she suddenly appeared at the kitchen door and looked out in surprise. I glared at her, and she went back to work in a hurry. Mr. Snyder smiled again and Miss Tuttle nodded, with one eyebrow raised disapprovingly.

After I told Mr. Snyder I would contact him in a few days to give him my decision, they finally left. I could have kicked myself. Before that day, I'd had no intention whatsoever of returning to the fold so soon, or ever for that matter. But I couldn't turn down such a good opportunity for regular income, in spite of what I told Mr. Snyder about final decisions. And I could tell from Mr. Snyder and Miss Tuttle's faces that my career as art teacher and story reader would be finished before it started if I didn't join the faithful once again.

At any rate, my spur of the moment decision made Jane happy. She'd been pestering me since she moved in with us to go to church for Chris' sake, at least.

"I can't bear the thought of that precious child growing up to be a heathen," she told me more than once, with her finger wagging in my face. "And it wouldn't hurt you any, either."

When Sunday rolled around, I dressed in my best clothes a bit grudgingly and got Chris ready to go. I hoped he would sit still. Jane wanted to go to Christian's old church, but that I refused to do. So we went to the Presbyterian Church that I'd grown up in. The last I knew, Mother had stopped attending when my father died, and I didn't have to worry about meeting her there. Besides that, none of the parishioners had seen me since I was a little girl and wouldn't recognize me. There was a certain amount of comfort in anonymity. I decided that we'd sit in the back and leave as quickly as possible.

When we walked through the door, my heart sank as I recognized Miss Tuttle sitting about three rows from the front. She turned around and gave me her anemic smile and a gracious nod of the head. I returned it as best as I could. For all her propriety and manners, Miss Tuttle was a sharp individual, and I knew I wasn't fooling her one bit. The minister preached a terribly long-winded sermon about irresistible grace and the deceitfulness of the depraved heart. Jane looked on in rapt attention while I kept a nervous eye on Chris's fidgeting. He'd never had to sit still so long in his life.

I breathed a sigh of relief as we filed out of the church. It hadn't been entirely miserable, I had to admit. There were a couple of sweet elderly women sitting in front of us who turned around and smiled sympathetically at me from time to time. They were quite taken with Chris and told me how glad they were that we'd come. The music from the organ and the choir had been beautiful, and I began to feel pleased with myself for doing something religious once again. With one Sunday behind me, I was certain it would be easier next time.

Now, my next project was to win over Miss Tuttle at the library. I got up early the day I was to go and entertain the children and went over all the supplies I had in my bag to make sure I hadn't forgotten anything. Book, paper, and several pencils—all was in order. I thought the children might like to watch me draw pictures.

I decided that for this first time, at least, it would be better to leave Chris at home with Jane. Perhaps I would bring him another time, if there was another time.

"Be a good boy," I said, kissing the top of his head. "I'll be back by lunch time, Jane."

"You're nervous," she stated.

"I am not," I protested.

We stared at each other for a few seconds then we burst out laughing.

"I'm nervous," I admitted. "I can't imagine why. It's just a large group of children, that's all."

That's what I told myself as I waited for them all to arrive, seated in a corner with my book in my lap. They came in with their mothers, some skipping and prattling confidentially at me and others hanging back shyly, trying to decide whether I was safe or not. At the appointed time, they sat down on the floor in a semi-circle and looked expectantly at me. Behind them sat their mothers in chairs and behind them stood Miss Tuttle in the corner, watching me like a hawk. I sat up straight and smiled. I wouldn't be intimidated.

"Good morning," I began.

None of the children spoke, but there was a loud sniff from a runny-nosed boy to my left and an, "Ouch!" from a little girl to my right who'd gotten her finger stepped on.

"Well, now, when I was a little girl, I was taught that it's only polite to speak when spoken to." I began again. "Good morning, children."

There was a volley of good mornings and hellos.

"That's better," I said, looking down at them from my elevated position in the chair. "I don't like this chair. I think I'd rather sit down there with you. May I?"

Miss Tuttle disapproved I could tell, but the little people looked pleased by the prospect. So I sat down, folding my legs to the side. Then I opened my book and read. It wasn't entirely smooth sailing. I had to stop and quiet down a few noisy ones, but overall, it went well.

When I'd finished, I held up the first picture in the book and asked, "Do you know who drew this picture?"

"No," they chorused.

"I did," I announced.

"Oooohh!" was their sweet response.

"And now," I said, pulling out my paper and pencils, "raise your hand if you'd like me to draw your picture."

I was busy drawing for an hour, making quick sketches of each child. Children are easy to please in many ways. In my opinion, the sketches weren't even that good since I had to do them so quickly. But the children were fascinated to watch me sketch and thrilled to take home a picture of themselves. And while the children were occupied with this, the mothers looked on at me as if I were an angel from heaven. I was keeping their children out of mischief for a few hours while they enjoyed some rare and precious adult conversation.

As the children left, I packed up my supplies, feeling satisfied with the way things had turned out. Miss Tuttle approached me with a check in her hand, and I could see a new-found respect in her eyes. It was certainly not amiability, but at least there was respect.

"Well done, Mrs. Brown. You have quite a way with children. I can tell you, it isn't easy to keep interest among such a large group of children, much less order."

"Thank you, Miss Tuttle."

"Perhaps you'll come again next month?" she asked.

"Yes, I'd like that."

The next day I called Mr. Snyder at his office and told him that I would teach the art class in the fall. He was delighted and thanked me over and over again. I was more than relieved. If my book didn't sell many copies, I still had something I could fall back on. Financial security came just in time. A week after I called Mr. Snyder, Jane handed me her bank book and showed me the balance on her savings account. This was the money that we'd been living off of, at least partly. It was now zero. But with a mixed sense of confidence and fear, I told Warren that we no longer needed the pension provided for us by the men at the Gazette.

"I have work to do now," I told him smiling.

"And I'm sure there will be more," he returned.

My heart was lighter than it'd been for two years. We were about to begin a new decade, 1920, and it seemed to me as if I was starting a new life. There was more drawing to be done, more books to be written, and more stories to be read.

One sunny afternoon, I sat upstairs looking out the window, waiting for Chris to wake up from his nap. I reflected on my life—where I'd come from and where I was now. Things hadn't turned out at all as I thought they would when I married Christian or even when as little girls, Genie and I planned our futures.

"I want to do something important someday, Genie," I remembered telling her, "something no one has ever done before."

I smiled as I remembered that. I'd said that so many years before, thinking that somehow I could earn my mother's love. I hadn't earned it and I was sure that I would never earn it. I knew that now. But had I really done something important, something no one had ever done before? I supposed that I had to a certain extent. I made the day a bit brighter and happier for a couple dozen children. That was important to me. I drew a picture of a little boy named Jimmy with his fox that no one had ever drawn before.

"Do you think you'll be happy then?" Genie had asked me that day.

There were reasons to be happy now. But I couldn't say that I was really happy—not entirely. If Christian were still with me, if I could've lived those few weeks before his death over again differently, perhaps I would be. But there was no use looking back at what I used to have. Right now, I had a little boy whom I loved tremendously, and I was busy and full of ideas. I supposed that would have to suffice for now. I trusted that happiness would come again later.

Chapter 18

Mr. Snyder was a man of lovely ideals. When the fall term began, I discovered that he not only believed that instruction in the arts should be a routine part of every child's education, he also believed it should be a mandatory part. Every single child at that school from the age of six all the way up to fourteen was required to participate. Wednesday was the day appointed for art class, and I found myself spending the entire day at school between the hours of eight in the morning and three-thirty in the afternoon.

I soon discovered that although teaching may be an inspiring and glorious line of work, it was still, after all, work. Most of the younger children approached the subject with gusto, the girls in particular. But the older ones, the boys especially, weren't quite so enthusiastic about paints and pretty pictures, and it was all I could do to drag them along the road to creativity with me.

That first day was exhausting. I was under the impression that since I'd managed so well reading stories to little children at the library, art class would simply be a theme and variations on that experience. But it wasn't. I'd left one important element out of the equation—art tools in the hands of six and seven-year-olds. I spent the morning running about, trying to stop squabbles, prevent children from writing on the walls or each other, all the while I maintained organized chaos instead of absolute mayhem. And I did it all without having a complete grasp of whose name went with what face.

"You there, sit in your chair..." I'd call out.

"Don't wave the paints around, dear..."

"For shame, we don't hit one another with rulers!" I'd declare, trying to restrain them.

It wasn't that they were particularly naughty, I reflected, as they trooped happily out the door at the end of the hour. I just hadn't devised the right system yet. I fell into a chair and surveyed the damage. There were pencils, paper, and paintbrushes strewn all over the floor. A ghastly smiley face painted on paper in red, orange, and yellow leered at me from where it had been plastered to the back of a chair with glue. Glasses of murky rinse water sat here and there on the desks. One had dumped over and was dripping at regular intervals on the floor. I looked at the time and sprang to my feet, setting things right before the next troop descended upon me. Yes, I decided I'd have to devise a good system without delay.

The next group of children to arrive that morning was the eight to ten-year-olds, and they were much more docile and used to sitting still. I breathed a sigh of relief to see things moving along smoothly. After lunch I taught the eleven to twelve-year-old group, and it was very much the same story.

When the oldest group arrived, however, I felt a bit of a knot in my stomach. The girls came in groups, smoothing their hair while trying to catch their reflections in the window. The boys slouched in, the popular ones winking and cutting up for the girls with some of the others scowling and muttering things under their breath like, "Sissy stuff," and "My kid brother plays with paint." I just sighed. Rome wasn't built in a day, I reminded myself. Then I straightened my shoulders and began.

I came home that afternoon, thoroughly worn out. I picked up Chris and collapsed into a chair, thinking about how to conduct an orderly class. That evening, as I got dinner ready, Jane sat Chris down in his chair and tied on his bib. He immediately began reaching for anything and everything on the table and knocked over a glass of water.

"Christian Brown!" Jane reprimanded him. "What have I told you? You fold your hands and wait like a gentleman."

"I sorry," he said, ducking his head and folding his hands. He looked longingly around at all the good food, but he didn't move an inch until Jane had said grace.

"Well, of course!" I blurted out in my epiphany.

"Hmm?" Jane asked.

"I just realized, if he can do it, so can the children at school." I saw how to bring order to the chaos. The next Wednesday, I was prepared when the littlest children arrived. First of all, I temporarily retired the paints and replaced them with pencils. I also kept all the art supplies with me instead of placing them on the desks, and that was only one of the changes I made.

When the children came running in noisily, I raised my voice and said, "Stop!"

They froze, looking at me in a bit of a daze.

"Now," I said, returning my voice to its normal, modulated tone. "Go outside, and come back in without running and talking." To my delight, they obeyed. "Excellent," I praised them. "Sit down, put both hands on the desk in front of you, and fold them. Look straight ahead at me."

When I had everyone's attention, I smiled. "Very good," I declared loudly. "This is how you'll come into class from now on."

I breathed an inward sigh of relief. With the noise and chaos gone, I could think straight. I began by passing out paper and pencils, drawing straight lines and circles on the black board and having them imitate what I'd done. On the whole, things went much more smoothly and stayed that way the rest of the year. Certainly, there were times when they forgot and had to be reminded, and naturally there were always the mischievous or naughty ones that needed a bit more discipline. But they came around.

With the older children, discipline wasn't as much of an issue. My problems with them stemmed from sullen attitudes, lack of interest, and peer pressure. What I needed most was patience and perseverance to help them see the worth of an art skill and the fun of it all. I determined to help them put away their worries about what their friends were thinking and simply make something beautiful. Already, there were a few bright, talented, and level-headed youngsters that I had great hopes for.

Thankfully, art classes only accounted for one day of my week. But the other days were fast filling up too. I began to receive calls from libraries and schools in other towns and even other counties, asking me to come and read my book, and then draw for the children. At first, I always agreed. It seemed like such a good opportunity. But soon, my days were so full of traveling or teaching that I scarcely had a chance to be with my little boy or work on my next project. I realized I had to do something to slow down. I decided I'd only travel one day a week and leave the remaining days to be spent at home, working on my new book and caring for Chris.

After I published the first book, the next idea soon popped into my head. It was so obvious that I wondered why it didn't come to me sooner. From the time Chris had been a newborn until now, I'd filled pages full of drawings—Chris sleeping at 2 months old, Chris sitting up smiling at Georgette, Chris pulling himself up to stand next to a chair. I had all the material for the next book already finished. I'd title it *The Adventures of Little Chris*. I had only to perfect my drawings, and that's what I worked on all through the fall and winter.

Meanwhile, my little boy was growing up. He reminded me so much of his father. His eyes, especially, were the same. Someday, they would make some girl fall in love with them as I had with Christian's. He had the same sweet way about him too. I noticed it especially in the way he treated Georgette. So many children are inept in handling animals and end up tormenting them, many times completely by accident. But he was so gentle and careful with her that I never had to say a word of caution to him.

He began talking early for his age. Perhaps it was because Jane and I read to him so much. Seizing the opportunity, Jane taught him to say his prayers as soon as he could string words together in sentences. Once he'd learned them, he faithfully remembered to say them every night before he went to bed. I would come and watch from the doorway as he recited them, kneeling by the bed with Jane. When he was finished, Jane would pull back the covers for him and say goodnight. I always stayed by the door until he got in bed and turned towards me with a big smile.

"Mama!" he'd call, opening his arms wide until I came to him and hugged and kissed him goodnight.

"I love you, Chris," I'd always say

"I love you, Mama," he'd say in response.

The first time he said that to me, I was in great danger of weeping for joy. And every night after that, my eyes became misty when he repeated those four words. It was silly of me, I dare say. But I knew better than most what a rare and precious thing love was, having only received it from a few people and much later than any child should have. When I looked into his eyes and saw his trust and confidence in me, I was determined that he'd never lack for my love. Heartache would come to him later, I was sure. After all, that was the one thing life guaranteed. But perhaps he'd be better prepared and grounded for it than I'd been.

Jane was indefatigable in her efforts to teach him from the Bible, much more so than she'd been with me. I think she felt as if she'd failed me. She knew I only went to church for her and Chris' sake and to keep up appearances for my work. Truly, I made no secret of it to her. But even though I didn't join in her efforts with Chris, I let her do what she liked with him in terms of religion. It couldn't harm him. In fact I thought it might compel God to look on him with favor. As for me, I was still a hopeless cause. I was certain that I was out of favor with God, and what's more, I had no desire to remedy the situation. I only wished to be left alone and live the rest of my life as happily and quietly as I could.

Things were shaping up in that department. I was beginning to make some headway with my art classes, and several students were doing quite well. In February 1920, I sent *The Adventures of Little Chris* to the publisher, who'd practically guaranteed to publish anything I gave him after the success of *Jimmy and the Fox*. I was receiving quite a lot of recognition in my own small town and in the surrounding areas. I made a few investments with the excess money I was making, and I must say it was a lovely feeling to have excess money.

I bought my first automobile that summer, and we had a grand time driving out into the country for picnics and hikes and things, just the three of us. Sometimes Warren came along, which made it all the merrier. He played rough and tumble with Chris, helping him burn off all the energy he'd accumulated from being cooped up in a little house with a stodgy old woman like Jane and a quiet, studious mother like me.

I had my small circle of close friends that I kept in touch with, mostly the Woodwards, Genie and Lawrence, and Warren. In addition, I had many acquaintances that I enjoyed talking to on a daily basis, people like Mr. Snyder and the local grocer. And, of course, there were the others that I tolerated as best I could, such as Miss Tuttle and my neighbor, the widow Finley and her brood of noisy children.

All in all, life was easier and much more pleasant than it had been in a long, long time, and I was content with it. I could imagine myself continuing with my work for many years, watching Chris grow into a man, settle down with a nice girl, and start a family of his own. It was a beautiful picture in my mind. I didn't know then that I would never see it come to pass. In one afternoon, the picture was shattered.

It was October, one of the last warm, sunny days before the frosty cold hit us. There was a warm breeze blowing, and Jane had thrown open all the windows in the house to let the fresh air in. The school term had begun, and I was sitting down at the table, experimenting with some paints and getting my thoughts together for the next week's art classes. Chris was buzzing around the house in his energetic two-year-old way, jumping on and off the easy chairs, tunneling under the table, and running into the kitchen to beg a snack from Jane, who was busy making supper.

"No, Chris. It'll spoil your appetite," she told him.

He ran back out to me and grabbed my arm just as I was dipping my brush in the rinse water.

"Come play outside with me, Mama!" he begged, tugging on my arm.

The glass overturned and cloudy water spilled everywhere.

"Oh, Chris!" I exclaimed, jumping to my feet and soaking the water up with my rag. "You mustn't jolt me when I'm working."

The watercolor I'd been working on was spoiled, and Chris' face fell when he saw what he'd done.

"I'm sorry, Mama," he said.

"I know you are, sweetie," I sighed, wiping his hands off. "Just remember to be more careful next time. Now, I want you to go upstairs and look at books quietly until supper time, alright? It won't be much longer now."

I kissed the top of his head and sent him upstairs with a light smack on the bottom. I hurriedly cleaned up the rest of the mess and started over. I wanted to finish my work before Jane set the table. In a few minutes, I was so absorbed in what I was doing that I lost track of time. I just barely heard a rush of air, like a sigh, and then a soft thud outdoors a few minutes later. I chalked it up to a branch falling from one of the trees in back of the house and continued with my work.

Jane came out and began setting the plates on the table. I quickly cleaned up my mess and helped her finish, bringing food out and looking for a clean bib for Chris.

Jane called up the stairs, "Come down now, Chris. It's time to eat."

There was no reply, but I knew he'd be down directly. He never wasted time getting to the dinner table. When he still hadn't come by the time I'd filled a pitcher of water and set it on the table, I called him again.

"I wonder if he fell asleep up there," Jane mused.

"He may have. Most likely he's just playing hide and seek," I said, smiling. "I'll go get him." I turned toward the stairs and hollered with a tease, "Chris, I'm coming to get you!"

I felt the breeze from the windows as I climbed the stairs. I looked in Jane's room first, peeking under the bed and in the wardrobe. There were a few picture books strewn on the floor, so I knew he had to be close by.

"Where are you, Chris?"

He wasn't in there so I looked in my room. I checked under the bed and was about to look behind the door when I stopped in my tracks, my heart racing. The chair from my desk had been pulled right up under the open window. The breeze fanned my face and sent the curtains dancing. I swallowed hard, went to the window, and looked out. At first I didn't see anything, and I was momentarily relieved. Then I saw a hand and his little face, lying perfectly still, almost covered by the overgrowth in the flower bed down below. In panic, I turned and ran down the stairs.

"Jane, come quickly," I screamed. "He's fallen out the window."

I reached the flower bed before Jane and stood looking down at him. His head was resting on a rock, one leg bent underneath him. A small pool of blood was widening around his head. My knees shook and buckled. I couldn't see if he was breathing or not.

"Don't try to move him, Elizabeth," Jane called as she ran to me. She put her fingers lightly on his neck, just under the jaw bone and felt for his pulse.

"Is he alive?" I cried.

"Yes, his heart's still beating, but it's very faint. Run in the house and call the doctor right away. You're faster than me."

I stumbled into the house and rang the doctor. When I spoke, I willed my voice to be steady and told him exactly what'd happened. I hung up and paced distractedly about the house, torn between the desire to be with Chris and the agony of seeing his broken body. I picked the telephone up again and dialed Warren's office.

It rang and rang as the receiver shook in my hands.

"Hello," I finally heard him say.

"Warren, it's Elizabeth," I began, but then my voice broke.

"Elizabeth, what's wrong?"

"Chris fell out of my bedroom window," I sobbed. "Please come."

Chapter 19

He lay so still on the bed. I knelt by him, clenching my hands together, as I watched one shallow breath after another. If I turned my head, I could see Jane sitting in the hall, silent tears rolling down her face, and Warren standing in the doorway behind me. The doctor wouldn't tell me if Chris would live or not, but he wouldn't leave the house either. He'd straightened Chris' broken leg and put it in a splint, bandaged his head, and then sat down to wait. Chris' head was swelling, I could see that, but instead of getting better, it worsened by the hour.

About midnight, I turned and looked at the doctor. "Please," I begged. "Just tell me one way or the other. Is he going to live or not?"

He cleared his throat, searching for the correct words. They were very correct indeed when he spoke them, but they fell like hammer blows on my heart.

"He's suffered a considerable amount of brain damage. If he should live, he'll never leave that bed or be able to communicate with you. If I were you, I'd pray for a miracle or a quick death." Then he put a hand on my shoulder. "I'm sorry, Mrs. Brown. I wish with all my heart there was some good thing to say about your son's condition, but I'd be a wretch to fill you with false hopes."

I swallowed and nodded my head. "Well," I said, "we can all watch over him as well as you, then. I wouldn't like to keep you here all night. Thank you for all you've done."

He shook Warren's hand, probably thinking him to be Chris' father, said a few words to Jane, and left.

Jane and Warren sat on either side of the bed with me all night, watching the rise and fall of Chris' chest. It was regular and shallow at first, but then it slowed with long pauses between each breath. Each time the breath went out of him, his chest would lay so still I thought he was gone, but then he'd breathe again. At five o'clock in the morning, he slowly exhaled. I waited and waited for his chest to rise, but it didn't. Jane wept while Warren drew the quilt over Chris' head. I couldn't seem to feel anything as I looked at the tiny lump under the quilt. I rubbed my eyebrows over and over, while I stared at the bed. I had to move. I had to go somewhere. I stood up, walked downstairs, and out the front door. I paced the yard, back and forth, rubbing my head.

I turned and saw my neighbor watching me through the window. Lights were beginning to shine through windows in houses up and down the street. People were waking up now, and there were too many people everywhere. I had to get away. I picked up my skirt and ran and ran, not knowing or caring where I was going.

In the back of my mind, I could hear Warren shouting for me to come back, but I kept running, sometimes tripping on the hem of my skirt or stumbling over cracks in the street. I ran until the town was behind me and the open country was ahead. Finally, my legs wouldn't hold me anymore, and I collapsed in front of a large tree in a grassy field, sobbing and gasping for breath. I lifted my head and looked around me. The sun was up in the east and just beginning to shed its beams over the grass, chasing away the dew. This was our place, the place we all went for Sunday afternoon picnics and outings. I could almost see Chris wrestling with Warren in the grass, while Jane looked on with a smile on her face. He was running to me, the wind blowing his hair around his face, my bright-eyed little boy. I sat in the grass, my head bowed, and words from that hated poem flooded my mind again.

> I sought no more that after which I strayed
> In face of man or maid;
> But still within the little children's eyes
> Seems something, something that replies,
> They at least are for me, surely for me!
> I turned me to them very wistfully;
> But just as their young eyes grew sudden fair
> With dawning answers there,
> Their angel plucked them from me by the hair.

For two years I'd shed all the love that I had to give on Chris. I lived for him when I wanted to die. I smiled for him when I wanted to weep. I worked for him when I wanted to close my eyes and sleep. It wasn't hard for me to do because I loved him. And now I wasn't to have even that. I wept, beating the earth with one clenched hand. I pushed myself off the ground and leaned against the tree, looking up through its branches to the sky above.

"God," I cried out, "You've taken my father, my mother, and my husband. Why my son? Couldn't you leave just one thing? He didn't deserve this! He's done nothing wrong!"

I don't know how long I stood there, pounding the tree with my fists and screaming at the sky. But then I heard an automobile pull up and a door slam.

"Elizabeth!" Warren called to me. "Come with me. Let me take you back home. You need rest."

"Go away, Warren," I cried. "Don't tell me anything. Don't come near me. You don't know what I feel."

He stood there with tears in his eyes, looking down at my bloody hands.

"Elizabeth, I loved him too."

I realized then that I was wrong. He knew exactly what I felt. I could see it in his eyes. I stumbled forward with a sob, and he caught me. He picked me up and put me in the car. I was too spent to resist even if I'd wanted to.

BY THE TIME THE DAY FOR HIS FUNERAL ARRIVED, I couldn't weep any more. I sat between Jane and Warren, feeling numb inside. Of the few parishioners I'd allowed to get near me, only about twenty or so came. But there were men there from the *Gazette* who'd known Christian, as many as could break away from work. They came in solemnly, looking terribly uncomfortable to find themselves in church, but I saw the kindness and sadness in their eyes and I appreciated it. I wanted to tell them how much, but I was too worn in body and spirit to think of anything to say. Miss Tuttle was there, watchful of me as ever, but for once I didn't care about what she was thinking.

After the burial, the minister stopped and spoke a few words of comfort to me. I barely heard him and only gave him a mechanical nod of my head. Before I went back home, I realized I'd left something of mine in the church and went in to look for it. As I walked in the door, I could hear Miss Tuttle talking in a low tone to a woman I hardly knew.

"What an unfeeling creature," she said quietly. "She sat there as stiff as a board, calm and composed. She hardly shed a tear. It's quite unnatural, if you ask me."

They heard my footsteps and saw me. The other woman looked ashamed, but Miss Tuttle just raised her eyebrow. I turned around immediately and walked out. Warren and Jane were waiting outside the door for me.

"I'll never go back in that church again," I said flatly. "Never!"

OVER THE NEXT WEEK, Jane and I slowly went through Chris' things. I only kept a pair of booties and a matching sweater that Mrs. Woodward had made for him. The rest of his clothes and toys were put in crates, and I sent them with Warren to the church. I hoped someone would be able to use them.

The numbness that settled over me after Chris died didn't dissipate in the weeks following. If anything, it grew. How can I describe the blackness? Life had lost its taste. Everything I drew seemed distorted and ugly to me. I couldn't bear to go out and meet the world. I stayed in my room almost all day and night, hiding myself from Jane and Warren, even though they needed comfort as much as I did. But there was nothing inside of me that I could give them. At night, I stared at the ceiling, sleepless. My mind worked far into the early morning hours. It had a will of its own, and I couldn't stop it. I thought constantly of ways I could've prevented the accident. I shouldn't have sent him upstairs alone. I should've had him read books downstairs. I should've checked on him sooner. I shouldn't have been so engrossed in my work.

After a week of this, I knew I had to get up and face life. I had to work again, or I'd become a burden on Jane. I had to have a reason to get out of bed in the morning. If I didn't have a reason, I'd give up. I must go back to my art class, I finally decided.

The next Wednesday morning, I stood at the front of the class by my desk, watching the littlest children walk quietly in as I'd trained them. They sat with their hands folded together, looking up at me expectantly. I cleared my throat and tried to speak, but I couldn't. My eyes roved over the pupils, gazing into one pair of bright, energetic eyes after another, thinking that this was where Chris would've been in another three or four years. I cleared my throat again.

"Good morning, children," I said, my voice sounding wooden and flat to my ears. "It's been quite a long time since we've been together, so I assume you've had ample opportunity to work on the assignments I gave you the last time we met. Please take them out and put them on your desks, and I'll come by and collect them."

I tried to look carefully at each picture, but I couldn't focus my thoughts, and I ended up simply marking an A on each one. The joy seemed to have utterly gone from my work, even from seeing the children each day. But I knew I must continue.

Requests came in every day for my appearance at this library or that school to read my book and draw for the children. I accepted as many as I could. There was no need for me to be at home any more. Many of those appointments even took me out of state, and it wasn't long before I rarely spent more than two or three nights a week in my own bed. I was beginning to be quite well-known across the country, and the balance in my bank account was steadily increasing.

"Jane," I announced one day, "I'm going to hire a girl to come to the house every day and help with the housework." I told her my plan on one of the few days that I found myself at home.

"There's no need for that, Elizabeth," she protested. "I'm capable of handling the house."

"I know you are, but you've worked hard all your life, and I want you to be able to relax now. You're past seventy, and I think it's only fitting."

She fussed and fumed, but I insisted and she gave in eventually. The truth of it was that I felt guilty. I was away so much of the time, and when I was home I withdrew into myself. I couldn't seem to reach out to her anymore. It was as if there was a door that had shut in my heart when Chris died, and I couldn't let anyone in even if I wanted to. I learned to turn on a switch so I could be affable and cheerful around the schoolchildren because I had to. But I was careful to avoid attachments. They were too painful. I felt badly about it, especially when Warren came to visit. He was so kind to come, but I always ended up pushing him away.

Sometimes he looked straight in my eyes and said, "Elizabeth, talk to me. Talk to me about the weather, anything at all. I need to hear your voice."

I would try for a few minutes and then lapse into silence again.

At any rate, I thought that if I hired a nice young girl, she could be company for Jane while I was absent literally and figuratively. I advertised in the paper and interviewed quite a few girls. The one I finally settled on, Violet Withers, wasn't quite what I had in mind. She was extremely quiet with a bit of a sullen look about her eyes. But after a few days of trial employment, I quickly realized she was much more capable and efficient than any of the other girls had been. I hoped she'd learn to be more open and friendly towards Jane in time. I continued to stay to myself.

And then Genie paid me a visit one day. She arrived looking as sweet and kind as ever, her belly swollen with another baby. I opened the door and forced a smile.

"May I come in?" she asked hesitantly.

"Are you sure you want to?" I returned, trying my hand at a bitter joke. "Everything I touch seems to break."

"Oh, Elizabeth," she said, taking my hand. "Jane called and told me all about it. That's why I'm here. But if you're not up to company, I'll go away."

"Come in and sit with me awhile, Genie. I'm glad you're here. But I warn you, I've not been very companionable the last few weeks. Would you like some tea?"

"Don't go to any trouble for me," Genie protested.

"Oh, it isn't any trouble. Not anymore." I turned and called out, "Violet!"

She presented her expressionless face at the kitchen door and waited for me to speak.

"Please bring one cup of tea out as soon as you can."

She nodded and disappeared.

"You see, it really isn't any trouble," I said again. At Genie's surprised look, I continued, "I hired her to take over the heavy work for Jane. I have to be away so often."

"I see. And where is Jane?"

"She's out, taking advantage of her freedom, I suppose. She wanted some new yarn."

Violet came with the tea and set it on the table, then turned around and left just as Genie was thanking her.

"She's very quiet, isn't she?" Genie remarked.

"Silent as the grave," I answered. "But she's quick and efficient and doesn't give us any trouble."

After a few minutes of silence Genie asked, "And how are you holding up, Elizabeth?"

"I try my best not to talk of that, or I simply won't hold up," I replied with a short laugh. "I've arranged my life so that most of the time I'm too busy to think.

"I have been praying for you ever since I heard."

"I don't know why," I said, impatiently. "In my experience, prayer has never prevented horrible things from happening."

I half expected her to reprove me, but she didn't. Instead, she took another sip of tea, her hand shaking a bit.

"I'm sorry, Genie. As I told you, I've not been companionable lately."

"It's all right," she said.

"I hate to disappoint you, but I'm done with God. I was done with Him a long time ago when my father died. I tried going back to church for a while, but it was against my better judgment. He's really done nothing but bring sorrow and disappointment to my life, so I'm done with Him."

"Elizabeth," she said, "I wish you could see Him as I do. But I can't make you understand."

"When is your baby due, Genie?" I asked pleasantly and she stopped short.

I couldn't bear to hurt Genie, but I could tolerate what she was saying even less. It made no sense to me. When she and I parted at the door a half hour later, she looked distracted and downcast.

"Don't trouble yourself with me," I said. "I'll manage. I always have."

I only wished I could believe that.

Chapter 20

Life went on and, as I expected, for another three years it went on without any major changes or events. There was nothing to make one day any different than the next. But I changed, almost imperceptibly. I think it all began with Chris' death. It was odd how it all happened, and I wasn't sure that I liked it. It seemed to be taking place outside of my control.

My work, my name, and my influence were spreading. There was no problem there. I never had to worry about where my next job would come from. Children liked me, and their parents liked me. Educators liked me. Most everyone liked me and my stories and my drawings. I had speaking engagements lined up for months in advance. A year after Chris died, I'd written and illustrated another children's book. I'd labored long and hard through much trial and error to develop the personae that was the most effective for my kind of work—quick and bright with a no-nonsense efficiency. Quick and bright because it made the children feel happy; no-nonsense efficiency because then they knew they must mind. I was good at what I did. It was my job, after all.

But I wasn't really quick and bright, no-nonsense and efficient. I was tired and weary of life. That's why I kept such a stringent schedule. When I was busy, I had no time to think about how tired I was. But when I returned to my house for a few days of rest, it all came home to roost—the fatigue, the grim formality I assumed to keep friends at bay, the bitter sarcasm, and the solitude I escaped to. It was the only way that I knew to take control of myself. Memories of my husband and little boy hovered around the margins of my mind at all times. I was afraid that once I admitted weakness and accepted sympathy, I'd fold and crumble beneath the weight of my memories.

I knew I'd be broken, unable to continue in the stream of life. That stream required that I either flow along with it as quickly as it persisted in taking me, or else stop and be drowned. And so, arriving home from being absent for a week or more, I'd say a few words to Jane and then shut myself in my room. There I'd work on sketches and ideas, only occasionally coming down for meals.

I didn't correspond much with Genie or the Woodwards, and I never encouraged them to visit me. Only Warren was persistent enough to come uninvited. Somehow, he always knew when I'd returned home from a long trip.

"Where's the hermit?" he'd thunder at Jane from the front door. "Elizabeth. Where are you?"

I'd sigh in response from where I sat at my desk and throw down my pencil. If I didn't come down to him, he'd march upstairs and pound on the door until I came out. There was no way to avoid him.

"Honestly, Warren, must you bellow so? You're loud enough to wake the dead!"

"Ah, there's miss sugar and spice, herself," he'd counter, smiling sweetly.

"Well, what is it? Do hurry, I'm very busy."

For all his jolly bantering, I could tell my barbs hurt him, though he tried not to let it show. It bothered Jane too. She never reproached me about the way I behaved. She only looked worried and sad. I hated myself for it, but I couldn't stop by any conscious effort. So I stayed away from them as much as I could. I took long rides on my bicycle into the countryside in all kinds of weather, carrying my sketch book and pencils in my satchel. Out there, in the middle of nowhere, I couldn't hurt anyone and no one could hurt me. I lost myself in observation, keeping absolutely still for hours on end, just so I could watch a deer grazing only a few yards away or a beetle climbing a blade of grass.

Some talk about the peace of being close to nature. I didn't go to nature for peace. There was no peace and no rest in my heart wherever I was or whatever I did. There was no peace at home among all the memories of happy times gone forever. There was no peace in observing a bird of prey swoop down from the air and snatch up a mouse or a rabbit. But something compelled me to go where people were not, where there were no prying eyes and no judgment. And when I sat huddled up in the pelting rain of a thunderstorm, the numbness left me and I could feel again. Rather, I allowed myself to feel when no one could witness my weakness. Sometimes I was shocked by all that I could feel when the pain and weeping swept over me. I could feel, but there was no comfort. Like the man in the poem,

> I drew the bolt of Nature's secrecies.
> I knew all the swift importings
> On the willful face of skies;
> I knew how the clouds arise
> Spumed of the wild sea-snorting;
> All that's born or dies
> Rose and drooped with; made them shapers

Of mine own moods, or willful or divine;
With them joyed and was bereaven.
I was heavy with the even,
When she lit her glimerring tapers
Round the day's dead sanctities.
I laughed in morning's eyes.
I triumphed and I saddened with all weather,
Heaven and I wept together,
And its sweet tears were salt with mortal mine;
Against the red throb of its sunset-heart
I laid mine own to beat,
And share commingling heat;
But not by that, by that, was eased my human smart.
In vain my tears were wet on Heaven's grey cheek.
For ah! We know not what each other says...

I DRIFTED THROUGH THE DAYS, on my guard at all times, and life went on. At the end of three years, two things happened—I cut my hair and Warren asked me to marry him. I suppose I should've seen it coming, the way he'd sit there on my easy chair, just looking at me with that strange expression in his eyes. It didn't matter how difficult or cold or indifferent I was, he was always there or leaving or about to come. It was aggravating, but it never occurred to me that he came because he loved me. But when I bobbed my hair, it all came out.

Everyone was doing it. But I didn't do it because everyone was doing it. I'm really not sure why I did it. It happened when I was away from home one fall day. I'd just finished giving a presentation at a school in New York City. There were a few hours before my train left for home, so I wandered up and down the streets, looking in shop windows to pass the time. I came across a barbershop, and through the window, I could see a young girl in the chair getting her hair cut and styled. I went in, and before I knew it, I was sitting in the chair. Down came my long blond hair. With a few snips, it lay on the floor around me. I paid extra to put a bit of a wave in. When I was all finished, I got up and looked in the mirror. I wasn't entirely sure that I liked it, but it did make my head feel remarkably light and buoyant. I shrugged my shoulders and put my hat back on.

"Thank you very much," I said to the barber, putting a few more dollars into his hand by way of a tip.

"Thank you, Mrs. Brown. It was my pleasure."

I walked out and headed towards the train station, nearly forgetting what I'd just done in my haste to catch the train. I arrived in the late afternoon and walked home from the station. As I approached the house, I saw Warren's car parked nearby and sighed. There were good smells coming from the kitchen when I walked through the door. Warren jumped up from his place by the fire to greet me.

"How was your trip, Elizabeth?"

"Fine," I responded. "Violet!" I called, taking off my coat.

She came out of the kitchen, carrying some plates to put on the table. Jane was right behind her and smiled hesitantly.

"Hello, Elizabeth. How are you?"

"I'm well. Violet, hang up my things, please," I said as I removed my hat.

Violet, expressionless as usual, followed my directions silently, but Jane gasped and Warren's lips parted in dismay.

"Whatever is wrong with you?" I asked, looking from one to the other.

Jane covered her mouth with one hand and pointed at me with the other.

"Elizabeth, your hair," she answered in shock.

I reached up with a hand and felt my shorn locks. "Oh, that," I replied. "I cut it."

They continued to stare at me. Warren didn't say a word, but his face said a good deal and I was annoyed.

"Don't worry," I said calmly. "I haven't taken to brewing liquor in the shed out back. It's just hair, for goodness' sake."

"Your beautiful hair," Jane breathed out, and there were actually tears in her eyes.

"Well," I said, briskly, "I believe I'll go out for a walk until we've all recovered from the shock. If you'll excuse me," I bristled. Then I turned on my heel to go.

"But Elizabeth, supper's almost ready, and we've made your favorite meal," Jane protested.

"I'm not hungry," I said, closing the front door behind me.

I had my sketch book with me, so I got on my bicycle and peddled out of town to my usual spot. I propped the bicycle up against a tree and hiked out into the woods. I sat down amidst the undergrowth and became absorbed in making a detailed drawing of a crimson maple leaf on the ground. A grey rabbit came hopping close by, his little nose twitching and turning. I sketched madly to catch him on paper before he went away. A short while later I heard noisy footsteps, twigs snapping, and dry leaves rustling. The rabbit took off out of my sight about the time Warren's large figure came into view. I sighed and waited for him to arrive.

"Hello," he said, taking his hat off and sitting heavily on a log.

"How did you know where I was?" I asked.

"Oh, I've seen your bicycle back here many times before. I thought maybe you'd be here tonight too."

"What do you want?" I asked tersely.

"I wanted to talk to you," he said, picking at the felt around the band of his hat.

"About what?"

"I'm not sure how to begin."

"While you're collecting your thoughts," I said, reopening my sketch book, "I'll continue with my work. I'm busy."

"You're always busy," he remarked.

"Yes."

For a long time, there was no noise but the scratching of my pencil on paper and the occasional chirp of birds getting ready to bed down for the night.

"What's happened to you, Elizabeth?" he asked. "You never used to be like this."

"Like what?" I asked somewhat distracted.

"You…well…you're not interested in your friends anymore…you treat Jane terribly…" he stumbled, searching for the right words.

"And I cut my hair like a naughty girl. Did you come all the way back here to say that? I can do without the fatherly scolding, Warren."

"Maybe not," he said, rising and looming over me. "Maybe that's just what you need. Go ahead and be sarcastic with me if you must, but don't treat Jane that way. She's given up six years of her life to come and live with you for no pay and no reward. She does it because she cares for you dearly, Elizabeth, and the last couple of years, you've treated her like a clod of dirt under your foot. I've tried to be patient with you because you've had a hard time of it lately, but no more. I'm sick and tired of the way you're acting!"

His voice had risen to a shout, and he kept leaning closer and closer to me until his face was just a few inches away from mine. His eyes snapped and the veins stood out in his neck. I'd never seen him that angry, much less at me. And it made me angry. As he shouted, my head shot up, and I could feel the muscles in my back tightening while I sat up straighter and straighter.

By the time he'd finished, I was clenching my jaw and glaring back at him.

"If you think that tirade is going to melt me into a puddle of tears like a shrinking little violet, you're very much mistaken," I said quietly. "Big, tough man," I added with a sneer.

He didn't move a muscle while he stared into my eyes.

"Your little superiority act doesn't fool me one bit, Elizabeth," he said, just as quietly. "I've seen it all before, and it's just that, an act. You might have fooled and manipulated Christian and made him miserable and unhappy, God rest his soul. But I'm not nearly as good and sweet-tempered as that man was, so you can go to the devil as far as I'm concerned."

Christian. I flinched at the blow. I could feel the anger draining out of me along with the blood from my face. I couldn't look Warren in the eye anymore, and I lowered my gaze to the ground.

"I shouldn't have said that," he said immediately. "I'm sorry, Elizabeth. I shouldn't have brought that up."

"It didn't really work," I said, twisting my fingers in my lap. "I couldn't get him to do what I wanted. He always did what he thought was right."

"Confound it, Elizabeth!" he shouted, throwing his hat on the ground. He paced back in forth in front of me. Stooping down, he picked the hat back up, smashed it on his head, and threw himself against a tree to think.

"I came here to say something, and it wasn't all that," he began again. "Lord knows I just ruined it. But I guess I'll say it anyway. I came here to ask you to marry me."

"What?" I gasped, "Whatever for?"

"For the reason people usually want to get married," he laughed in exasperation, "because I love you. But now you hate me. I guess I don't blame you."

He knelt down and took both of my hands with a sheepish sort of grin.

"But I do love you. I love you when you're happy. I love you when you're mad at me. And I growled at you just now because I love you, and since you're going to say no anyway, I'll tell you what I think about your new hair style. I hate it. You're a beautiful girl with or without long hair, but I still wish you hadn't cut it."

I laughed a bit helplessly. "I can't marry you, Warren."

He let go of my hands and sat down in front of me, pushing his hat forward to cover his eyes.

"And it's not because I hate you. You want a nice, sweet wife, a little kitten to nestle up to you when you come home from the office every night. I used to be like that. But recently, I've forgotten how to sheath my claws. I'd just make you unhappy with my superiority act, as you call it. I don't want a husband or any more children to worry about. Christian and Chris are gone, and I can't bear the thought of anyone taking their places. I don't think I can love anyone like I loved them. You don't want me, not really."

"I know exactly what I want," he replied from underneath the hat. "If I can't have it, then I can't. Only, let me be your friend. Don't shut me out anymore, Elizabeth. Don't shut Jane out."

"Warren you don't understand..."

"What is it that you want? What are you going to find out here away from the people you love? What are you running from, Elizabeth?" he asked, urgently, pushing his hat back.

"The hound," I said laughing.

"What?" he answered with surprise.

"The Hound of Heaven," I said lightly. "He's been chasing me ever so long. And I've been trying to find something else, anything else, besides Him."

"Elizabeth, you're not making any sense."

"Well," I smiled, "Call me superstitious, then. I've pursued lots of things all my life. The normal things, you know. Love, mostly, but also fame, recognition, and while I've been chasing after them, the Hound of Heaven's been chasing after me. It's a strange sort of dog, always at my heels, but just in front of me too, snatching things away from me. He's everywhere at once."

Warren listened, his brow furrowed.

"You know, Warren, I've caught everything I set out to catch. But the Hound of Heaven took all the things I wanted the most and left the rest behind." I stopped and pointed my thumb over my shoulder. "He's just behind me now. He's going to catch up with me soon, and then I suppose I'll find out just what it is that He wants from me."

Warren licked his lips nervously and cleared his throat.

"Maybe you should take a rest from your work for a while, Elizabeth. Go somewhere quiet."

"I'm not going crazy," I told him. "I'm quite sane. I'm so sane, Warren, that sometimes I wish I could live in a pleasant little delusion for a while, just to give me some relief from reality."

The sun was setting as we talked, and I could barely see his face in the shadows. I stretched out my hand towards him, and he caught it. The truth was, I was afraid and I didn't know how to tell him.

Chapter 21

I tried to improve after my talk with Warren, I truly did. But it was hard. There was very little that I enjoyed in life, and there was nothing to look forward to anymore. I was old and worn and bitter. But I was only twenty-five, and there was still a lot of life to be lived. So I tried my best to engage Jane and Warren in conversation as much as possible. I still made my solitary visits to the countryside and stayed for many hours at a time. It was mostly because little things would remind me of Chris and Christian, simple things like the scent of their favorite foods or curtains fluttering in the window. Then I'd begin to wonder why I was alive and resent the endless cycle of working to make money, spending the money, and making more money so I could live. *Why do I do it when there seems to be no point in living?*

When the blackness closed in, I wanted to scratch and bite everything and everyone around me. It was better for all parties if I went alone somewhere until I could be civil again. But the fact remained that life had its demands, and I couldn't disappear at will whenever I felt the gloom coming on. There were times, to my great shame, when I took out my frustrations on others. I still managed to keep things under control when I was with my art class or away on business trips, and I practically strangled myself to keep from snapping at Warren or Jane. That left only one person to bear the brunt of my anger and that was Violet.

I'd never liked her in the first place. I didn't like the way she averted her eyes when I tried to talk to her. Her silence and sullen deference rattled my nerves, and it bothered me that I could never read her face like I could with most normal people. She kept a perfect, blank veil over it. She was irritating to begin with, and when I was in a foul humor, she was ten times worse. And she never did anything wrong, nothing that I could put my finger on. Even when I reprimanded her for the most ridiculous trifles, she didn't retaliate.

Only once did I ever see anger in her eyes and that was only for a moment. I came upstairs to get something one day and as I walked into my room I saw Violet leaning over my desk paging through my sketchbook, a feather duster hanging limp in one hand.

"What are you doing with my book?" I demanded.

She slowly turned around, not saying a word. I crossed the room, pulled it away from her, and put it in the drawer with my journal.

"You have no business nosing through my things."

"I'm sorry. I didn't mean any harm. It was open on the desk and I liked the pictures."

"What are you doing in here?" I asked.

"Straightening up. Jane asked me to dust."

"Well, in the future, I'll thank you to keep out of my room. I'll do any straightening up that's needed."

And there it was, just the faintest flicker of anger passing through her eyes.

"Yes, ma'am," was all she said before she turned and left.

I didn't like her at all.

"YOU KNOW SOMETHING, Elizabeth? Not that I miss it or anything, but I haven't seen Mr. Stonely's column in the paper for a couple of weeks," Jane remarked one Sunday afternoon.

"Haven't you?" I asked, pulling my gaze away from the fire.

It was a chilly November day, and we were both sitting as close to the fireplace as we could. It was Violet's day off, and I'd been feeling unusually calm and tranquil. But now I was thoroughly alert.

"No," Jane replied. "Odd, isn't it? Perhaps we're finally to be rid of that man."

"Yes. I suppose" was all I could answer.

"Are you all right, Elizabeth? You don't look quite like yourself."

"Oh, I'm a little tired. I think I'll close my eyes for a few minutes, if you don't mind."

My thoughts were racing. I hadn't paid much attention to Mother's writing for quite some time. I'd been so wrapped up in my own troubles. Over the next few Sundays, I checked the paper myself to see if Mr. Stonely would reappear, but he didn't. Now I wanted an explanation.

"Warren," I said casually one evening, "has the *Gazette* discontinued Mr. Stonely's column? I haven't seen it for a few weeks." He'd stopped in, and we were all eating dinner together.

"Why do you ask? You have a taste for that sort of thing?" he asked, looking keenly at me.

"Certainly not," I laughed, "but when such a firebrand disappears without warning, I can't help but notice."

Warren shook his head, wiped his mouth with a napkin and said, "No, we haven't discontinued it, but Mr. Stonely hasn't sent anything for a while."

"I wonder why," Jane mused.

"Mmmm...it was something to do with failing health, a heart complaint or something. I don't recall, exactly."

I didn't dare ask any more questions for fear Warren would begin to suspect something, but I wished I knew more. How bad was Mother's condition? It had to be bad to keep her from what she wanted most to do. Should I visit her? Would she even agree to see me? What if she were to die without my ever seeing or talking to her again? I didn't know what to do so I did nothing, but she was in my thoughts constantly. I kept on with business as usual while I waited for some news or word from her.

"Mrs. Woodward called while you were out, Elizabeth," Jane said to me one day after I had returned from teaching my art classes.

"Did she? What did she want?"

"It seems that Genie's little boy, Jimmy, contracted polio a month ago and he's not doing well at all."

"Jimmy?" I repeated, picturing that vivacious young fellow in my mind. "Is he out of danger yet?"

"Yes, but both legs are paralyzed and he's confined to bed. I think Genie would have told you herself, but she's had her hands full caring for him and the rest of the children."

I sighed and consulted my calendar. I pursed my lips as I ran a finger over the dates, trying to find an empty slot in my busy schedule. I finally paused on the next Monday.

"I believe I'll call and cancel my engagement for Monday. I could drive to Genie's and be back by evening. Maybe I can do something to help."

"I think that'd be a fine thing," Jane said warmly.

"Well, after all they've done for me, it's the least I can do."

I didn't tell Genie that I was coming. I didn't want her to go to a lot of trouble for me as she was sure to do if I called beforehand. I only hoped I could do something for her and not get in the way. I took the two books I'd published since the first one. Jimmy had many, long weary days in bed ahead of him, and I hoped my books would help pass the time.

Lawrence answered the door, their youngest child in his arms.

"Elizabeth," he said, smiling. "Come in. What brings you to our doorstep?"

"I heard about Jimmy, and I wanted to see all of you," I said, noticing the lines that had deepened on his face since the last time I'd see him. "I brought some books for Jimmy."

"It's very kind," he told me. "Genie's lying down for a nap."

"Don't wake her," I urged. "She must be exhausted. You look tired yourself."

He nodded. Then pointing to the sweet girl in his arms he said, "Our youngest, Lillian," kissing the little girl's cheek. "I don't believe you've met."

"She's lovely," I said, reaching out to touch her curly head.

"Elizabeth. Is that you?" Genie asked from a doorway, rubbing her eyes. "It's so good of you to come."

She looked too thin. But her wonderful smile and sweet way was still intact.

"Might I see Jimmy?" I asked. "I brought him something."

"Of course, come upstairs," she said, leading me by the hand.

I don't know what I expected to find when I reached the top of the stairs, but the sight of him brought unexpected tears to my eyes. Genie and Lawrence had situated the bed so that Jimmy could see out the window easily without craning his neck. He lay there quietly with his hands folded on top of the blankets, looking out the window and not heeding the noise of our footsteps. His skin was so pale, it looked almost transparent. The rosy-cheeked, energetic little boy I remembered was gone.

"Jimmy, you have a friend here to visit you," Genie said, and he moved his head listlessly to look in my direction. "Do you remember Elizabeth?"

"Mm hmm," was his mumbled reply.

"Hello, Jimmy," I said, moving a chair beside his bed.

I smiled and smoothed the hair away from his forehead. He gave me a little smile in return.

"You said you'd come and see me," he stated.

"Yes, I did, didn't I?" I said, surprised that he'd remembered. It had been at least four years ago. "Well, it took me a while, but I'm finally here. I'm sad you're not feeling well."

He shrugged but didn't say anything.

"I brought you a present," I said brightly, pulling the two books I'd brought for him out of my bag. "I hope you'll enjoy these."

He paged through them curiously. The last book in particular, caught his interest, and I knew why. It was filled with pages and pages of drawings from nature, the fruit of my solitary ramblings outdoors. But after a while, he closed it and pushed it away from him.

"Don't you like it?" I asked.

"It's nice" was his weak reply.

Out of the corner of my eye, I saw Genie put a hand to her eyes and quietly leave the room.

"I can't play outside anymore," he said, putting his arms behind his head and staring back out the window.

"Yes, I know," I said, seeing the outline of his two motionless legs under the blankets.

There was such a terrible finality about it. I couldn't tell him that, yes, he couldn't play outside right now, but he'd soon be well. I couldn't tell him that life confined to a wheelchair wouldn't be so bad, and that he'd get used to it in time. There wasn't much to say at all, so I just sat with him, stroking his hair and humming until he fell asleep.

I found Genie crying into a handkerchief in the hall.

"I am sorry, Genie," I whispered, putting my arm around her shoulders.

I spent the rest of the day with them, doing little things. I helped Genie in the kitchen. I brought Jimmy's lunch to him on a tray and sat beside him while he ate a few mouthfuls. I washed dishes accompanied by Genie's sad humming. Then later, I sat and sketched Lawrence with Lillian in his arms while listening to Rebekah practice a poem she was to recite at church the next Sunday.

"'I have no wit, no words, no tears; My heart within me like a stone, Is...is...'" she faltered.

"Numbed," Lawrence helped her along.

"'Numbed too much for hopes or fears. Look right,'" she looked to her right at me and gestured with her hand, giggling a bit self-consciously as I smiled at her, "'look left, I dwell alone, I lift my eyes, but...but...'"

"Dimmed with grief," Lawrence reminded her.

"'...dimmed with grief, No everlasting hills I see; My life is in the falling leaf: O Jesus, quicken me.' A better Resurrection, by Christina Rosetti," she announced as she finished.

"Very good, Rebekah," Lawrence praised.

"Papa, what does the 'falling leaf' part mean?"

"Hmmm, that's hard to explain."

"It's like today, Becky," Genie said from her corner where she sat mending Lawrence's shirt. "Look out the window. Doesn't today look sad? The leaves are all dying and falling to the ground. Sometimes people feel sad like that, like a leaf falling to the ground."

"I don't," Rebekah said, whirling in place, pleased to see her dress fanning out around her.

"Good," Genie smiled. "But someday you might, and then you'll understand."

At that moment, I wasn't sure which was worse—my own struggle or watching Genie's. I was powerless to relieve my own much less hers.

I left in the mid afternoon. It was a long drive home, and I had plenty of time to think. I'd always thought of Genie as a happy person, and she was. But happiness alone couldn't explain what I witnessed in Genie and Lawrence's house that day. There was something beyond a cheerful disposition, something that ran much deeper, that held them up. The same thing, the same light that beamed from Genie's face as a happy little girl was still there in sadness while she cared for Jimmy as a disappointed mother. Perhaps over all these years, I'd been too quick to explain the inexplicable with a word like happiness.

"THERE YOU ARE, Elizabeth," Jane said anxiously as I stepped into my home. She had the earpiece of the telephone to her ear and said into the receiver, "Here, she just walked in the door. Elizabeth, a lawyer is on the line, your father's lawyer."

"What?"

"That's what the man said. Are you going to stand there gawking or speak to him?"

"But..." I stammered while I hurriedly took my coat and hat off and shoved them into Violet's hands. Then grabbing the telephone, I said, "Hello?"

"How do you do," the man responded. "This is Elizabeth Millhouse Brown I'm speaking to, is it not?"

"Yes, that's me."

"I have some very important business to attend to that has to do with you. I wonder if you might meet with me the day after tomorrow at your mother's home."

"My mother's home? Maybe it would be better if you came to mine."

"Well, I could, I suppose," he said. "Your mother suggested we all meet together."

I put my hand on my forehead and glanced wildly around at Jane.

"Mrs. Brown, are you there?" he was asking.

"Oh, yes. Yes, I'm here."

"Will you be able to come?"

"Yes, I'll be there."

"Then we'll expect you at three o'clock."

I hung up and slowly turned around to look at a wide-eyed Jane. Violet stood quietly by the closet with my coat and hat still in her hands.

"I'm to meet with my father's lawyer at my mother's house. Whatever can it mean?"

"Perhaps you're finally going to get the inheritance you're entitled to," Jane said.

"I don't understand," I said, pacing slowly around the room. "She really must not be well."

"How do you know?" Jane asked.

"Well, Warren said that…" I stopped short and rephrased. "I don't know for sure. It's just a feeling I have."

"What nonsense," Jane replied. "Come and eat your dinner before you get anymore odd notions."

It'd been six years since I'd parted with my mother. Six years of independence and after all this time, I was still terrified of her.

Chapter 22

Mother had always hated tardiness, so I arrived half an hour early. The old house looked about the same as it had the day I left it six years before. But I was different. I realized this as I stood on the walkway looking at it, a light snow dusting the well-trimmed lawn. With six years removed from that austere place, I no longer felt the dread of it, and I could simply look at it as a large, nice-looking house. I smiled at the strangeness of the thought. Then I sobered when I thought of my mother and realized that I hadn't changed that much after all. I walked to the front door and knocked.

"Hello, Rachel," I said when she opened the door.

"Hello, miss," she answered as she smiled a bit. "I've been expecting you."

She took my coat and my hat and hung them up, stealing glances at me from time to time.

"I read about your husband and your little boy in the paper. I'm so sorry."

"Thank you, Rachel," I replied as I hung my head.

"I read your books too," she smiled. "We always knew you'd make something of yourself. You were always such a bright thing."

"We?" I asked, probing a little.

"Well, the cook and the gardener and I."

"I see," I nodded. "Thank you. I suppose I ought to go see Mother. Where is she?"

"She's in her room with the lawyer. She's not well, Elizabeth."

"Is she very bad?" I asked.

"Well, I'm no doctor, but it doesn't look good to me. It's her heart. It's just given out on her, and she doesn't have much strength."

I nodded again. "Does she," I began and then stopped. "Does she ever talk about me?"

"No, not to me," Rachel said, putting a hand on my arm. "Come now. You'd better not keep her waiting."

When I entered the room, I barely noticed the man sitting beside my mother's bed. My eyes locked with Mother's. She was sitting up in bed, wearing her spectacles. Her hair was pinned up neatly and her hands were folded in her lap. Through parted lips, she took quick, almost jolting breaths. She held my gaze steadily without smiling or frowning. She had a few lines on her forehead, but she looked remarkably young. Her hair was the same blond with only the slightest hint of grey. She was still beautiful.

"Hello, Mother," I said in scarcely more than a whisper, the old, familiar dread of her taking hold of me.

"Hello, Elizabeth," she said in the voice of an old woman, frail and feeble. "Sit down."

The lawyer stood, shook my hand, and then I sat. "Shall I begin?" he asked, looking at both my mother and I.

Mother nodded. "But don't bother reading the document," she said with an impatient wave of the hand. "I don't care to hear it. Just tell my daughter the amount of money she's to receive from her father."

"Well then, Mrs. Brown, your father stipulated in his will that when you reached the age of twenty-five, you were to receive one million dollars." I didn't register any response at the news so he asked, "Mrs. Brown, are you listening?"

I was still looking at my mother so it was hard to tell if I heard what he said.

"I don't understand," I finally said. "When I left to marry Christian, you made it seem as though Father left all his money to you. And you told me you were cutting me off financially."

"First of all, Elizabeth, when we had words that day, I never said my husband left everything to me. Incidentally, he did, and I have no intention of reversing the decision I made six years ago in regards to you. The inheritance you receive today is not from my husband. It's from your father."

"My father...your husband, what are you talking about?" I asked, my voice rising.

"Very simply, my husband, James Millhouse, was not your father."

"Then who was?" I demanded, standing to my feet.

"I don't wish to speak about it."

"Mrs. Brown," the lawyer soothed, "if you'll just sit back down while I explain the legalities, I think I can answer your question in due time."

"I don't care about the legalities!" I said, waving my hand at him. "Mother, I don't want to hear it from him. I want to hear it from you."

"Elizabeth, please..." she dropped her head and stared at her hands. "You should leave now, both of you."

The man stood up and gently took my arm.

"Come, Mrs. Brown," he said. "We can talk at length in the parlor if you'd like."

I pulled my arm away staring at my mother's bent head. My eyes blurred with tears, and I knelt down beside her.

"You can't just drop something like this on me after all these years and then turn me over to a stranger to explain it," I said. "I can't believe that you had me come to your house today for nothing when I could very well have met with this man at my house. There must be something you have to say to me."

"Come now, Elizabeth. Let's have no tears," she said, refusing to look me in the eyes.

"Mother…" I began to plead. But my hands fell to my sides. Then out of the corner of my eye I saw something familiar. On the stand beside her bed was a stack of books and underneath them all was a thin one, the title just visible. It was one of my books, my first book, *Jimmy and the Fox*. I turned to her again.

"Please, Mother," I begged, putting my hand over hers. "Please, don't turn me away again. I have to know who I am."

She took her hands away and folded them. My heart sank.

She turned to the man and said, "Would you be so kind as to leave us alone for a few minutes?"

"Of course, I'll wait outside until you want me."

When he'd gone, she looked up at me and shook her head.

"Get up and sit in a chair. I'll not have any daughter of mine groveling on the floor."

She was still my mother and so I obeyed.

"Your husband is dead," she said, and I couldn't tell if she was asking or stating a fact.

"Yes," I answered.

"And you had a child. A little boy I believe."

"Yes," I answered again.

"Also dead?" she inquired.

I nodded.

"When Christian Brown came to me, asking for your hand, he had the look of death on him already. I knew he wouldn't last long."

"It was the influenza," I said.

There was a long silence between us.

"Well," she began again. "You want to know everything so I'll tell you. I've never told anyone before, but I suppose you have a right to know since it involves you."

She looked pointedly at me and said, "But it isn't nice."

"I don't care. I want to know."

"My parents died a few years after I was born. So my grandfather took me in. You never knew him. He doted on me and spoiled me terribly. My grandfather did me a grave disservice by giving me anything I asked for and letting me have my way in everything. By the time I reached the age of fifteen, I was a naïve, undisciplined, and headstrong coquette. And my grandfather did a poor job of protecting me. It was a great joke to my grandfather and my uncles, all the male relatives in my life really, to watch the young men in the neighborhood flocking to the house to call on me. My grandfather would pinch my nose with a hearty laugh and tell me what a heartbreaker I was. So I continued in my silly flirtatious ways, unchecked. After all, to my grandfather, a woman's only purpose in life was to be charming, to attract a man, and become a pretty little ornament in that man's parlor."

I listened in fascination as she spoke. She painted such a different picture of herself than the one I saw before me.

"The only thing that kept me from becoming a fool in every way was my desire to learn. You're very much like me that way, Elizabeth. I read everything I could get my hands on. When I finished my general education, I begged Grandfather to let me go on to high school. He just laughed and asked me why I wanted to bother my pretty little head about Algebra and Latin. So I did the best I could with what I had." She laughed to herself as she thought about it.

"I shouldn't give myself too much credit. I was silly and frivolous. Oh, I enjoyed the power I had over men. I liked the way they sought me out. Most of them, I didn't care two cents about. I just liked having them make a fuss over me and do everything I told them to. My husband, the one you called Father, was one of them. He was at the house nearly every day of the week, looking forlorn and lovesick because he was smitten with me. He asked me to marry him four or five times, I believe. But I turned him down, sometimes before he could even get the words out of his mouth. He was so serious and I couldn't abide him. Besides, getting married, settling down with one man, and having babies sounded boring. I was having too much fun to think about that. But then he came to town." Her voice hardened, but her words were short and clipped.

"You mean my father?" I asked.

"Yes. Dean Masterson was his name. I saw him at a party first. He was the most handsome man I'd ever seen. It wasn't just good looks, though.

There was something about him that was different than all the rest. All he did was look at me once, and I melted inside. He made all the others look like a troop of little boys. I'm not even sure how. Nobody seemed to know much about him except that he was wealthy or would be when he got his inheritance. It was said that he lived abroad and was unmarried. But that was enough information for my grandfather to allow him to call on me.

"For once in my life, I was enamored with a man. He came to see me every day, and we visited in the parlor. He said the most beautiful things and had the most perfect manners. We went for long walks and buggy rides. Due to his old age, my grandfather often forgot to send a chaperone along with us, and I didn't remind him. My feelings only grew as I spent more time with Dean. I believe I'd have done anything he asked of me short of jumping off a cliff. My grandfather had no idea of the dangerous situation I was in. I lacked self-control. I was too willing, and we were too often alone.

"At the end of that summer, he told me regretfully that he had no choice but to return to Europe. Business called him. Once again, we were out in the country in a buggy alone. I immediately dissolved into tears, and he proclaimed his love to me. He promised that once he received his inheritance, he would come back to the States and marry me. And then he asked the unthinkable. He wanted me to give him what society and the church said I couldn't until I had a wedding ring on my finger. At first I refused, not because I was so conscientious, but because I was afraid of discovery. He begged me and made all kinds of flowery speeches, promising undying love and devotion. It didn't take long before I gave in. I gave myself to him heart and soul. He took from me what I could never have back, and then he left the next day. I didn't hear from him ever again."

I sat perfectly still, gazing at the stranger in front of me. All the while, she looked back into my eyes, for once giving me her undivided attention. It was like a dream, and I couldn't quite grasp what she was saying. I didn't want to.

"I was such a fool," she said, shaking her head. "I was stupid but not so stupid that I didn't realize I was carrying his child a few months later. I wrote to Dean Masterson five times and sent it to the address he'd given me, but he didn't reply to any of my letters. By then I was terrified. I had no one to turn to. If my grandfather found out, he'd be furious. Yes, furious, in spite of the fact that he winked and laughed at my flirtatious behavior. I knew that once my condition was known, I'd be thrust out of society, scorned, and held up to other young girls as a terrible example. I could forget marriage and financial stability all together. What respectable man would have me after that?

"Then, one day while I was looking at the newspaper, Dean's name popped out at me. The article reported Dean's success on Wall Street. Apparently, he'd recently raked in a large sum of money. I didn't pay much attention to that. The last sentence is what I read over and over again in disbelief. 'Mr. Masterson and Elaine Masterson, his wife of five years, reside in London.' I fainted right there on the sofa. When I came to, the maid was fanning my face and my grandfather was pacing the room, waving the paper around his head, ranting and raving about scoundrels meddling with his granddaughter. After he calmed down, he patted me on the shoulder and told me to forget all about Dean Masterson. There were other fish in the pond.

"I was devastated. He'd lied to me in every way possible. He wasn't waiting for an inheritance, and he had no intention of marrying me. He used me, and I stood by and let him."

Then she laughed, "No, I didn't stand by. Even now I try to defend myself. I didn't stand by; I actively participated."

"You were very young, Mother," I said, trying to control my voice.

"Don't cry for me," she said. "I don't need your pity. I was an idiot and I deserved what happened to me. But I resolved that no man would ever make a fool of me again, ever! And I might add that no one has since that day."

I looked down at my hands and waited for her to continue.

"But I must finish so you can leave. A few days after my discovery, James Millhouse came to call. He told me that he heard about what had happened, and he wished he could get his hands on the fellow. It was then that I saw my way out. I would marry James. I knew it wouldn't take much doing. He was obviously smitten with me. Personally, I couldn't stand him, but I needed safety. I needed a wedding ring on my finger, and quickly, if I was to avoid discovery. So I petted him and hung on his every word, all the while despising every moment of it. He proposed to me a week later. He was quite surprised when I insisted on marrying immediately. So was Grandfather, but I was used to having my own way, and as usual, I got it.

After the wedding night, I never let James come near me. I couldn't bear it. He tried to win me to him but eventually gave up. My pregnancy became ever more obvious, and seven months later you were born, well-developed and perfectly formed. James knew you couldn't possibly be his. He was extremely angry when he realized what I'd done, but I knew my secret and my position in his home was safe. He was a proud man, and he wouldn't want the thing to be known and blight his name. We went on living in the same house, quite unhappily I might add, until his death. Now you know everything."

My strength seemed to have gone out of me; it was such work to lift my head and look at her.

"I'm a bastard then," I stated.

"If you must put it that way, then yes. I believe that's the correct term," Mother replied, returning my gaze. "Don't look at me that way, Elizabeth. You asked for the truth, and I gave it to you."

"My father...did he ever see me? Did he say anything to me in the will?"

"No, he didn't," Mother said. "I fancy he suffered a few twinges of conscience before he died and left the money to you to atone for his misdeeds. You weren't the only one, I'm afraid. In fact, he mentioned two other illegitimate children in the will alongside you."

"I wish he hadn't left me anything," I said through my teeth. "The one I called Father will always be my father."

For a long while there was no sound but the ticking of the clock. I stared at the carpet until it became a blur.

"Why did you send me away all those years ago, Mother?"

"For many reasons, I suppose. I was busy with my writing, and I didn't want a child underfoot. I'm not motherly, Elizabeth, I never was. I never wanted children, you know. Besides that, I soon realized you were highly intelligent and I wanted you to have an excellent education. I wanted you to have the opportunities I never had. I thought that would be the best thing I could do for you. My husband, James, thought it was unnecessary. He was quite displeased with the whole idea. He seemed to think I wanted you far away because you reminded me of Dean. Your eyes are just like his. But as you weren't James' child, I had my way eventually. When he was dying, he begged me to bring you back home for a while. I don't know what came over him. He'd never taken much of an interest in you before. Well, I relented then because he wasn't barking orders at me. I saw no harm in it."

She paused for a moment as if to gather her thoughts before continuing.

"I don't regret what I did, Elizabeth. You were better off at school. I was right about Christian, too. You'd have been better off not marrying him. You know I'm right. I don't believe you understand what you were given."

I stood up slowly, shaking my head.

"No," I said. "It wasn't right. It was wrong of you."

I walked to the door and looked back at her.

"I always thought I was a mistake," I mused. "I'll go now. That way you won't have to look at me anymore."

I put my hand on the doorknob.

"Elizabeth," she called out to me.

"Yes, Mother."

"I don't blame you for hating me."

There was such a strange look on her face. She looked unsure of herself, like a child waiting for approval. It made me hope.

"I never hated you, Mother," I said through my tears. "I just wanted you to love me."

She laid her head back on the pillows.

"May I come again?" I asked.

"If you like," she said, mask in place once more.

Chapter 23

I did come again. In fact, it was the next day. But by then, she was nearly unresponsive. She seemed to take notice when I entered her room, but not when I left several hours later. Rachel called to inform me of her death the next afternoon.

In her will, she was true to her word and left not one cent to me. The house was to become a refuge for women who'd fallen into hard times, and all the money would support that charity. She'd written in her will that she didn't want a funeral and wouldn't be using the plot that my stepfather had paid for. She'd bought her own plot, located several yards away from his. Instead of her grave stone saying, "Here lies Mrs. James Millhouse," the stone simply read, "Elizabeth Mansfield," which was her maiden name.

I stood looking down at the stone and the fresh mound of dirt already beginning to freeze. I felt guilty, somehow. Guilty, I suppose, because I thought I ought to be mourning her, this gigantic personality that had loomed over every part of my life. What I felt instead was difficult to pinpoint. Perhaps it was weariness, confusion, a resignation to a fact I couldn't ignore. I held the obituary in my hand, but there was no need to read it. I had it memorized, especially the last sentence, "She is survived by her daughter, Elizabeth Millhouse Brown."

"So this is where the line ends," I whispered. "Poor Father, yours ended long ago. You were kind to love me a little, in spite of it."

I heard the crunch of gravel and turned to see Warren walking towards me. He took off his hat and stood beside me soberly. I threaded my arm through his.

"Don't ask me what I feel," I said, looking up at him. "I don't even know. How do you mourn for a stranger?"

"She must have had some regard for you, to leave you something," he said.

"Yes," I lied calmly. "I suppose she did in a way," remembering my book in her room.

He nodded quickly, but I remember he looked disappointed in my answer.

After a while he cleared his throat and said, "I'm afraid I'll be going away for a while."

"Going away?" I repeated in surprise, "How long?"

"Just a few weeks," he said hurriedly. Then he smiled, "It's rotten of me, but it makes me feel pretty good to see you so unhappy about it."

"Oh, Warren," I groaned as I let go of his arm and walked to the other side of the grave.

"I'm sorry," he replied, "I do feel badly about going, especially with your mother dying and all…"

"I'll be fine."

"I'm sure," he responded.

I looked back at the stone rather than him.

"Anyway," he continued, "I haven't had a holiday for a few years, and I've been told to take a rest. I'm going to visit my sister in New York. There's a new fellow that can take over my work for a while."

"That's good," I commented. "You deserve a rest." With that, we began to walk home.

"You know," he said, looking sideways at me, "there's something about death and dying that makes me want to confess my sins."

I smiled a little and shook my head. "Please don't," I pleaded, "at least not to me."

"I wasn't quite forthright with you when you were trying to get your first book published."

"It's no matter," I shrugged. "It's published, isn't it?"

"Yes, but…I never did tell you who I sent it to the last time. Well, it's like this. Being in the position I'm in at the *Gazette*, I have access to the addresses of a lot of influential people."

I nodded absentmindedly.

"So, I sent your work to someone I thought would be sympathetic to a young woman trying to make her way in the world. This person wasn't always well-thought-of, and so I didn't tell you who it was. I was mostly worried about what Jane would think."

He paused and I walked ahead, my mind full of other thoughts.

"I sent it to Alexander Stonely."

I stopped and turned around to stare at him.

"What's wrong?" he asked, earnestly searching my face.

My mind was whirling. *What did he know?* I couldn't ask him without giving myself away.

"You're upset," he commented.

"No. I'm surprised, that's all," I said, smiling weakly.

I began to walk again, trying to hide my anguish with action. "It's all right," I finally answered. "I'll always be grateful for what you did for me. Let's not talk about it anymore."

Before he left me at my door, he gave me a phone number where I could reach him if I needed to.

"Be sure to call if you need anything," he urged.

"What could I possibly need? I'm a millionaire now," I said. "Have a wonderful time, Warren."

Once at home, I said the necessary words to Jane before I escaped to the solitude of my room. Jane was so sympathetic to my "loss" as she called it and so kind that I was afraid I might spill the whole ugly tale to her. And then what would she think of me? I wanted so much to tell someone, to get rid of the weight I carried on my shoulders. But how could I?

I sent it to Alexander Stonely, I kept thinking.

I sat at my desk, staring out the window far into the evening. I could see my mother's face as she told me the story behind my life, looking into my eyes so impassively. And yet, she knew everything there was to know about me. The success of my book wasn't my doing, it was hers. She made me what I was. She'd decided what kind of person I would be, perhaps before I was even aware of the world, and then set about to ensure the success of her plans. Now, here I sat, the finished product. I was a well-educated, independent woman with no husband or children to hamper me. I relied on no one but myself for a living.

I could pull myself up by my own bootstraps and do whatever I wanted to do. And I was alone, cut off from my friends by the secret she'd told me. There were many similarities between my mother and I. Against my will and through circumstances beyond my control, I'd become like the person I disliked the most. I'd become my mother.

Everything was a muddle. Somehow, I'd disliked her and loved her at the same time. *Did she love me? Did she care for me at all? Or was I simply an interesting experiment?* "It's enough to make one weep," I finally said aloud, my eyes as dry as they could be.

I wrote the whole story out in my journal, down to the minutest detail, thinking I would get rid of my load on paper since I could tell no one else. I fell into bed exhausted but unable to sleep. I couldn't quiet my thoughts, but I closed my eyes in desperation. I had a speaking engagement the next morning, and the sun would rise whether I slept or not.

I performed my job the next day and came home to all the petty cares and annoyances that constitute daily living. Jane reminded me for the tenth time about the leak in the roof that needed patching. I'd missed my appointment with the dressmaker, and Violet hadn't shown up at the house all day.

"Don't bother about her. We'll just get another," I said.

"Yes, but what if she's sick?" was Jane's concern.

"Violet? I doubt she's been sick a day in her life. She's just that ill-tempered."

I attended to everything Jane asked that afternoon, feeling distracted, tired, and irritable. Then I sat down to think over lesson plans for the art classes the next day. I didn't have a moment to myself before bedtime. I left the house early in the morning so I could stop by the library to speak to Miss Tuttle about an error on a check she'd given me. It was cold and foggy, and in my haste to get warm indoors, I hardly noticed the newsboy on the corner shouting out the morning's headlines.

"Miss Tuttle, you forgot to sign the check you sent me the other day," I said through my shivering. "Would you mind signing it now?"

She didn't say a word to me when I gave it to her, but she looked so strangely at me, I began to wonder if I'd forgotten to put on some important article of clothing.

"Is there anything the matter?" I asked.

She shook her head and signed the check. She pushed it hastily across her desk at me and turned around to rummage through a filing cabinet.

"Well, thank you. Good day," I said, but she didn't make any comment in return.

I went slowly towards the door, but it was strange. I knew she never really liked me, but she'd never been impolite to my face. I turned around to look at her as I was passing through the door. She'd been joined by another woman, her assistant, and they both stared at me with disgust. I was puzzled and a little worried. All the way to the school, I tried to understand what I'd done wrong, but I could think of nothing.

When I reached my classroom at the usual time, there was a piece of paper tacked to the door that read, "All art classes canceled today."

No one had contacted me with such news. I quickly made my way to Mr. Snyder's office and rapped on the door. He didn't answer so I searched the halls for him. I finally saw him disappearing around a corner and called his name. He didn't seem to hear me so I ran to catch up with him.

"Mr. Snyder, wait. What's all this about canceling my classes?"

He turned reluctantly to face me. He looked odd, not at all the same open, enthusiastic Mr. Snyder I was used to.

"I'm sorry, but it was necessary to do so. You must understand why," he said, looking everywhere but in my eyes.

"No, I don't," I said in alarm. "Please explain."

"You mean, you haven't seen this yet?" he asked, holding up the front page of the *Gazette*.

I snatched it from him, my heart sinking as I read it.

Things Not What They Seem:
New and alarming information
about a popular children's author revealed.

Due to an anonymous source, it's recently been discovered that Elizabeth Millhouse Brown, author of *Jimmy and the Fox, The Adventures of Little Chris,* and others, is not only the illegitimate child of a well-known multi-millionaire, but is also the daughter of Alexander Stonely. It would appear that Mr. Stonely never existed in actuality but was the pen-name of one of the most prominent citizens of this town, the late Mrs. James Millhouse. The same Mrs. Millhouse (Stonely) was a catalyst to Mrs. Brown's success, seeing to it that her daughter's first book was published in one of the most prominent houses in the country.

One would be inclined to overlook Mrs. Brown's unfortunate birth and connections if her character were more admirable and suited for a young child's example. According to the aforementioned anonymous source, however, she professes to be both "angry with God" and "disgusted with religion in general." As recently as four years ago, her marriage was strained almost to the breaking point when she objected to her husband's church attendance. It was shortly thereafter that he became seriously ill and died.

I forced myself to read on. Everything was there. Every horrible, sordid detail was there. My hands slowly dropped as I looked up at Mr. Snyder.

"It's true, isn't it?" he asked.

I nodded, pleading with my eyes, "Yes…it is. But…"

"I'm sure you see that I have no other course. I've already been bombarded with telephone calls and visits from enraged parents. What can I do? You mustn't blame me for it," he said, nervously. Then he took my arm and escorted me to the door.

"Now, please go before someone sees you here. I'm sorry; I truly am. But the board is going to have my head as it is. You really must leave. Perhaps later, when all this calms down..."

But I wasn't listening. I walked out the door in a daze. The town was fully awake. Was it just my imagination as I walked home, that people stopped and stared at me? Did women scuttled by, looking at me out of the corners of their eyes? Why did my grocer, the one I'd always spoken to as I passed by, hurry inside his shop when he saw me coming? And there was Mrs. Finley, staring at me through her window, pushing her curious children away as if I could pollute them with my eyes. I ran inside, slamming the door behind me.

Jane was waiting for me. She had the newspaper in her hand and her face was white.

"Elizabeth," she faltered. "I've been reading and hearing such awful things. Who would spread stories about you and your mother?"

Unfortunately I couldn't answer her.

"What...what are we going to do?"

"They're not stories, Jane," I said through my teeth. "It's all true. I'm illegitimate. My mother was Alexander Stonely. I do hate religion. I did torment poor Christian when he converted. Everything's accurate. Go on and leave now before I stain your reputation."

She sat down and cried.

"Why didn't you tell me, Elizabeth?" she asked. "You could've told me."

"I didn't want anyone to know. I was ashamed. I'm still ashamed."

"How did all this come out, then?"

"I don't know!" I shouted. "I'm not God."

"Think, Elizabeth. Someone's responsible for this."

The telephone rang and Jane answered it. There was an angry babbling on the other end of the line, and Jane reached for my date book. Another engagement at a school was canceled. I turned and ran up the stairs. I pulled open the drawer in my desk where I kept my journal, but it wasn't there. I tore open all the drawers and emptied them, scattering papers and drawings everywhere. But there was no journal. Then I remembered that I'd left it on top of the desk, wide open for anyone to come in and see. Violet would have seen it.

"It won't help to lose control of your temper, Elizabeth," Jane said from behind me.

But my anger was already raging and I turned to explain who the traitor was.

"It was Violet who gave the paper all that information. My journal's gone. She's the only one who could've taken it. She never liked me."

"That's a theft. I'm calling the police," Jane said.

I laughed as I stood in the middle of all those papers. What did it matter now? The damage was done. I drew the curtains, locked the door, and sat down against it in the dark as I waited for the story of my horrible life to spread.

Chapter 24

How long did I sit on my bedroom floor, shivering in the dark? I don't know. I seemed to lose all sense of time and surroundings. I couldn't seem to conjure up any one clear thought. I was only aware of a terrifying silence and the vague impression that I ought to jump out the window, but that it wasn't high enough to do the job properly. It'd been high enough for Chris, but not for me.

Throughout the day, I heard knocking at my door and Jane's anxious voice begging me to come and eat something, to speak to her at least. But my overtaxed brain twisted even that and sent my heart to beating wildly. I envisioned crowds of angry women rushing at me in righteous indignation, skirts billowing. I clutched my knees to my chest, trying to hide myself until the danger was past.

When the dawn came, I hadn't moved, and I watched the coming of the morning with almost more dread than I had the approach of darkness. Sometime later, I heard the front door open and slam shut. Jane was crying and frantically explaining something to someone. I heard running up the stairs and felt a loud knocking on my door.

"Elizabeth!" Warren shouted. "Open the door."

His voice jolted me out of my living nightmare, and I struggled to find the words to answer him.

"I came as soon as I heard. I fired the guy who let that story go through. If I'd been there, I would've stopped it, I swear. Elizabeth, answer me. Let us know you're all right."

I heard him breathing heavily in the hall. I heard Jane's smothered sobbing as well.

"None of it makes any difference to me," he continued. "I knew who your mother was, anyway. We were friends. I've known everything all along except that you were born illegitimate, and I don't care a hoot about that. Come on, Elizabeth. Open the door."

I began to cry, my body shaking.

"Elizabeth, don't do anything to hurt yourself, please! I don't know what I'd do if anything happened to you."

He was beginning to panic, and I could hear it in his voice.

"You better talk to me or, so help me, I'll break this door down!"

"Warren," I managed to say while crying but laughing a bit, "you can't go around breaking doors down all the time."

I could hear him letting out a sigh of relief. He put his hand under the door, and I put mine over it.

"Why don't you come out?" he begged.

"I can't right now. I must be alone. Go away for a while. Please, I won't hurt myself, I promise. I never break promises."

There was a long silence and then he said softly, "All right then. Take as long as you need. I'll be waiting for you downstairs."

I reflected that it was good that Warren had come because now my mind wasn't quite so cluttered. I could think a little. And then I wished that I couldn't think. The hopelessness of my situation was far too evident. I was tempted to call Warren back to me as his footsteps receded down the stairs. And then, there was that poem again. At every turn in my life it mocked me.

Naked I wait Thy love's uplifted stroke.
My harness piece by piece Thou hast hewn from me,
And smitten me to my knee;
I am defenseless utterly.
I slept, methinks, and woke,
And, slowly gazing, find me stripped in sleep.
In the rash lust head of my young powers,
I shook the pillaring hours
And pulled my life upon me; grimed with smears,
I stand amid the dust o' the mounded years—
My mangled youth lies dead beneath the heap.
My days have crackled and gone up in smoke,
Have puffed and burst as sun-starts on a stream.

Father was gone, Christian was gone, Chris was gone, and now Mother was gone, whatever that meant to me. I had my million dollars, but what did that matter when the good opinion of the world, the world that I knew, was gone forever. There was nothing left, nothing but Jane and Warren and a crowd of people that had turned against me in a short period of twenty-four hours. Perhaps Genie and the Woodwards had finally become shocked and dismayed enough to cast me off. Perhaps Jane and Warren would become embarrassed and leave after all. Considering everything that had happened to me in my short life, nothing seemed impossible but good and pleasant things.

This was where it ended. There was nowhere else to go. No place to escape to. The Hound of Heaven had finally caught up with me.

"God, why did you do all this to me?" I whispered. "Was it really necessary? Have I been so evil and wicked that I truly deserve it? There have been worse people, far worse than me, who have lived pleasant lives. I've never killed anyone or stolen anything. You sowed the seeds of all that's happened before I was old enough to kill or steal. Why do You punish me for the things I can't control? Haven't You given me good reason to hate You?"

As always, my answer was an empty silence. I stood up and paced the room, back and forth, back and forth, pausing then pacing again. I must have driven Jane and Warren mad with my pacing. After a while, I began to think of things. Memories began to flit through my mind, things I thought I'd forgotten. There were snatches of songs, conversations, young and familiar faces, places, and events. They were things like:

"All things bright and beautiful, the Lord God made them all..." sang the girls at school. Genie was among them, smiling.

"Elizabeth— my God is bountiful... That's what your name means. Did you know that?" Mr. Woodward had asked me.

"Pray to God about your trouble, Elizabeth. He loves you," Mr. Woodward urged me.

"Does He? No. No, I don't think He does," I responded in my little girl voice.

There was my father's face, quiet and pale, "I'll be a better father. I'll begin now."

"Goodnight, Papa," I'd answered. "I'll see you in the morning."

And there was Mother coldly saying, "He's gone now. There's a black dress laid out on your bed. Go put it on."

It was as though I lived out the life in the poem as it declared,

I fled Him, down the nights and down the days;
I fled Him, down the arches of the years;
I fled Him, down the labyrinthine ways
Of my own mind...

Thou shalt love the Lord thy God... rang in my thoughts, over and over.

Then I thought of the dog in the Woodward's field, the one chasing the rabbit. The rabbit hanging limp in vise-like jaws.

There was Christian, kneeling in front of me in the snow, "Don't cry. I love you. I'm going to marry you."

"Thou shalt love the Lord thy God with all thy heart..." I remembered chanting with the other girls at school.

"Elizabeth, as your mother, I insist that you listen to me..."

"I feel no obligation to listen to you or heed your advice. You gave me a roof over my head and food to eat and clothes to wear, but you didn't love me."

"Thou shalt love the Lord thy God with all thy heart and with all thy soul..."

I heard Christian pleading with me, "Elizabeth, be reasonable. This doesn't have to ruin our marriage; it can make it stronger. Please listen to me."

I heard my own voice saying, "Oh God, if I find Christian safe and well, I promise I'll never make him unhappy again. I'll even be a Christian if that's what he wants. I swear it."

Then the poem again,

> But with unhurrying chase,
> And unperturbed pace,
> Deliberate speed, majestic instancy,
> They beat—and a Voice beat
> More instant than the Feet—
> "All things betray thee, who betrayest Me."

I saw Christian holding out his Bible to me, hands trembling, "He...loves you."

"Thou shalt love the Lord thy God with all thy heart and all thy soul and all thy mind..."

I remembered tucking little Chris into bed and hearing him say, "I love you, Mama."

I saw Chris' bleeding head and his last breath.

I saw poor Jimmy, lying in bed, and Rebekah reciting, "My life is in the falling leaf, Oh Jesus, quicken me."

"I wish you could see Him as I do," I could hear Genie's voice again. I could see her sitting gravely by, painfully aware of her crippled son lying in bed above her but still so calm, so kind. "But I can't make you understand," she finally said.

"Thou shalt love the Lord thy God with all thy heart and all thy soul and all thy mind. This is the first and great commandment. And the second is like unto it, Thou shalt love thy neighbor as thyself." I was haunted by that Bible verse. It wouldn't leave me in peace.

The memories seemed to come so thick and so fast that I couldn't take them all in. It was too much, too overwhelming. And then, very suddenly, I saw myself as a little girl standing in front of a mirror after my father's funeral wearing a black dress. It was at that moment I'd said to God in my heart, *I hate You!* I winced at the memory, as the full weight of my words struck me. I'd always told myself that I hated God because of what He'd done to me and allowed me to pass through. I'd always hated Him because he'd withheld His love from me.

But it now occurred to me that perhaps I was looking at things backward. *Was I angry with God because He didn't love me or was God angry with me because I didn't love Him?* If I'd been born into a loving family, had lost no loved ones, had no disappointments in life, would I have loved God then? I wanted to affirm that I would've, but I doubted myself. I doubted myself because of who I was fundamentally and who Christian and Genie and Lawrence and Mr. and Mrs. Woodward were. I couldn't ignore the difference between them and myself and the way in which they'd all responded to similar disappointment.

I couldn't fool myself into thinking that my life had been more difficult than my friends any longer. As a young lad, Christian lost both of his parents and struggled along in poverty for several years before he married me. Those last few weeks of his life, he faced my cruelty with kindness. He wasn't bitter like me.

When crippling illness struck Genie and Lawrence's firstborn, they didn't become angry. In every word and action they mirrored Job's words in that ancient book, "Though He slay me, yet will I trust in Him." And the Woodwards were two people who would've and should've made beautiful parents but were childless. I was sure it was a disappointment to them. But instead of resentment, they radiated love to me and everyone around them, devoting their lives to other children.

If my life had been easy and pleasant, maybe I would've thought fondly of God. I'd have reflected on Him as the nice old man in the sky who took care of things on earth. But love Him with all my heart and soul and mind? I might have liked Him, but I thought it more likely that I would have been indifferent to Him. Now I saw that both possibilities were heinous crimes in the light of the first and great commandment.

"But You took so many things away," I then said, trying to justify myself.

As if to answer me, He seemed to parade through my mind, all the things He'd given to me. I had the best education a girl could ask for, free of charge. I had the Woodwards who loved and mentored me. I had two beautiful years of marriage with Christian that produced my sweet little boy. I had faithful friends who'd suffered much as a result of my bitterness, two of which were waiting downstairs, standing by me through everything. My mother had cared enough to anonymously help publish my first book, paving the way for future success. I'd never suffered from cold or hunger. I never lacked for the things I needed. My delicate health had vanished with adulthood. The list went on.

I bowed my head and wept as words from the poem played themselves in my mind. For the first time, I understood what they meant.

> Now of that long pursuit,
> Comes on at hand the bruit;
> That Voice is round me like a bursting sea:
> "And is thy earth so marred,
> Shattered in shard on shard?
> Lo, all things fly thee, for thou fliest Me.
> Strange, piteous futile thing!
> Wherefore should any set thee love apart?
> Seeing none but I makes much of naught" (He said),
> "And human love needs human meriting:
> How hast thou merited—
> Of all man's clotted clay the dingiest clot?
> Alack, thou knowest not
> How little worthy of any love thou art!
> Whom wilt thou find to love ignoble thee,
> Save Me, save only Me?"

Then I said aloud the final lines of the poem,

> Is my gloom, after all,
> Shade of His hand, outstretched caressingly?
> "Ah, fondest, blindest, weakest,
> I am He whom thou seekest!
> Thou dravest love from thee, who dravest Me."

I felt the full weight of my guilt and in that moment, I admitted it.

"Oh, God," I gasped, "Forgive me."

At that moment, tension drained away and an inescapable fatigue settled over me. I stood up slowly, feebly, and I unlocked the door and laid down on my bed, clothes and all. My eyes shut. Sometime in the night I was vaguely aware of being lifted and put back in bed, the covers tucked in around me. My sleep was dreamless, full, and deep.

Chapter 25

The first thing that I was aware of when I opened my eyes in the morning was light and then warmth. The sun shining through my window was almost blinding, and I closed my eyes again, bathing in it. I opened my eyes and saw that a snowstorm must have passed through the night before. The roofs of the town were covered with a foot of snow. There were three extra blankets on my bed. Jane must've put them there to keep me from getting chilled in the night. I was warm and I felt so safe. I was afraid to move, afraid to spoil the beauty of it. I let my eyes wander around the room, watching the sun beams play on the wall.

Then I noticed that there was a man sitting in a chair at the end of my bed, reading. He hadn't yet noticed that I was awake. His chair was turned sideways, and I could only see his profile. But what a familiar and friendly profile it was. He had on rumpled trousers, his gray hair was not quite tidy, and he squinted down at the book he read because he'd forgotten to put on his spectacles. I smiled and my eyes became quite misty.

"Mr. Woodward," I whispered.

He turned with a smile and put aside his book.

"There's my Elizabeth," he said, seeming to forget that I was a woman grown. "How do you feel?" He moved his chair closer and I took his hand in both of mine.

"Oh, Mr. Woodward, you came all this way to see me?" I paused as all the events of recent days came flooding in and then they burst out as I asked, "Are you sure you don't hate me now that everything's known?"

He smiled and nodded, "I'm sure. I brought something to cheer you up," he said, placing a small paper bag in my hands. "They don't make mints like they used to, but these will have to do."

"Oh, thank you!" I said, somewhere between a laugh and a sob.

"Now, no more crying," he said. "We've got to get you feeling better again."

"Where's Warren?" I asked.

"He went to the police station. He'll be back in a while."

"The police station?" I echoed in concern.

"Jane called the police about your missing journal. They went to Violet's lodgings the other night, and she and most of her belongings were gone. But she left the journal behind. The police wanted to talk to you, but as you weren't well, Warren went instead. I think their main question is whether you want to press charges or not."

I let my head sink back in my pillow as I considered the news.

"No," I said. "What's the use? Let her go. I only want my journal back. She got a nice kick in my shins, though. I expect that I deserved it after the way I treated her."

"I think that's a wise decision. You can let the police know when you're feeling better."

I stared past him out the window as my troubles began to crowd in on me once again.

"Warren put a stop to any further stories with you as the subject," Mr. Woodward said eventually. "It seemed to me as I spoke with him this morning that his chief frustration is that he can't put a stop to the ones circling in other publications."

"Dear Warren. He's so good to me. How is Jane?"

"She's asleep. She's had quite a time of it, answering all the telephone calls."

"Poor Jane, I hope she rests well."

I twisted the edge of the bedsheet into a little knot and smoothed it out again.

"Mr. Woodward, I can't bear the thought of being whispered about, pointed at, and avoided for the rest of my life. If that's what I have to face from now on, I think I'd rather stay in this room til doomsday."

Mr. Woodward looked thoughtfully at me for a moment and then said, "Remember, Elizabeth, the manner in which you came into the world was no fault of yours. Your father and mother hold responsibility for that, and there's no need for you to be ashamed. The same goes for your mother's dual personality—this Alexander Stonely business. You're not to blame for that. She'll answer to God for whatever wrongs she committed."

"And Violet will answer for hers, and I'll answer for mine," I thought out loud.

"Yes," he answered gently. He paused for a moment as if in thought. I expected him to point out the wrongs I was responsible for. I almost wished he would, but he didn't. Instead he continued on another track.

"People have very short memories. It's both a blessing and curse, I suppose. We're always and forever forgetting the things we ought to remember and remembering the things that are of no consequence. Give it a little time,

Elizabeth. They'll forget. And even if they don't, they'll soon realize that there are far weightier matters in this world to fret over. It won't be easy for you at first, but it will pass. I have no doubt that many children will enjoy your books for years to come."

I nodded in appreciation. I felt that what he was saying was true. But something else was weighing heavily on me. My mind was working quickly, trying to think of a way to tell him my most recent discovery. I bandied it about in my mind from different angles and then simply told the truth.

"Mr. Woodward, I've been wrong," I said.

I put my hand over my eyes to hide my tears. I'd tried to keep up appearances for so long. Now, to my dismay, I'd suddenly lost my stiff upper lip.

He didn't speak, but only waited for me to continue.

"I've been angry at God. I've hated Him for so many reasons. But I don't have any right to be angry and hateful. I know that now. You and Mrs. Woodward always used to tell me to love God and pray to Him. You used to tell me that God loved me. Do you think…?" I said, pausing to get my voice under control. "Do you think He'd still have me after the way I've treated Him for twenty-five years?"

"Yes. I know He would," Mr. Woodward responded. "He went to a great deal of trouble on your account, Elizabeth. Do you think He would die for you only to throw you away now when you've decided you want Him after all?

"I don't know," I said. "I don't know anything anymore."

"'I have loved thee with an everlasting love: Therefore with loving kindness have I drawn thee.' That's what He said to the children of Israel after they'd ill-treated Him for hundreds of years. What's twenty-five years compared to that, Elizabeth?"

"But how can I make it all right? How can I do enough good to make up for it?"

"You can't, Elizabeth," he said with a smile. "He doesn't ask you to. He only asks two things."

"What are they?" I asked, as if my life depended on it.

"He asks you to go to Him in faith and follow Him."

"That's all?" I looked desperately at Mr. Woodward, trying to understand this riddle. "Why would He want me to do that? I have nothing to give Him."

"My dear girl," Mr. Woodward said and there was such kindness in his voice. "He knows that already. He doesn't want anything but you."

"He knows everything about me. He must know, more than all those people out there reading the newspapers. And He still loves me?" I asked in wonder, more of myself than Mr. Woodward.

"Yes," he assured me with comfort.

When I heard that, I laid back on my pillow, my tears blinding me.

"I want to respond to Him," I said after a long pause, "but I'm afraid I'll fail again. I'm afraid I'll do wrong."

"You will," he answered with a grin.

"But what will I do then?"

"You'll go to Christ again, a thousand times if you must. Once you first go to Him with a willing heart, you'll never stop and He won't mind. You see, you can only fail if you don't go at all. So will you go?'

In my mind, I could almost hear the Hound of Heaven say,

All which I took from thee I did but take,
Not for thy harms,
But just that thou might's seek it in My arms.
All which thy child's mistake Fancies as lost,
I have stored for thee at home:
Rise; clasp my hand, and come!

Letting all the truth fill my mind, I found myself wanting His love and care more than anything. Then slowly, I nodded. "I'll go," I finally said.

I'm glad Mr. Woodward gave me no foolish promises. I'm glad he didn't tell me that I'd never be unhappy, that I would soon forget my past life, or that I would never fail and disappoint my friends or myself again. He only promised what God promises. He promised that God would be my father, a father like neither of my earthly fathers. He promised a friend in Jesus who would be closer to me than a brother or a sister. He promised that Jesus would carry my prayers to God and speak them for me when my lips were unskilled. He promised that God would change me, gradually but surely. He'd take away my sharp tongue, my unkindness, my hard heart, and replace it all with His love, gentleness, hope, and mercy.

It was good that he made no silly promises because my troubles were far from over. The hateful calls kept coming in and oftentimes reduced Jane to tears. I lost very many speaking engagements. During the next weeks and months, I learned the hard truth that most friendships and even friendly acquaintances last only as long as good fortune does. It caused me to cherish true and faithful friends all the more. The Woodwards, Genie and Lawrence, and Jane grew so dear to me. They had very little to gain but the bad opinion of others by staying true to me. And Warren was the dearest of them all. He'd known nearly all of my secrets for so long without ever judging me or turning away.

A FEW DAYS AFTER MR. WOODWARD LEFT to "rescue my wife from that horde of little girls," as he put it, Jane allowed me to come downstairs by the fire. She encouraged me to bring my sketchbook on the condition that I allow her to tuck a blanket around my legs to keep off the chill. What with the heat from the fire and the wool blanket, I was well-nigh to roasting. I didn't feel much like sketching, and I was happy when I heard Warren's familiar heavy tread on the walkway outside.

"How's the invalid?" he asked, throwing off his coat and hat and sitting in the chair opposite mine.

"I'd be better," I answered, "if Jane would let me get up and do something, anything. I feel like a fool sitting here like someone's infirmed old grandmother."

"Well, you certainly don't look like anyone's grandmother to me," he said and winked.

"Oh, go on," I said, the heat rushing to my cheeks. I chalked it up to the fire being too hot.

He chuckled, then stretched his legs out in front of him and rested his head back on the chair.

"How are you, Warren?" I asked. "Your eyes are all puffy and red."

He sighed, "Last night, I realized there was so much work to get done after the hullabaloo of the last several days. So I just stayed up and finished it. I knew I'd never catch up otherwise."

"Oh, Warren, you've had so much trouble on my account."

He opened his eyes and looked at me.

"You know nothing I do for you is any trouble. It never has been, and it never will be."

I dropped my eyes to my hands and began rubbing the binding of my sketchbook with my thumb. Warren sighed again. When I looked up, his eyes were closed once more.

"Warren?" I asked softly.

"Mmmm?" was his only response.

"May I ask you something?"

He just nodded.

"Remember when I locked myself in my room a few days ago, and you told me you knew everything and it didn't matter to you? You said you knew who Mother was, that you two were friends. How long...I mean...how long have you known?"

"Shew," he reacted with a sigh, "that's a long story, Elizabeth."

"Tell me, please."

He leaned forward and put his hands on his knees.

"Let's see. It was about ten years ago that I came to this town and began my job at the *Gazette*. I was about your age, the biggest, smart-mouthed young fool you've ever seen. I got myself into all kinds of trouble that year," he laughed, shaking his head. "They say fools rush in where angels fear to tread. I suppose that was exactly what happened when I managed to meet your mother, only it ended well instead of in disaster as it should have.

"The fact of the matter was that I didn't like it that we knew absolutely nothing about this Alexander Stonely fellow. Oh, I suppose at one time the editor before me had known about it and simply forgotten to brief me on the situation before he left. But at the time I came, no one knew who Alexander Stonely was. He was a regular columnist, but I never laid eyes on him. His articles arrived at my office every Saturday afternoon without fail. And every month we sent a check to a post office box right here in town, so I knew he lived nearby.

"I decided I'd do a little journalistic investigating. I began to deliver the check to the post office in person, and then I waited to see who'd pick up the mail. That was difficult enough in itself. I never saw anybody pick it up, never. I decided that he was one smart guy, that Stonely. I asked the postmaster when Mr. Stonely usually came to pick up his mail, and he told me he'd never seen him either. He said a woman, who looked to be a housekeeper or maid because she often wore a uniform and apron, would come at odd times to pick up the check."

"The check?" I asked, pricking up my ears.

"Yes," he replied, "The only thing Mr. Stonely ever received was a check from the *Gazette*." I started to lean forward as my interest rose quickly.

"Well, naturally, I was even more determined to get to the bottom of things. So as often as I could, I'd have my assistant take care of matters for me at the office while I watched Mr. Stonely's box. After a week, my persistence finally paid off. I saw your mother's maid, Rachel, unlock the box, take the check out, and leave. I followed her to your mother's home and watched her go inside. I stood outside for a few minutes, then I straightened my tie, marched up to the house, and knocked on the door. Rachel answered.

"'I'm here to see Mr. Alexander Stonely,' I announced, handing her my card.

"You should've seen the look on her face, Elizabeth. I just about strangled myself to keep from laughing. She asked me to wait a moment and then bustled off with my card in a hurry. In a few more minutes, she came back and showed me upstairs to your mother's room. There was your mother sitting calmly at her desk, writing.

"She looked up when I came in and said, 'You wanted to see me, Mr. King?'

"Then, I suppose you should've seen the look on my face. I'd never been so shocked in my life. She just looked expectantly at me, sitting there like the Queen of Sheba, while I recovered myself. Suddenly the whole thing struck me so funny, I began to chuckle. I can't swear to it, but I believe I saw just the faintest hint of a smile on her face.

"'Won't you sit down, Mr. King,' she then said with the greatest of poise.

"Now, I don't know how she did it, but somehow she convinced me to keep her identity a secret. Being the sophomoric idiot that I was, it probably wasn't difficult for her. I got such a kick out of the whole thing. It was such a good joke that I decided to go along with it, regardless of how hard she was on my sex. We shook hands on it.

"'Do we have an agreement?' she asked me pointedly.

"'It's a deal, Mr. Stonely,' I said. 'Or may I call you Alex?' I then added with a smile.

"'You can leave now and let me get back to work,' she said wryly.

"I laughed at her dismissal of me and turned to leave.

"'Mr. King,' she said without looking at me. 'You're a very refreshing person. Come and see me again sometime. But carefully, mind you.'

"Then I laughed incredulously at her deception. The whole thing was almost too hard to believe."

"She'll never cease to amaze me," I said shaking my head. "Well, go on. This is so interesting."

"I'd visit from time to time, just as she suggested," Warren continued. "Sometimes I'd bring her the check in person, cautiously as she'd asked. I never spent more than ten or fifteen minutes with her at a time. We'd chat briefly then I'd leave. It was another three or four years before I knew she had a daughter. But, before that, of course, Christian began working for me. Oh, how sorrowful the day was when he started walking around all starry-eyed, talking about some beautiful girl named Elizabeth he'd taken a fancy to. I suffered through enough of his word pictures about your eyes and your hair and your smile…"

I smiled as I thought about Christian. I'd never heard that before.

"Oh, he was in a bad way, but I didn't pay much attention to it. Then one day in May, I strolled over to the house to bring the check as my habit was, but your mother seemed unlike herself, like she was distracted. I'd learned by then not to pry into things that weren't my business, so I didn't mention it. But she did.

"'Well, Mr. King,' she said to me, her back to me as she stood and looked out the window, 'my daughter's going to be married today.'

"'I didn't know you had a daughter,' I answered, 'but I wish you joy.'

"'She's been away at school for several years. She only recently came back. She was going to college so she's not home often,' she said. 'There's a picture of her in my top drawer there. You can look at it if you like.'

"I opened the drawer and that's when I first saw you.

"'She's a lovely girl,' I said, and I meant it.

"'She's marrying one of your men. Christian Brown is his name. I forbade her to do it.'

"I didn't know quite what to say so I didn't say anything.

"'I gave her a choice between him and me, and she chose him. As a result, I disowned her.'

"After a long pause, she asked, 'Christian Brown doesn't look well. What do you know about him?'

"'Well, he's a good fellow, one of the best…" I began.

"'No, that's not what I meant. He looks sick.'

"'He had quite a bout with pneumonia around Christmastime,' I answered, 'but he seems to be recovering well.'

"'Hmmm…' was her only response.

"'I suppose I ought to get back to the office,' I said, trying to make my exit.

"'Would you do something for me, Warren?' she asked.

"'Yes, of course.' I assured her.

"'Keep an eye on them for me, would you? But don't let them know I asked you to.'

"'If you like, certainly,' I said, turning to go. But then I stopped and said to her, 'I hope you and your daughter can work out your differences someday. Life's awfully short, you know.'

"'Thank you,' she said, briskly turning from the window and sitting back down at her desk. 'But it isn't likely. I believe it's for the best.'

"So I did what she asked of me. Christian and I were already on friendly terms so it wasn't difficult. The problem came when he died. I intended to go about looking after you in a calm, business-like manner. But I found that the more I came to know you and Jane and Chris, the more I grew to love and care for you. You became close to my heart."

There was so much for my mind to process in Warren's story. A few things were beginning to make sense. I turned my face away, trying hard not to cry.

"Warren, that pension you gave me after Christian died," I said. "It didn't come from the boys at the office, did it?"

"No, it didn't," he admitted quietly. "I kept her abreast of all the goings-on in your life. I told her when Christian died. I mentioned to her that maybe you'd be in contact with her since you had no one to provide for you now. I'll never forget what she said.

"'Not Elizabeth,' she declared. 'She wouldn't even if she were starving. She's just like me, stubborn and determined.'

"She said it with such pride, even as she made arrangements for me to give you a monthly allowance.

"'You'll see,' she told me. 'Elizabeth won't beg from anyone. You'll be hard pressed to get her to take this. You'll have to come up with a good story.'"

"Do you think she was proud of me?" I asked, "Really?"

"Oh, I know she was. It was plain to see," Warren assured me. "I'll never forget the day I brought your manuscript for her to look at. She paged through it with a smile growing on her face.

"'Well, Warren, what did I tell you?' she asked. 'Didn't I say she was a smart one?'

"She backed your book with her own money, Elizabeth. I really didn't do that much."

"And what about Chris?" I asked, my tears overflowing. "What did she say about little Chris?"

"Well," he chuckled, "she was a little put out that you'd had a boy, but told me she supposed it couldn't be helped. She did tell me that if he took after you and his father, he ought to be a handsome fellow when he was grown. She didn't say a word when I told her about his death. She just nodded and stood looking out the window until I left."

Now I couldn't speak. It was too much to bear. Finally I asked, "Why didn't you tell me all this before? All this time…"

"I had a promise to keep," he said. "She wanted it that way."

"Yes, I suppose you had no choice," I said.

"I wanted to tell you so many times. You'd let little things slip and then look so worried," he said, putting a hand over mine. "I hoped you'd learn to trust me enough to confide in me. Then I could be a comfort to you without breaking my promise. I tried to ask questions that would give you an opportunity to tell me, but you didn't."

I bowed my head in shame at his comment. "Warren, you almost make me believe my mother did love me."

"She was a strange woman, but yes, I believe she did."

It broke my heart when I heard him say that. I think of my mother every day. I think of her abandoned, left to fend for herself while carrying a selfish man's child. I think of her alone in her room, day in and day out, writing and writing. I think of her facing death alone with no one to comfort her. I've thought of that every day since then. I'm afraid I'll think of it every day for the rest of my life.

Chapter 26

"Jane, you must wake me up in time to go to church tomorrow," I announced one Saturday evening.

We were sitting at the supper table, Warren, Jane, and I. They looked at me in shock.

"You told me you'd never set foot in that building again," Warren said, fork suspended in midair.

"I know. But I've changed my mind," I said with some boldness.

Jane was beaming.

"Elizabeth, I don't... Well, the last thing I want to do is discourage you in your new-found faith, but are you sure that's wise? Going out so soon after all that mess in the paper could be difficult. I can see the gossip now—that you're just trying to get back into everyone's good graces by going back to church. I don't think anything of the kind, but you know how people talk."

"I know," I replied, "Maybe I'm crazy, and I can't say that I'm not nervous. But I've had a long time to think, and I've decided that if God knows everything about me and loves me, then I should do the right thing and not care what people think. God's opinion is what matters the most anyway. Don't you think, Warren?"

I looked up at him expectantly, hoping he would agree with me. I did want Warren's good opinion. After all, I wasn't perfect.

He smiled at me and gave my shoulder a squeeze. "What time is the service tomorrow?" he asked. "I'll go with the both of you."

As it happened, there was no need for anyone to wake me up. I woke before the sun. I couldn't stay in bed a minute longer. I got up and washed, then made the bed. I stood in front of my mirror, brushing my hair until it shone. Jane had been so distressed after I'd cut it that I let it grow out again. I took great care to arrange it well. It wouldn't do to go to church with messy hair. I buttoned my dress with trembling fingers. I was terrified inside.

Before leaving, Mr. Woodward had spoken some comforting words to me and I remembered them now.

"Elizabeth," he said with a gentle tone, "don't let what people do or say defeat you. You're a child of God now. Do what becomes a child of God, and He'll attend to the rest. Remember what the apostle Paul said, 'If God be for us, who can be against us. He that spared not his own Son, but delivered him

The Pursuit of Elizabeth Millhouse

up for us all, how shall he not with him also freely give us all things. Who shall lay anything to the charge of God's elect? It is God that justifieth. Who is he that condemneth? It is Christ that died, yea rather, that is risen again, who is even at the right hand of God, who also maketh intercession for us.'" Then he assured me, "No one but Christ has any right to condemn you, and He doesn't. Not anymore."

"Who is he that condemns me?" I whispered over and over to myself trying to still my fears.

When I was ready, I opened the curtains and sat down at my desk to look out the window and watch the world wake up. The sky was still dark but for a faint glow in the east. If I craned my head to the left, I could see a light on in Mrs. Finley's house, and the children tumbling out of bed to be scrubbed and pressed and shined for church by their mother's nervous hands. A door opened to the right, and I heard a sloshing sound as a housewife threw out a pan of dishwater that must have sat out all night. These were the good respectable people of my town. Were they still thinking of my disgrace? Nervous energy coursed through me, and my fingers began to rap an unsteady rhythm on the desk. And then I stopped.

Looking up at the brightening sky, I said, "I feel the necessity of doing this. I am determined to do it. But I'm afraid, Father. Help me."

It was a beautiful sky. I took some paper and pastels and set to work with quick strokes of my hand. As I worked to put the sunrise on paper, I began to hum a familiar tune, something I must have learned at school. And then I began to sing the words.

> Oh, love that will not let me go,
> I rest my weary soul in thee,
> I give thee back the life I owe,
> That in thy ocean depths it's flow
> May richer, fuller be.
>
> O Joy that seekest me through pain,
> I cannot close my heart to Thee;
> I trace the rainbow through the rain,
> And feel the promise is not vain
> That morn shall tearless be.

O Cross that liftest up my head,
I dare not ask to fly from Thee;
I lay in dust life's glory dead,
And from the ground there blossoms red
Life that shall endless be.

I heard my door open and Jane came in. I turned and smiled at her. She put her arm around my shoulder as I worked and sang. I looked up at her, and she was smiling and dabbing at her eyes.

"It's all going to be all right, Jane," I said.

We walked to church, the three of us. It wasn't far, and the fresh, cold air felt good on my face. As we went along, I saw many people that I knew, driving or walking to church. After seeing that I was among them, many averted their eyes and walked quickly on. Some ignored me altogether. But there were the others, those precious few who stopped to give me their condolences on the passing of my mother and my recent misfortunes. Among them were those two dear old souls that sat in front of me the Sunday that Chris, Jane, and I came to church after so many years of absence. They recognized me right away.

"Why, Mrs. Brown," the littlest one exclaimed, "are you going to join us again? We've missed you ever since...well, ever since your little boy's funeral. What a sad day that was."

"Yes," I said, looking down into their sweet, wrinkled faces. I was ashamed to find that I couldn't remember their names. "Yes. But here I am again."

"Good," said the other, "You must sit with us in our pew."

"Aren't you that *Gazette* editor?" asked the little one, frowning at Warren.

"Well, yes," Warren said uncomfortably.

"I think it's a shame what you people printed about Mrs. Brown," she said, shaking her finger under his nose. Her head barely reached his elbow, but that didn't concern her any. I had to turn my face away, the picture was so amusing. "Putting out people's lives for everyone to read," she continued. "It's a lot of silly sensationalism. I think it's terrible."

"I quite agree with you," Warren replied soberly. "My only comfort is that it didn't happen on my watch. I was away at the time. But now that I'm back, I intend to do my utmost to prevent the same type of thing from happening again."

This satisfied her, and we continued on together. As we came closer, I saw my nemesis standing just outside the door. Miss Tuttle watched me approach, speaking quietly to a woman beside her. I felt a knot tightening in my stomach as we drew nearer. I could just imagine what she was saying. I was so angry I stopped walking for a moment. But I could feel Warren's eyes on me, watching what I would do.

If God loves me, He must also love Miss Tuttle, was my only thought. *So I must love Miss Tuttle. But I can't.* I was failing already.

"You will," I remembered Mr. Woodward saying. "You'll come to Christ again, perhaps a thousand times if you must... He won't mind."

Help me, I prayed silently as I took a deep breath and stepped forward. I paused in front of her and smiled.

"Good morning, Miss Tuttle. Isn't it a lovely day that God's made?"

She stood in place, looking aghast. Then she turned and hurried inside. I looked after her sadly, because in that brief span, I understood what a miserable, unhappy woman she was, and I felt badly for her.

For the next hour I sat in rapt attention with Warren and Jane on one side and the two grand old ladies on the other. The minister preached about the righteousness of Christ, and for once in my life I found him neither long-winded nor boring. I doubted that he'd improved in speaking skills as much as I'd improved as a listener. We sang the old hymns, but they all seemed new to me. I'd never really paid much attention to them before.

When the service was over, I stayed in my seat while the congregation filed out. Miss Tuttle wouldn't look at me when she passed. Poor Mr. Snyder gave a nervous twitch in my direction, which I believe was supposed to be a nod.

"Coming, Elizabeth?" Warren asked.

"You and Jane go along. I'd like to talk to the minister. I won't be long."

I waited until everyone had left before I approached him to shake his hand.

"I'm Mrs. Brown. Elizabeth Millhouse Brown, that is. May I talk to you a moment?"

He smiled and motioned for me to be seated. I sat down in a pew and cleared my throat a bit nervously. I felt I ought to talk to him, but I wasn't exactly sure what I wanted to say.

"I imagine you've read about me in the paper recently," I began.

"Yes, I have."

I looked down at my hands and then plunged forward.

"Reverend, over the last week, I've had a serious change in heart." I paused, biting my lip. "I'm not sure, but I think I've become a Christian. That is, I hated God before and now I love Him. I don't love Him very well, but a little. Not as much as you do, I'm sure, but I'm new at it still."

He was smiling and nodding at me as I spoke. He was a nice man. I wondered why I hadn't noticed that before. He asked me a few pointed questions about how I'd come to that decision, and I gave him my answer.

"Yes, Mrs. Brown, I believe you've become a Christian," he said, and then added sincerely, "I'm glad to hear it."

"Yes, well," I said, "it wasn't easy for me to come today. But I wanted to."

"I expect it wasn't. It was courageous of you."

I sighed with relief, glad that he seemed to understand.

"And may I say," he continued, "that you mustn't worry about how much or how little you love God. If you're His child, your love for Him will grow. He'll see to that. In the meanwhile, read your Bible and come and worship as much as you're able and hear the things of God taught. I believe many things will become clear to you that way. But if ever you have questions, please, always feel free to ask me."

"Oh, thank you, sir," I said with a smile. "Well, good afternoon."

I did what he said, and I've continued to do what he said. It's been three years since that day and every year, I understand more than I did the year before. I've become quite a different person.

Life has evened out a bit. Gradually, people began to speak to me again. Several people, in fact, have apologized for the way they treated me back then. Book sales are beginning to pick up. Mr. Woodward was right. People do have short memories. And even if they don't, most of them have the good sense to realize what's important to fret over and what's not. Unfortunately, there are also the people who seem determined to remember. Miss Tuttle still won't speak to me anymore. Occasionally, a rumor will begin about me and spread around town and then begins the arduous task of undoing it. Every time, I soon discover that the rumor has Miss Tuttle as its origin. It does no good to be angry about it. I've learned over the past few years that I must answer to God for my misdeeds and leave the misdeeds of others to Him.

Mr. Snyder called me rather sheepishly a few months after everything happened and asked if I would resume art classes, so I did. As for the widow Finley, after much hard work and persuasion, I finally convinced her and all of her children to come to my house for dinner one evening. Though it's not a warm friendship, at least things have improved enough for her to feel quite comfortable running over to my house and borrowing the occasional egg or a cup of sugar.

I never saw Violet again, and I doubt I ever will. She did me a great deal of harm, but in a way I should thank her. Ultimately, she was the catalyst that brought me to Christ.

I'm nearly at the end of my story, as much as I've lived of it, at any rate. Warren is the one who encouraged me to write it. He thought that if people heard the story from my perspective, they would be more apt to understand and less likely to judge. But only God knows what the outcome will be.

He's an interesting fellow, that Warren. After my initial shock and when my world seemed to stabilize a bit, he pulled back for a while and let me deal with difficult situations by myself. Before, he'd have rushed to my defense and tried to protect me. At first I wondered why he wasn't rushing to my aid. Then I suspected that he was watching me to see how I'd handle things. A few days ago, without explanation, he told me that he'd decided to become a Christian too.

When I asked him why, he said in his gruff, straightforward manner, "I couldn't do much else, after seeing a miracle take place in front of my very eyes." He meant me, of course.

I'm sitting at my desk this evening, putting the finishing touches on this manuscript. Warren just left for the evening. There was quite a spring in his step, I must say. He asked me to marry him once more, and this time I accepted. Really, how could I have turned him down? He's my best friend after all. He's determined to be married within the month.

I just smiled and said, "Yes, dear."

He's a dear man, and he'll be a good father. Yes, I said a father, for I'm still young. There's still time for a home and family, and it'll be a true family, one like I had only briefly with Christian. The only difference this time is that God will be the center of our family, not me.

There's one thing more that I pray for. Above all things, I pray that God will give me a daughter. I want a chance to raise a little girl differently than I was raised. If He gives me my request, our little girl will have a mother and a father who will love her and love each other. She'll be confident of it. She'll know from the very beginning that God is love. We'll show her with our lives. And we'll name her Elizabeth, because I know now that my God is bountiful!

About the Author

Amanda Barber is the author of numerous short stories and essays. In 2009 Amanda collaborated with her brother, Justin Barber, to produce an album of original compositions with a complimentary narrative, entitled Children's Suite. Early in 2011, she wrote and co-produced a radio broadcast which aired on 106.7 FM Radio Harbor Country, Three Oaks, MI.

Amanda has a keen interest in writing for films. In the summer of 2011 she wrote a short film script called, The Wednesday Morning Breakfast Club. The film is currently in production and is tentatively set for release in the summer of 2013.

Amanda's interest in writing began at Christmas of 1997 when she pulled a journal out of her stocking. She began her writing career by chronicling all her Christmas presents in the first entry. From there, she branched out into short stories and novelettes. It was in the fall of 2009 that she took one of those novelettes and developed it into this novel, *The Pursuit of Elizabeth Millhouse*.

Amanda is first and foremost a Christian, and her writing reflects this. It is her desire to provide captivating fiction that entertains while it encourages other Christians to hold to the truth and keep close to God.

In her spare time, Amanda loves to read, sew, cook, go for long walks, and spend time with friends and family. Music is a great love, as well. She plays the violin in the Kalamazoo Philharmonia, teaches private violin and piano lessons, and listens to classical music.

CPSIA information can be obtained at www.ICGtesting.com
Printed in the USA
BVOW081550190613

323661BV00002B/35/P

9 781581 694567